the Treasure Keeper

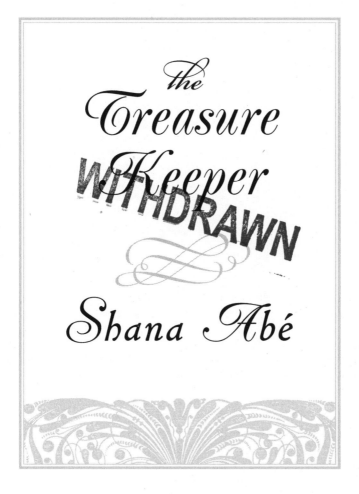

the Treasure Keeper

Shana Abé

BANTAM BOOKS

THE TREASURE KEEPER
A Bantam Book / April 2009

Published by Bantam Dell
A Division of Random House, Inc.
New York, New York

Book design by Catherine Leonardo

Bantam Books and the rooster colophon are registered trademarks of Random House, Inc.

Library of Congress Cataloging-in-Publication Data
Abé, Shana.
The treasure keeper / Shana Abé.
p.   cm.
ISBN 978-0-553-80685-4 (hardcover)
ISBN 978-0-553-90593-9 (e-book)
1. Changelings—Fiction.   I. Title.
PS3551.B329T74 2009
813'.54—dc22
2008041389

Printed in the United States of America
Published simultaneously in Canada

www.bantamdell.com

10 9 8 7 6 5 4 3 2 1
BVG

For two truly amazing ladies: Annelise Robey and Andrea Cirillo, who have always been so smart, and so kind. Thank you for your guidance, for your patience, and for all the years of encouragement.

I also offer my most heartfelt gratitude to Shauna Summers and Nita Taublib, who keep me on track and always have great ideas.

Thank you to my family, too. Of course.

And to Sean, who accepted my dare and so got to be a dragon.

PROLOGUE

Something Dark is coiled around your heart. Something scaled and glistening, and ferociously beautiful. It has been with you all your days and nights, all your years, in all your thoughts, shaping every single movement: your hands, your lips, your respiration. It lives because you live. It lives because magic is real.

It gives you grace when Others are clumsy. It gives you strength when Others crumble apart. It gives you animal splendor, and cunning, and the means to walk the earth on two legs in open disguise. You are secret smoke and claws, a cocked ear to the music of metal and stone, fangs and luminant eyes, wings for flight. You are the zenith of creatures; you are the hunter and the reaper, and all the Others—whether they witness your true face or not—instinctively glance away when you pass.

Their skin crawls; they don't know why. Their souls heave a shudder.

It is because of you.

Yet you are not above the laws of the universe. As with every facet of life and death and even magic, there is a price for glory,

1

and that price for you is this: The Dark Thing eats through your blood and tendons like acid. Although for the sake of your very existence you must restrain it, it demands constant release. Sometimes the physical need for Change racks you so fiercely you are lost; you cannot taste your food or wine, you cannot suck in the filthy city air, you cannot move or speak or look even the lowest urchin in the eye until you surrender and cut the Dark Thing loose.

Because you're not like the slow and dense Others who trudge through their tiny lives just beside you—no, not at all.

You are a dragon.

Drákon.

Did it hurt, your first time? Of course it did. It hurts us all, even me. This is how it happens: You're minding your day, or drowsing through your night. You're young, you're strong, and the sun threads gold through your hair, and the moon celebrates the luster of your skin. You are standing or seated or incumbent, you are breathing or talking or eating. The only necessary constant in every instance is that your eyes be open, because it won't happen without your sight. So the world spins on the same as every other day, every other night, and between one contraction of your heart and the next, you are devoured.

You're vanished. Jewelry flashing and falling, your garments drifting into a heap on the floor.

It's that swift.

Without your will, your human-shaped body has Turned into something else, something diaphanous. Ephemeral.

You are smoke.

And aye, it *hurts*. It's as if with the Turning of your flesh your very essence is scraped away raw, skin ripped from sinew, sinew torn from bones. You want to scream but you no longer have voice; no one hears. You're alone. Even if you're surrounded in that one lethal instant by those whom you love, you're alone, because their hands only slip through you. There is nothing they can do to help. You *must* Turn again, you must fight the agony and Turn back to what you were before—or else you're truly gone.

Too many headstones dot our burial grounds from children who die just like that, bright lives snuffed into wisps of vapor that rise and thin and never return. No coffins to bury, no bodies beneath the sod.

But you lived, didn't you? You knew what to do, and you lived, and after that…the pain diminished. By your third or fourth Turn, you had control, and all you felt was searing joy.

Are we not magnificent?

You won't remember our origins. None of us do, except perhaps in the most fevered of clan dreams. But I know our past, a very good deal of it; certainly more than you'll hear from anyone else.

We're not from here. We are not native to this soft and mild green isle. Ages ago we were churned to life from the molten union of earth and sky, from smoking lava and diamonds and a crescent range of faraway mountains that are now called *Carpathians*.

It was a good place for us. The magic that whipped us into perfection had also perfected our home: thick misty woods, glacier-fed rivers roaring hard and clear, melting into streams. Mounds of pine needles and sweet resin throbbing in the trees and delicious animals that fled too slowly at our approach.

Gold sifted through the streams, swirling into pools with beckoning laughter. Veins of copper and silver fingered up, up through the bedrock, trying to reach us. Diamonds speckled the forest floors, so fat and numerous we could pluck them like summer berries for our pleasure.

Each one welcomed us. Each one begged for our touch.

So we thrived. We hunted and soared and eventually built a castle for our clan, one set upon the highest, bleakest peak, carved from pure quartzite, studded with gems. We named it *Zaharen Yce*. The Tears of Ice.

Imagine it a moment, sparkling in the sun like distant pillars of salt, the songs of all the stones lifting and calling and weaving lush dreams around you from dawn to dusk and back again.

Close your eyes. You can almost hear it, can't you? So can I.

Humans, as you know, perceive little beyond the most primitive of sounds. But they are spawn of the earth; they crave diamonds and rubies and precious metals nearly as much as we do, although for different reasons.

Zaharen Yce drew them to us like a flare.

Siege after siege befell our people. Arrows. Ambushes. Poison left to steep in the rotting carcasses of our once-abundant prey; *drákon* too starved and desperate to detect it.

We lasted as long as we could. We had much to defend, after all. Much to lose.

And yet… we did lose.

Now we live here. Now we look like them. We wear corsets and silks, powdered wigs and rapiers. We attend cotillions with rouge on our cheeks; we sip tea and port and ale and try never to breathe very deeply when surrounded by the stench of mankind.

Consummate actors, we *drákon*. To ensure our survival we've learned to mimic *la crème de l'humanité,* and we do it with such skill and guile we deceive nearly everyone, betimes even ourselves.

But we are not humans, and *nearly* everyone is not everyone. Those are the Others who hunt us still.

CHAPTER ONE

Journal of Mlle. Zoe Cyprienne Lane
Presented to Me Upon the Occasion of My Thirteenth Birthday
Myers Cottage, Darkfrith
York, England
May 1, 1766

No rain.

Cherry Cake with Breakfast. Spotted Scones and Cider after Supper.
From Mother: The Journal. An Embroidered Tucker.
From Uncle Anton: A Tome of Verse: *Songs for Gentle Girls.*

From Cerise: An Ink and colored Portrait of my favorite rooster, Maximillian. (*From me to Cerise*: A Polished Silver Nugget in the Shape of a Heart from the River Fier.)
From Lord Rhys Sean Valentin Langford, second son of the Alpha (!): A bouquet of Pure Whyte Roses (the marchioness's garden?). A Small Carving of Maximillian from Pine (bloodstain on the left wing? dirt?). A Woven Ring of his Hair (!!).

Roses to Mother. Hair Ring to the dust bin. I rather like the carving.

Journal
June 13, 1766

No rain. Quite hot.

Lessons to-day in the village from the Dreaded Council for All *Drákon* Children. (I do think that at Thirteen Years of Age One ought *not* to be called a Child, and ought *to* be excused from these events, but the Council Begs to Differ.) I don't know why they bother repeating the same shabby old rules year after year. We've heard them enough by now to choke on them: We must not *Leave the Shire*! We must not *Speak of the Gifts*! We must not *Reveal our Secrets to the Others*! We must *Think Only of the Tribe*!

Rhys arrived late, as ever (no one even chided him. i suppose it must be lovely to be a Lord), and insisted upon squeezing into the seat next to mine. Then he kept pretending to tip his Inkpot upon my skirts when None were Looking. Vexing. I don't care what he said afterward, I don't believe he would have stopped without my kick to his shin. I will Concede, however, that it was unfortunate the Ink spilled upon his breeches instead.

Cerise claims She Saw it All. Grew very red and said that I was a shameless flirt. I told her to find a looking glass before casting names at me. Everyone knows she's a Goose, no matter that she's the elder by three minutes.

I cannot fathom a person less Likely to be my Twin.

Perhaps she is a changeling.

Journal
June 19, 1766

No rain.

Full moon, couldn't sleep. Mother made me extinguish the lamps early. The smell of smoking oil simply fills my face; I can hardly breathe with it. When I opened my window the stars tried to siphon me up into the sky. Saw Uncle Anton flying, the marquess, Mr. Williams, Mr. Grady, at least five more. We are so very lovely by moonlight. I do hope—I do I DO HOPE I shall fly too someday. I know that females no longer Turn into dragons, not since the marchioness, but I could be the first. I want it so much.

I shall be pink and gold and silver. Those are my favorite colors. I shall have a mane of glorious silk.

Rhys boasted he can already Turn. Liar. Lord Rhys of the manor house surviving his first Turn? I certainly would have heard about *that*.

June 21, 1766

Cloudy.

With Rhys in the woods. Should not have gone there with him, but he said he would prove he could Turn. And he did.

Thirteen is young. I suppose he's a half year older than that but most in the Tribe Turn after they are sixteen at least. I have time yet before I need worry.

His eyes are very green. I wonder that I never noted it before.

June 24, 1766

Still Cloudy. No rain.

Rhys says the most foolish things. My hair is like Ivory. My voice is like Dusk. My eyes are like Pitch.

Pitch. Indeed. I told him that comparing my eyes to the color of tar was uncouth.

He changed it to Obsidian and Tried to Kiss me again. I did not Let him.

June 25, 1766

Wind Rising. Clouds Darkening.

He keeps trying to get me to Go Back to the Woods with him. I know it's a Terrible Notion. But I want to. He tracked me to-day to the Lending Library, which very much needs to have its windows wiped. It was murky and we—

I do not know why I feel these things around him, my stomach up-set and my heart pounding all queer. It's quite unpleasant, actually.

He's Graced me with a Pet name. No one's ever done such a thing before. "ZEE." As if my given name is too difficult to manage, all two syllables of it.

Zee.

His smile is so fetching. He never bothers with a hat or gloves so his skin has tanned with the sun. I did not go with him to the Woods.

Cerise more and more waspish every day. She has at least Five beaux. I can't imagine why she would begrudge my One.

June 26, 1766

Storm to the East. Not here Yet.

I had a Dream Last Night that he came to my window as a dragon, dark glimmer and gold. I dreamt the dragon was tap-tapping on the glass, like raindrops, steady and soft, but when I woke, he was not there. Only those storm clouds, and not a drop of rain.

The air feels so heavy I could tear at my hair.

Addendum

HE LOVES ME.

!!!!!!

He wrote it on a slip of paper during Council Lessons. Pressed it into my hand as we were Leaving, along with a rose petal he had hidden in a pocket.

Lord Rhys Langford of Chasen Manor Loves ME, of all the maidens of the shire. Me, the daughter of the seamstress. Me, who once put a clot of mud in his tea when he wouldn't stop teasing me about besting him in Latin *and* Arithmetic. Me, and I'm not even Pretty. Cerise says my eyes are too strange and my lips are too big and I'll certainly never Develop as she has.

Me.

What a load of piffle. All that just to steal a kiss in the woods. It's really rather pitiful, isn't it?

(I shall save the petal here, between these pages.)

Addendum Addendum

Cerise found the paper. I had dropped it by accident in the Hallway after Supper, and came upon her just as she was picking it up. I could hardly disguise from Whom it Came. Master Baird says Rhys's penmanship flows like a Sultan's robes in the wind, right off the edges of the page. Most Distinctive.

She was red again, even more red than her hair. She was trembling. I stood there and felt as if a great hammer had smashed upon my head.

Cerise is in love with *Rhys. Enormously* shocking!

But she is. She's weeping in her room right now. I can hear her through the wall, though she's trying to be quiet.

August 1, 1766

I've thought on it a great deal. I've thought and thought.

Cerise and I have been at odds nearly our entire Lives. She is Comely while I am not; she is well liked while I am not. She is fashionable, and droll, and buxom, while I am ... not. It's a very great Wonder that we should have shared a womb at all. But I look at the portrait of Maximillian she made for our birthday, now hung above my bed. I look at the lines very carefully drawn, and how steady her hand was with the colors. How she got every stripe in his feathers just right, and the red comb, and the cock of his head. I think about how long it must have taken her to complete it, especially since Maximillian despises Cerise and must have spent a great deal of his portrait time hiding behind the coop.

She is my Twin. When she weeps I feel it to my bones.

August 2, 1766

Cloudy. Warm.

I told Rhys to leave me be. I told him I did not love him. I gave him back his carving of Maximillian, just so he knew I was Sincere.

August 4, 1766

Cloudy. Hot.

He persists.

August 19, 1766

Cloudy. Hot, hot, *when* will it rain?

He leaves gifts for me on my sill. He follows me about. When I walk to the village, he is there. When I walk to the downs, he is there. When I feed the chickens, he is there, and it is a Very Big Fuss because now that he can Turn, all the animals scatter in fear of their Lives. Mother Heard the Fuss and now she's cross at both of us. The hens won't settle if he's near; they remain frightened for days. No eggs.

I hardly think it's fair *I* was punished for that. I'm *trying* to get rid of him.

September 1, 1766

I had the same Dream last night. Rain was softly falling, and he came to my window, tapping on the glass. Only this time when I awoke, it was so hot I was perspiring, and the rain was really, truly falling, drawing into silvery tears down the panes.

And behind the tears was the dragon, watching me with glowing green eyes.

No Dream.

I walked to the window and looked back at him. His scales were slick and shining, an emerald so dark it was nearly black, and his talons and mane and wings were metallic gold. He looked from me to the brink of the eastern forest over his shoulder, then back at me. I understood him as clearly as if he had spoken the words.

Come with me. Come to the woods.

Instead, I pulled the shutters across the window, latched them, and returned to bed.

December 24, 1769

Snowing!

It's wonderful to have everyone around in one house, even if it is for just a few days. I love the scents of the holidays, cinnamon and roast goose and pine needles covered in ice. Mother's cough has improved. Even Cerise laughed at the runny mess I made of the plum pudding.

Saw Lord Rhys back from Eton today in the village, shopping, I think. He was there with all three sisters and his brother, and their father. The Marquess of Langford tipped his hat to me and wished me a very Happy Christmas. I, of course, wished them all the same.

February 2, 1773

Cold and Sunny.

I cannot fully describe my emotions on this day. I'm very happy for Cerise, of course. She deserves every Felicitation and it's a joy to see her so flushed and pretty. Thomas is no doubt a good man, a strong dragon, and their child will be doubly blessed.

I can't imagine having a baby. I can't imagine being wed. I think of Love and feel only a rather empty sense of curiosity. I've been kissed before, and I liked it. I've been squired before—to dances, to soirées—and I liked that too. But I feel so strange these days. I look up at the sky and I feel as if I have forgotten something important.

Not the Turn. I suppose I never really believed that would happen. Yet when the clouds gather and blow, it almost seems like they're taking a part of me with them. I long for the rain, all the time, and I don't know why.

Hayden James came by today for tea bearing a posy for me and a bouquet for Mother's sickroom. He's blond and tall and quite handsome. But he spent an entire two hours talking with me about the weather. Even I was bored.

⚮

May 11, 1774

Temperate. Clear.

I should have anticipated this. I mean, I did anticipate it. I just never truly believed he would work up the nerve to ask.

Hayden is very dear. I do like him. Perhaps I even love him. I enjoy his quiet company, and his thoughtfulness, and the way his eyes light up to the most perfect blue when he smiles. I appreciate that he still brings lilacs to Mother's grave, and that he worries about me living alone here in the cottage. It's very kind, if unnecessary. I have my work (although I am a poor substitute for Mother's skills), and family about. I have ones who care. We are a tribe, after all, and no one is ever truly alone in Darkfrith. Just ask the Council.

I suppose that if I am to note that Hayden's character is rather reserved, I must also truthfully declare that his manners are always the pinnacle of courtesy. If his demonstrations of physical affection for me are somewhat . . . restrained, at least I know he values my virtue.

I've tried to close my eyes and picture him in the cottage with me, taking tea with me every day for the rest of our lives. Our sons and daughters around us, yellow-haired and merry. What a relief it would be to finally slip into the domestic ease enjoyed by the rest of the tribe.

Madam Zoe James. *Madame Zoé James.*

He is a fine man. I must think about how to answer him. My least desire is to hurt him.

⚮

May 12, 1774

Rhys. Langford. Is. An. Ass.

Saw him at Market this morning in the village. Heavens knows what he was doing at Market, since he surely never has to purchase anything of his own. There are servants to shop for him, after all. No doubt he's just been sent down from Cambridge (again) and decided to rake up some trouble here at home for a change.

(What would I *give* for a chance to leave this shire and attend school! You can bloody well wager I'd not get caught doing *any-thing* to send me back here, but of course only the hallowed family of the Alpha is allowed to leave!)

He spies me before the bakeshop buying bread and saunters over. Yes. Saunters. He wears his hat cocked back and his brown hair un-tied and his breeches too tight and has this *smile,* this so Charming and Sweet smile, as if he's just happened upon a Dear Bosom Friend. Which I am not.

"I understand I am to congratulate you," he says.

"Oh?" I reply, because I can't imagine to what he's referring. Cerise's second child? Surely not Hayden, as I have not yet spoken with him.

18

"Indeed," he says. "Hayden James, eh? Decent sort, if a bit dull. I wondered if any of the fellows here would ever pluck up the courage to end your reign as the Old Maid of the Shire."

I did not throw my bread at him. I merely gave him my coolest smile and answered, "As long as it wasn't you. Oh, but that's right—you did try, didn't you?"

And then I sauntered away.

❧

May 13, 1774

Cloudy. Drizzle.

We have set the wedding date for June of next year.

❧

May 28, 1774

Something grave has occurred. I don't know what. There's a hum racing through the shire, through the tribe, an awful sort of excitement. I know there was a letter delivered today to Chasen Manor. Susannah Cullman, the third scullery maid, caught a glimpse of it on the salver before it was delivered to the marquess and is telling everyone it was stamped from a foreign land, written from the hand of a princess. And then I heard it was actually from Lady Amalia, the marquess and marchioness's youngest daughter (who, as everyone knows, was supposed to be at boarding school in Scotland).

Whatever it is, it's not good news. I was in the garden pulling weeds when I first felt it. It was clement today, sunny with the smallest of breezes. I was on my knees in the bed of mint and thyme, enjoying their fragrance and the warm pungent dirt, listening idly to all the little rocks beneath me when all at once, without warning, a great cloak of Deep Blue Darkness rose up to wrap around me. I don't know how better to depict it: soft, encompassing, infinite. I froze, trapped in my body; I could still feel the tips of my fingers and my toes, my face, that one particular bone of my corset that is pushing out of its seam into my ribs—but everything else was gone. I was suspended in indigo space. There might have been stars, but the sensation of blindness filled every sense. No smells, no sight, no touch or taste. Utter, perfect silence.

A cold wind shivered over me; my skin prickled like I was stark naked in snow. I caught the scent of pure panic, of fear. There were still no sounds around me but the *feeling of danger! discovery! hide!*

And then three single words, echoing as if coming from the center of a great bell, yet very clear: *Lia. Maricara. Drákon.*

When I drew breath I was back in the garden. I held a mint leaf in my hand, torn from its branch. The leaf was crushed, and the smell of the damaged leaf—the sight of the green juices upon my fingers—nearly turned my stomach.

I don't know what that was. I don't know what to think.

May 30, 1774

Hayden has the ear of the Marquess of Langford. He's of a good family, reliable and trusted, and came to me late tonight after an emergency meeting with the Alpha & Council to tell me what he could of what's occurred.

I can hardly pen the words. There is *another* tribe of *drákon*! None of us ever, ever *once* suspected such a thing. They live in Transylvania, in the far, far hills. They are hosting Lady Amalia even now, though God knows how she got all the way out there, or even how she found them at all. And here is the most amazing news of all: They are ruled by a princess—a female! Princess *Maricara* of the Zaharen.

It's a strange and marvelous miracle, that there are more of us. That a woman could lead.

Hayden disagrees. Grew rather fussy about it. Pointed out the danger behind this discovery, that this new tribe threatens our existence. That they may be wild, or feral, or taking risks that could be of immense danger to us, leading to our exposure. I admit I didn't really consider that. . . .

Told him he was right. Offered him tea and gingerbread (only a very little scorched!) and watched his natural Mild Humor return. He unbent as far as to kiss me Good-Night. On the lips. Very nice.

I did not mention the incident in the garden. It seemed insignificant, in light of everything else that has occurred. Perhaps I'll bring it up later.

It was probably my imagination.

✍

June 5, 1775

This was to have been my wedding day. Feels like Every Other Day. Nothing special. Worked tonight with Cerise in their tavern; they do need the extra hands. It's a dirty, messy job, and my gowns end

21

up reeking of tobacco and ale and gin. I don't enjoy it. But she's always so grateful for the help. And in truth, I appreciated the distraction, although Cerise could not know why. I never told her the exact date.

Hayden says perhaps soon, perhaps even next year. He's still so worried about our future. Says until the threat of the other *drákon* is contained, it would be Irresponsible in the Extreme to Wed (he means, I know, to Breed). He's deeply involved in the Council's plans for these "Zaharen" *drákon*. I do wish he'd tell me something of it. But he won't. Or can't. One man has already left the shire, and no one has panicked about it, so he's not a runner. Luke Rowland, about our age, unwed. It isn't hard to conjecture he's been sent after the rogue dragons. But again, no one will discuss it.

Today by the rye fields we shared a picnic I had prepared—my private little No-Wedding Feast—and Hayden murmured something about how my hair shone like moonlight under the bright sun. Which didn't even make sense, if you consider it. Managed not to laugh or cry. I only tipped my head and asked him calmly, "Well. Are you free June next, Mr. James?"

He understood me. He's very wise when he wishes. He took my hand and kissed it and said, "My heart is yours today, June next and the next, and always. It is more my body which concerns me."

I replied, "And me," which was really rather bold of me, but he only smiled.

"You are my love" is all he would say.

That tells me practically nothing, does it?

March 28, 1776

He drops by every afternoon for tea. He is absent all the rest of the time. I have told him I need more, but he only averts his eyes and repeats the same word: "Soon." I know he is vital to the plots of the Alpha and the Council, to our future as a tribe. But he is vital to me as well.

I don't have "soon" any longer. I am not a wife. I am not an un-matched dragon maiden. I am affianced, and alone. Always alone. It's a bit too much like purgatory.

August 3, 1777

Today I was washing dishes in the tavern and the Most Peculiar Thing happened. I wasn't paying much mind to my work—really, who enjoys washing dishes?—I was looking out the window to Cerise's little garden, admiring the green, the cuttings she's planted, Mother's lavender growing still, despite the damp, in the far corner, when I felt a faint, faint tingling across the skin of my hands.

I looked down, and—

I don't know what happened. I don't dare even put it into these pages.

It was lunacy. It was not real.

November 15, 1777

It was Worse than I anticipated. I did not cry. I fancy Cerise cried for me quite enough when I discussed this with her yesterday. But my eyes were dry, as were his when I informed him of my decision this afternoon.

I simply could not go on like this. He is half a stranger, half my heart. I understand his hesitations. There are undercurrents at work of which most of the tribe remain remarkably unaware. I might be as well, but for him...and the blue-dark Feelings that cloak me from time to time. The sense of danger galloping closer; of rising, enclosing threat.

I never wanted this half-life with him, to exist strictly in his leisure time and Sunday shadows. I confess it: I want true love and diamonds and passionate declarations. I want a mate who breathes my breath and strokes my skin, who holds my hand without reservations, who returns home to me every evening with open arms and happy anticipation. I want to be able to look up at him with the same adoration I glimpse in Cerise's eyes whenever she glances at her husband. And I want to see that adoration reflected back at me.

As I look over the previous paragraph I realize how childish it sounds. I'm ashamed of my weakness, that I'm not good enough or kind enough or patient enough to wait for Hayden any longer. It's been over three years now without any promise of a wedding date. I cannot change what's in my heart.

But I was so nervous to speak to him, my hands shook. It was very hard to give him back his ring.

Naturally, Hayden was a gentleman about it all. He kissed me *adieu,* very gently, on the cheek.

August 24, 1779

Sunny. Scattered Clouds.

It's been so dry this year, so dry and warm. I remember how I used to watch the clouds. I was younger then. I dreamed more. I suppose I believed in more as well.

August 25, 1779

Gray day. Clouds thickening.

Cerise wants me to go up to the manor house for the Tribal Socials the marchioness hosts every month for the singles of the shire.

I told her exactly the truth. I'm twenty-six years of age. How foolish would I look surrounded by a flock of giddy adolescents?

She seemed about to grow teary again so I forced a smile and told her not to worry. I was well and happy alone. I didn't mind being an Old Maid (!!) and that matrimony and children were for the wildly beautiful and good, like her.

She gave me a very curious look. She said, "You are beautiful."

I laughed and replied, "You're my sister. I cannot rely upon your opinion."

She sat up straighter. "Zoe. You're beautiful. You're probably the most beautiful woman in the tribe, more beautiful even than the marchioness."

I laughed once more. What else could I do? But it only angered her further, so I lifted my hands in surrender.

"Cerise! You yourself once told me how odd I am. My eyes are too dark, my lips are too big. Even my hair is this peculiar color- less color. I have mirrors. I can see the truth. I'm far too strange- looking to attract *that* sort of notice from men."

She was quiet a moment. She was staring at me hard, the way she does when she's trying to understand one of my jokes, or a pun I thought particularly clever. We were in the tavern after closing, seated together beside the fire. A fine gentle glow danced along our skirts. Finally she said, "Are you blind? Really, truly? Are you blind?"

"No," I said.

"Then I must suppose you are merely stupid. No wonder Hayden walked away."

That made me blink! I stood. But she was Cerise, ever Cerise, and she did not give quarter.

"No one courts you because you frighten them. You have this severity about you. This ice-cold perfection. But there's no ques- tion of your looks, Zoe Cyprienne. You're a diamond. You're a pearl. Haven't you noticed how all the males who come to the tav- ern stare at you, how they quiet when you're near? I've spent my en- tire life longing for *half* your charms, insane with the knowledge

26

that you knew how much more fair you always were. Now...I can't believe you *don't* know it. Are you jesting with me? Because it's not amusing in the least."

"No," I said slowly, gazing down at her. "I'm not jesting."

We locked eyes. Hers are such a lovely whiskey-gold. I always wished for eyes like that.

"You're an idiot," she said.

"On that," I said, "we agree."

January 5, 1781

Cloudy. Light snow.

Went for a walk today. My legs were restless, and the blue-dark cloak of Nothingness seemed to hover uncomfortably close to the cottage. I needed to leave.

Blackstone Woods are perfumed and dense; one can nearly always find a path there to follow without running into company. The snow fell in tiny glimmers, sideways, embedding into the tree trunks, throwing sparkles across my shawl. It was silent and empty and starkly serene. Within an hour snow encrusted my skirts and began to fill my boots.

I paused to rest in a clearing of rowan and oak. It's one of my most favorite places in the shire. In spring it's carpeted in grass and clover. In the summer it flowers with bluebells and red campion.

The snow picked up, still sideways. I lifted an arm to admire it, inspecting the individual crystals caught upon my sleeve, in the woolen weave of my mitten. Then I took off the mittens, both of them, and raised my hands to the flakes.

My fingers were rosy with the cold. I spread them, watching the white little dots hit my skin and melt into moisture...and I realized it was happening again...

The snow struck my hands. The snow melted. And every place there was a drop of water—I was gone. I had vanished.

I stood very still and let it happen. I waited until my hands were entirely wet, and I still felt the cold, and the sting of falling ice. Yet my hands were invisible. Except for the rush of frost from my breath, I could see straight through them.

Invisible.

Have I lost my wits? This is not a *drákon* Gift; I've never heard of such a Gift. This is surely something else.

Perhaps I've been alone too long. Perhaps my mind has bent.

February 18, 1781

Cloudy. Dry.

I seem to have some control over it. I seem to be able to Will it or Not. Mostly.

Tonight I stood before my bedroom mirror and splashed my cheeks with water from the basin. This was my Twenty-Second experiment, and nothing happened, as usual. I was relieved. And I was discomfited. I had imagined that moment in the woods or I had not: Either way, it did not bode well for me. And then, as I was staring at my reflection in the glass, I noticed my eyes growing darker and darker—they are already black, so I don't know how else to describe it. And *then*—yes! It happened again. My cheeks and nose and chin were gone. Only my eyes and my forehead remained.

As I watched I saw that I actually began to flush visible once more, even though my face was still wet.

I Willed it.

Oh, God. Should I tell anyone? Is this a New Gift or an Ancient One? What does it mean for my future?

I know the Council edicts. Sweet mercy, we all know them. Save for the marchioness and her daughters, female *drákon* have been unable to Turn for generations. Now any female of exceptional Gifts is considered tribal chattel, to be given to the Alpha or his line. She will be wed and bred into his family, and to hell with whatever *she* thinks about it.

The marquess is already wed. His eldest son is engaged. That leaves just Rhys Langford. Arrogant, rakehell Lord Rhys, with his long dark hair and mocking green eyes. Rhys, who cannot help but send me a gloating grin every miserable time we cross paths. He's always escorting some starstruck lass; obviously I'm still the Old Maid.

Bugger. I'd rather take my chances alone. If I can avoid water I can hide this. I'm certain of it.

May 1, 1781

Happy Birthday.

The tribe on edge, worse than I've ever felt. The Marquess and Marchioness of Langford have broken our most fundamental law and stolen away to the human world, to hunt Lady Amalia. Luke Rowland—sent to find and parley with the Transylvanian *drákon*—has been missing without word over four years now. The man sent after him, Jeffrey Bochard, has also disappeared.

The deep blue cloak follows me about. If I pause too long, it sneaks up on me. If I try to sleep, it slithers up into my dreams. This afternoon it caught me in the parlor between footsteps: wrapping close at once, vanishing the world. Suspending me in silence and fear and anger and worry. I heard the men's names. I felt their families' despair. I felt—I know not. Whisper brushings, their spirits? They seemed so lost; it was dreadful.

And then the cloak dropped me back into the parlor, and I finished my step, and there was a knocking at my front door.

I did not want to open it. I knew who it was, and why he had come.

What have I done? I can't bear to see him depart alone in his heart, as those other two did. I can't bear to have him think I never cared.

30

I always did. And if this isn't love, well—does it matter? He deserves a wife. He deserves a reason to make it back home.

The Council will not send a married *drákon* man, so we'll wed after he returns from his mission to the Carpathians. Hayden promised.

And after that, I'll tell him of the dark cloak. Of the Gift. After.

Journal Conclusion

I'm very sorry, Cerise. I know you're going to read this and worry. I would, in your position. Although I think perhaps we've only recently begun to be real friends, I've never doubted the bond between us. And so I begin this final entry with my apology.

This is my sad, roundabout way of keeping you in my life, even if it's merely through memories scratched on paper. I've always been hopeless at organizing, as you know, and so there was never any chance I would manage to pen an entry every day. But I believe most of the important events of my past few years have been recorded here. Enough to give you insight into what I'm about to do next.

You know Hayden left the shire, and you know why. Calm, loyal, meticulous: He was considered our last good hope of reaching the Zaharen *drákon* and brokering a peace with them. And everyone in the tribe knows now that the Zaharen sent us their princess Maricara in turn, bringing her horrible news. That the *sanf inimicus,* those human hunters, have discovered us, have killed at least two of our three emissaries—although we don't know which two.

That they've breached the shores of England. That only weeks ago they kidnapped and tried to kill the princess herself, and Lord Rhys. At least Maricara escaped, though heaven knows what happened to Rhys. We've had no word.

The princess claims that Lady Amalia and her husband Zane, still in hiding, are working covertly against the hunters. That Lia was the one who recently stole little Honor Carlisle from her home here. That Zane has infiltrated the *sanf* by pretending to be one of them.

I admit it was that last bit that sparked my mind and opened my eyes. If Zane, a human, not even one of our kind, would risk his life to help protect us...

I'm far from impulsive. I hardly need mention that. I tend to consider matters very carefully before taking action. How often have you complained about how long it takes me to select even a pair of garters for my stockings? You above all will realize how much I've mulled this over and over.

My position in the tribe is low, as is my influence. If I thought it would do an ounce of good, I would go before the Council and tell them of my Gifts, offer myself as an *apparatus belli* against this group of Others who have possibly murdered my fiancé. But I think we both know how fruitless that would be. I'm female; I'm unwed; I might still breed. Nothing I could say would persuade them to view me in any fashion beyond those three overwhelming facts.

They would lock me away, by force if need be. They would do whatever they thought they must to keep me bound to the shire. Our history speaks most eloquently for itself.

I used to think the Council was a faction of stuffy old men, bleating stuffy old rules out of lethargy, or just blind fear. Time has tempered my opinion. Now I better understand why they've held so tightly to our traditions. We do need to stand united against these hunters. We need every weapon at our disposal, which is why I must go. I cannot Turn, but I have these Gifts. I *am* a weapon.

I never told you—or anyone—that after Hayden left, he would send me a note every week to let me know where he was, that he was well. It was something I required of him, and to his credit, he never failed me until his communications with the tribe ceased entirely. His last note placed him nearly to Paris, en route to Dijon. I'll start there.

I shall leave up to you whether or not to share this journal with anyone else in the tribe. I said good-bye to you and the children tonight in your beds, although you never saw me. It was a test, and I passed. So I must no longer delay.

No need to reflect upon all the horrors of tribal punishment should I get caught. We both know the consequences for disobedience of the laws, so suffice it to say, I do not plan to be caught.

I wish I could better explain to you why I'm doing this. I wish I had the wit or the words to describe to you why I'm chancing nearly all that I love with this decision. I must make do with this: You have always been the other side of me, my twin, my friend and rival. I've watched you blossom as a wife and mother without a scrap of envy. Yet it would be a lie were I to write here that I did not long for the same as you. Hayden was that promise for me, that hope. He was the key to my future here in Darkfrith: my husband and helpmate, the father of my children.

You will not be surprised, I think, when I tell you that I've always felt slightly apart from all the rest of the tribe, just a step out of tune with everyone else. Hayden offered me the chance to find my place in the music here. For perhaps the first time, I felt that with him, despite my differences, I could belong.

I do not know if this is the definition of true love. All I know is that I must find him. I must discover what's happened to him. I will bring him home again if I can.

For ages we've been instructed to guard our place here, to grow our roots into this soil. But against our will we've been thrust into this new age; the human world has evolved without us. The marquess and his wife, Lady Amalia, Luke, and Jeffery—all scattered to the winds.

And now Hayden has vanished. Rhys has vanished.

I'm going to vanish too.

Be safe, Cerise.

Forever love,
Your twin,
Mlle. Zoe C. Lane
August 1, 1782

CHAPTER TWO

Paris
September 1782

He'd been following her for three long blocks down the Seine. She did not walk quickly, which was one of the things he noticed first about her. Her pace was slow, often uneven; a demoiselle who perhaps had partaken of too much champagne with her dessert.

And she *was* a demoiselle—or at the very least, a demimondaine. The sheen of her gown—satin without question, glimmering taupe by the smoky light of the street lanterns. The coat of fine sky-blue velvet she wore over it, edged with silk tassels that swayed in time with her oddly graceful gait. Even her hat, wide-brimmed and elaborately feathered, ropes of paste pearls draped around the band, the bow tied smartly beneath her chin. If she was a prostitute, she was an extremely successful one. Everything about her spoke of Means.

No question, there were other pigeons to be found tonight. With its theatres and operas and vendors, the musicians playing ballads on the bridges, Tuileries was always the most likely place in town to bump into a careless soul who didn't keep a firm hand on his purse, especially after the shows let out. But there was something about this girl, some compelling, mysterious pull from her...once she'd caught his eye, he found he couldn't look away.

She had a reticule over her left wrist, blue like the coat, with nice thin satin cords. Good enough.

She kept her own head down, watching the gutters and paving stones of Quai des Tuileries instead of her surroundings, pushing modestly through the crowds. Every so often her face would lift; it was only then he'd gain a swift glimpse of her nose, of her chin and lips. Dewy youth, lush beauty. He very much looked forward to seeing the rest of her.

But for now, Basile maintained his distance. He would not be so imprudent as to risk a glance directly into her eyes. It would not do to let her know he was studying her, and besides, there were still too many people about.

Her wig shone beneath the lanterns as well, the powder like none he'd seen before. He was not a man of great fashion, but he knew enough about wigs to recognize that hers was expensive. Definitely human hair, not horse, very fair and almost eerily natural. It wasn't even gray, but instead a glossy, glinting white. Two long, perfect coils spiraled down her back, bouncing like the tassels with every step, most fetching against the blue. It drew a man's eyes upward, to the nape of her neck. To the way the coat hugged the pretty slope of her shoulders.

Ah, the rich. What pleasures were denied them?

And yet as far as he could tell, his demoiselle walked the Quai alone, without a maid, without a footman. Without even a cabriolet to follow at a discreet distance. If she was meeting a lover, she was clearly reluctant about it. Perhaps the man was a toad.

The thought made Basile smile.

Over the clatter of horses and mules and carriages along the boulevard rose the soothing smack of the river pushing at her banks, the occasional echoing *allô!* of the boatmen drifting below. The autumn night smelled of damp leaves and burning coal and steaming fresh manure. The clouds pressed low in the sky, shrouding the jagged points and peaks of the city in wet, misty soot.

The demoiselle slowed yet again. This time when she raised her head, it was to take in the sudden line of trees before her. They had reached the far end of the gardens of the Palais des Tuileries, enclosed by a wall taller than two grown men, the tips of chestnuts and black oaks waving their branches over it like hungry fingers in the night.

She muttered something he couldn't quite hear. It wasn't the first time she'd whispered words to herself, another peculiarity that had snagged his attention away from the pockets of the other nobles who packed the boulevards. It seemed to him that this time she asked herself a question. He watched as she gave a short nod—an answer to herself, no doubt—then strolled on.

The nearest gate to the gardens was yet another half block away; Basile knew it well. It was composed of thick rusty iron bars and a much more formidable new padlock, and sure enough, it was to there that the demoiselle wandered, weaving past a pair of interested army officers without even a sidelong look. The gate was in shadow. She walked close, one gloved hand closing upon a bar, and stood without moving.

Basile drew back to give her space, leaning a shoulder against the nearest lantern pole, glancing around them, considering the moment. It was growing late, and the hordes along the Quai were finally beginning to thin. A trio of merchants clacking their walking sticks strode past, arguing about cards and a woman named Ariane. From the other direction two sedan-chair men huffed along more slowly, cheeks and jowls flushed, the tall black lacquered wood of the box gripped between them beginning to bead with the moisture of the night.

A face peered back at him from beyond the window; kohled eyes, pasty flat skin; the lace curtain was quickly dropped.

When Basile looked again to the demoiselle, she was gone. The gate swung open, very gently, upon its hinges.

He straightened in surprise, then quickly looked around once more. But she hadn't continued down the Quai, and she hadn't retreated back toward him.

The gate still hung agape, a clear invitation.

So Basile accepted it. When he was near enough he discovered that the lock had been broken somehow, the bolt completely bent free of the base. The entire contraption had been dropped to the dirt just inside the gate. Very strange. The girl must have noticed the same thing and let her curiosity—or those voices in her mind—lead her into the gardens.

He'd been here before, of course. He knew all the best dark places of the city. The gardens of the old palace were officially forbidden to the common people who swarmed the streets surrounding them, but thrice a year the gates were opened for parades, and even the lowest of the city filth was allowed a visit inside.

Basile's mouth twisted into a smile. *Vive le Roi.*

The place was enormous, acres and acres of fountains and statues and hedges and trees. He'd lose her if he didn't hurry, so he stepped inside, melting at once into the gloom.

There were no torches lit along the neat rows of chestnuts and gravel before him, but he could nearly make them out anyway, the heavy black strings of trunks, the paler paths of crushed rock raked between them. He couldn't see the abandoned palace from here, not even a hint of the roof. There were no torches for it, either.

He stopped to listen. Trees creaking, almost no wind. The city past the walls strident enough, but quiet inside here, an unnatural hush. There would be insects at least, he thought, but heard none.

However—he did hear footsteps. Up ahead, to the right. Light, uneven.

He followed her as silently as he could, and that was very silently indeed.

One of the reflecting pools shone like a flat pewter disc through the nearest break in the trees. Basile found his gaze flicking to it again and again as he stole carefully forward, his eyes repeatedly drawn to that sole slick of light. He avoided a drift of withered leaves by a bench only at the last second, and just as he was inwardly cursing himself, dancing sideways to save himself from that one fateful loud step, a hand closed hard around his throat.

In front of him. And there was no one there.

He brought up both his hands to clutch at it. He felt the air squeezed from his larynx, trapped like a bubble tight inside his chest.

He was lifted high, entirely off the ground. His feet kicked out and met resistance: cloth, a great deal of it, like the skirts and petticoats of a gown. Basile rolled his eyes downward. It *was* a gown, taupe satin. It stood in the path without a body, without support of any kind. He could see clean down inside it. And beyond that, just beyond—a hat and coat against the base of a chestnut, tossed nearly out of view. A single dropped glove, still on the path.

Spots began to color his vision, bright light at last. He tried to cry out but only managed a wheeze; the grip on his throat did not loosen, but his boots hit the gravel again.

Beyond the spots—orange, blue, yellow—there was now a face

gazing up at him. A beautiful face, more beautiful than he'd ever seen. A face from a nightmare, perfect and wintry calm, surrounded by locks of silky, silvery white.

"Good evening," said the demoiselle in a stroking voice. "Were you looking for me, sir?"

Basile wheezed some more, and the young woman nodded, serious.

"Perhaps I've been looking for you as well."

She had an accent. The slightest, slightest accent, not local at all—

He gave up clawing at her hand and took a swing at her instead, but she only leaned back, avoiding his fist. Yet her hold did loosen, just a bit, and he was able to suck in a fiery raw breath. The spots began to pop and fade.

The woman's eyes were absolutely black. The pupils and irises both, and then more, all of her eye, both of them, all black and shining and liquid like the pool, but infinitely, ominously more deep...

Basile wet himself. He couldn't stop it. He felt the warmth trickle down his leg to his boot.

Voices. There were voices all around them, words he didn't understand, foreign words, English perhaps, and then words he knew: exchanges from earlier tonight, Nadette with the baby in her arms, shrilling *don't come home without livres,* Emile hailing him from across rue St.-Honoré, *come on, some wine, a little billiards, good fun. we'll find that girl at Café Caveau, she likes me you know*—

"No," said the demoiselle abruptly, and dropped him to the ground. "You're not the one I want, after all."

Basile had crumpled to a heap at her feet, but only for a second. As soon as he was able, he scrambled away from her, gasping and staring, his fingers gouging deep into the gravel. The woman gazed down at him without expression.

No, not a woman, he thought frantically, over and over, *not a woman, not a woman, a demon, a monster—*

"Still," she continued, sounding thoughtful, "it's not good for your soul to steal, is it? That *is* what you were planning. I think, Basile Coté, it's time for you to find a more laudable profession."

She walked away from him, moving nimbly now to the coat and hat she'd discarded before, gathering them into her arms, finding the lost glove too. She threw him a final glance from over her shoulder.

"Perhaps I'll be watching to see what you're up to, Basile. You never know."

And the monster walked off through the king's trees.

The Palais des Tuileries was known throughout certain quarters of Paris as the Grand Squander. It had been a royal residence once upon a time, but that was nearly a century past, and today it was merely an elaborate, empty reminder that the aristocracy could waste anything they wished, even a palace. The king and queen and their courtiers resided just outside the city in sparkling Versailles; Tuileries, with its vast drafty chambers and dim, dark-paneled hallways, was considered old-fashioned and unnecessarily dreary.

It was very nearly vacant. There were a few retainers still living on the lower level, along with a handful of retired court officials who no doubt felt the sting of their banishment very sharply. Royal soldiers still patrolled the grounds, but it was monotonous, tedious work, and more time was spent furtively hunched over dice than actually walking about. After all, who would want to break in? The most lively occupants of both the gardens and the palace were the rats.

Curiously enough, however, the rats were hard to find lately. They had fled, in droves, in the pit of the night not quite one week before, along with all the ravens that had been roosting in the trees and the wild geese and ducks nesting in the grasses. And the mice from the stables. And the colony of rabbits that had dug generations of warrens beneath the western amphitheatre and its verdant slopes.

There were no animals of any kind left in Tuileries, in fact, except for two.

One were the humans.

The other was creeping softly up the servants' staircase in the far southern segment of the left wing of the palace. The stairs were dusty, remarkably so, but there were no windows to illuminate the flight, and thus no easy way for anyone else to see her footprints. Still, she carried her shoes in one hand, hitching up her skirts and coat with the other, careful with the hems.

The silver-haired demoiselle emerged cautiously from the doorway that opened to the uppermost floor, easing around it soundlessly, although she knew the corridor before her was deserted. The entire wing, in fact, from top to bottom, was deserted; it was the main reason she had chosen this place.

The lack of human distraction.

Her eyes closed a moment; she tested the area, inhaling deeply, drawing the air over her tongue, using every sense she could, just to be certain. . . .

No. No people. Only dust, and her.

With the skies so overcast there was no moonlight to reflect off the walls and mottled green tiles of the long hall ahead of her, but that was fine. Zoe knew her way by now. Her feet in their stockings padded without noise along the marble. There had been a runner here once, but it had been removed, along with all the paintings and pedestals and even the chandeliers. No one, however, had bothered to strip the coved ceiling of its frescoes of hunters and horses and golden-crowned kings. There was even a panel of a dragon—dead on its back, with a knight standing over it and a sword angled through its neck.

Zoe didn't bother to glance up at it as she passed. She kept her gaze on the center tiles that stretched before her in a straight pale arrow, smoother and cleaner than everything else.

They led her to the fifth doorway on her right, the painted black-and-gray door, closed as she had left it. As all of them here were.

The hinges did not squeak. She had ensured that after her first night.

The apartment she'd chosen was cold, almost colder than the open night beyond its windows. She kept the heavy velvet curtains pulled shut across them, not just to keep in whatever heat she herself managed to generate—obviously she couldn't light a fire, even if the chimney would draw—but also to conceal the set of candles and the oil lamp tucked away in the bedchamber, her sole means of light.

The curtains had faded from maroon to reddish pink and reeked of old smoke, and there were moth holes cratering the trim, but they functioned well enough. On her second night here she'd left a candle burning and then slipped outside, and she hadn't been able to detect even a tiny glow from the gardens below.

Although the majority of the palace had been divested of its finery, this suite was still furnished, perhaps because it was not so elegant as some of the rest—or perhaps because the massive antique gilt bed squatting in the bedchamber and cracked walnut mirror across from it were too cumbersome to move. Even she had a hard time shifting the mirror to where she wanted it, and that was saying something.

The bed, however, dominated the room. It was heavily carved into a profusion of scrolls and garlands and swirling vines; the canopy supported a silk tapestry cover and drapes—also with moth

43

holes—featuring woven roses still so purple and fat and lavishly petaled they seemed ready to drip from the folds. The gilt was curling away from the wood around most of the edging; she crossed to one of the posts and pressed a thumbnail beneath a loosened flake, lifting it free.

The gold warmed her nail like a tiny, tiny sliver of a summer day, sending heat down into the bones of her hand. Zoe let out a sigh and the flake floated away, zigzagging down to the bare maple floor.

There had been no bedding left, but that was easily remedied. Chests of linens and coverlets were scattered throughout the occupied apartments at the far other end of the palace; she reckoned no one would miss a sheet here, a blanket there. The plain covers looked oddly out of place against the succulent colors of the rest of the suite, but they were comfortable, and that was all that mattered to her. She sank to the edge of the mattress and studied the mirror from the corner of her eye.

It had been removed from its hooks to lie propped against the crimson-papered wall, an angled tilt that caught the ceiling in its reflection, the nearest window with its curtains, three-quarters of the bed, and her. The crack had splintered the enormous square of glass into two nearly equal halves: on one side, shadow Zoe and the shadow chamber, a pale figure of a woman against a ruddy gloom, the faint foxing of spots near her shoulder trailing down in a curve to the frame.

In the other half, the room—bed and curtains and woman and all—had vanished.

The other half showed her the deep blue darkness. The cloak, and the ghosts within it, their edges smoking and writhing. Waiting. None of them crossed over to the normal side of the mirror; it was as if that shining, uneven crack was a mighty river they could not breach. The blue darkness dissolved upon its edge.

This Gift, whatever it was, was growing stronger. She didn't know why she saw ghosts in glass now, the cloak manifest. She didn't know why it was becoming easier and easier to draw the blue void of it near to her, to hear the whisperings from inside it. To use it to capture the thoughts of the living.

Perhaps it was Paris, or her, or both. Perhaps she was doomed never to dwell in true silence again.

Her eyes cut away. She didn't want to see it now, any of it. She didn't want to feel the lost souls caught in that blue. She'd been out all day, and now all she wanted was to sleep. If she'd had an extra blanket, even another sheet, she would have tossed it over the glass, but she needed what she had.

Tomorrow, then. Tomorrow she'd borrow another blanket.

Zoe stood and walked to the closet where she'd hidden her valise, and began to undress.

From the mirror lifted the voices, pleading, soft and indistinct. She bowed her head to watch her hands, frowning, focused on loosening her bodice. Without turning around, she murmured, "Not now. I'll try again tomorrow."

But she knew they wouldn't really quiet. They seldom did.

Once properly in her nightgown she bent down, scooped out a handful of jewelry from the valise, and went back to the bed.

She sat again upon its edge and began, piece by piece, to adorn herself for the night.

The choker of diamonds and topaz, strands of stones three bands wide.

The earrings of gold and coral. A bracelet of emeralds, and one purely of diamonds. Three bangles of gold.

A ring for every finger, gold, gold, gold. Even a pair of anklets, opals that sparked green and blue and pink from their milky depths.

When it was done, she blew out the candle. She inched down

between the chilly sheets and closed her eyes again, this time letting the metal slowly warm her entire being, her mind drifting with the songs of the stones, drowning Paris, drowning her, until at last she could sleep.

But the ghosts in the glass never ceased watching. They glided back and forth and back, drawn by the living radiance of the dragon who was their only voice in the Other world, their only eyes and hands and means of vengeance.

She slept with her back to them all night, as if she knew.

CHAPTER THREE

Legends of the Others often preach of how we hoard and guard our trove. They paint us as snarling fiends crouched over chests of stolen jewels, coins of gold and copper and silver piled recklessly about, plundered from terrified innocents. They say we like to dwell in caves—freezing damp caves, can you believe it?—and ruthlessly devour any humans who dare to venture near.

Yes, I know. That part might be somewhat true.

None of them realize the whole truth, though. Of course, we *do* guard what's ours. But we don't need to *steal* gems and gold. Not usually. We're given the Gift of their music, all the harmonies and chants and descants that soar to the stars, far more dulcet than any human composition. And in return, we give them the Gift of our protection. Our veneration. There's no stealing. If we unearthed all the diamonds and rubies and amethysts and emeralds—all the rocks and ore and crystals and boulders that constantly clamor for our attention—there would be little left to shore up the mountains of the world, would there?

So we accept only the very finest of these things for ourselves, to adorn our bodies and our homes, to keep close to our hearts.

And if the humans occasionally happen to beat us to the finest… well, I suppose nature should have given *them* fangs and talons to defend it.

One certain way to tell a *drákon* from an Other is the manner in which they wear their jewelry.

No matter how many gemstones embellish them, humans merely bear their weight.

A dragon may wear a solitary ruby tear, and still we sparkle with its might.

No doubt you've noticed how good you feel when you touch certain minerals and stones, the hum of their voices thrilling up your spine, surrounding your senses. Diamonds, so hard and cold and glittering, are the ones most like us, I think. Perhaps that's why we use them most often in our baubles; why they comprise the majority of the ancient treasure guarded by our tribe. Some of our diamonds are as old as our history itself. They have names and stories. They have heartbeats.

Think back. Can you remember a time, ever in your life, when you did not wear even a single diamond pendant around your neck? The Alpha ensures that every *drákon* child receives at least this one small gift at birth, the first of many to come.

We were clever to have settled in a place that offers us so much earthly wealth. The silver mines of Darkfrith are vast and deep, and keep us all well adorned. And really, who deserves those metals more than we? Who appreciates the cut of a sapphire, the clarity of an emerald, better than the dragon for whom they sing?

Now imagine being without your lovely gems. Imagine having to endure the loss of warm gold and cooling silver, of fiery copper too. Imagine all you have is darkness, and iron around your wrists.

And the shards of a once-mighty diamond that sing and sing and sing in your head, pushing out all your better thoughts, keeping you dull and alive and only very distantly wishing you were dead.

The diamond was once named *Draumr*. And the dragon trapped in its ruined world was named Rhys Langford.

I wish I could tell you only joyful stories of our history. I wish I could assure you that the many Gifts Nature has blessed upon you will be your salvation against all comers. Yes, we are More than the beings surrounding us. We are Better, and what graces we exhibit today we have earned, I promise you. Our sinuous beauty. Our native intelligence. Our ability to steal the shadows for a hunt.

But we are not invincible. And to prove it, Nature took the very same stars and lava and sky that melded and made us, and from them forged the most exquisite and sinister stone ever to come to be: *Draumr*.

Nature is the veriest Bitch sometimes.

Once *Draumr* belonged to a dragon-princess of the Carpathians, many centuries past. To be clear, it belonged to her Zaharen family, and then was stolen, and then, at the cost of her life, she stole it back. *Draumr* sparkled like a drop of arctic blue sky, frigid cold and absolutely flawless, nearly too wonderful to behold. Its name means *dreaming diamond*; and here's what more you do not know about it: It was the sole stone carved from this Earth that had the power to enslave us. Yes, enslave us. Anyone who held it could command us. Any low, simple human scum.

You may well imagine what disasters befell us *then*.

Why was it never destroyed while the Zaharen *drákon* still

possessed it, before it was ripped from our castle by human hands? There's no certain answer for us today. Perhaps our ancestors were more trusting than we, thinking no Other would dare to even attempt to take it. Perhaps they were overly confident, or overly foolish. I don't know. But it was taken, more than once, found again by us, and finally shattered into evil little pieces.

You'd think that would break its power, would you not?

You'd be wrong.

Even those tiny pieces, scattered and floating like thin blue needles through the warp and woof of the universe, have the power to harm us still.

Poor pretty Rhys. He found that out too well.

CHAPTER FOUR

The body of the creature was kept in the cellar. She was unhappy about that, because the cellar had been in full use before the thing had been brought here, and like any good cook, she regretted its loss. Unlike many other cellars, this one was pleasantly large and well designed, and tiled all the way around in limestone. A wine rack had been built along one wall, and on the opposite, convenient shelving for all the many cheeses and jellies and kitchen herbs she enjoyed. True, the darkest corner was constantly damp and had a patch of blackish mold, but she'd devoted two barrels of mushrooms growing in sand to it and they'd been doing very well, in fact. Everything had to be removed to the upper level once the creature came, and now the mushrooms had shriveled, and cheeses were cracking, and the herbs were beginning to taste more like grease than rosemary and fennel and dill.

But at least she didn't have to go down there any longer. She'd seen the body once, and that was enough.

It was kept in manacles that were oddly glinting, as if they'd been sprinkled with tiny blue stars. There was a blanket tossed over most of it, hiding the face, but just one glimpse of those gold-clawed, twisted hands frozen in the air had given her a nervous stomach for a week.

She let the others manage it. She had other matters to attend to.

He had been born into a world of glorious secrets: in a bed-chamber of ivory and gilt, in a mansion of glass and stone, to a sire and dam of unspeakable beauty and ferocious power, held tight behind their polished human masks. He was not born first or even second; Rhys was the third of five children, firmly in the middle, all of them different yet all the same. Blessed to be a lord, blessed to be *drákon,* he had celebrated his good fortune at full tilt for as long as he could recall. There had been no real reason not to. Unlike his father, he would never assume the honor of be-coming Alpha to the tribe. Rhys had an older brother to take care of that. Let the two of them put their golden heads together to wrestle the ancient *drákon* rules and traditions into the modern day. Let his mother and three sisters fuss over their human façade, planning balls and soirées and high teas like the fiercest of war generals.

Rhys's world was slightly . . . more feral than all that.

He was comely, because all the tribe were. He was aware of that, even as a boy. He'd been granted his father's ice-green eyes but his mother's deep chestnut hair, a decided advantage with the females in a clan of creatures that tended to be redheaded or blond. It didn't hurt also that he possessed a certain piratical nature—his eldest sis-ter had called him that once when he was eleven and she thirteen, *piratical,* to his enormous and open delight—that seemed to soften even the hardest of feminine hearts.

Most of them, anyway.

Despite his face and title, he'd found it rather easy to slip away from the undue notice of his parents and nannies and tutors. In fact, it became one of his more valuable skills, the ability to fade into backgrounds, to listen without speaking, to see what he wouldn't otherwise if he didn't stick to the shadows. He supposed it might have been a natural talent; his mother, after all, had once been one of the most notorious thieves London had ever known. Rue Langford alone would find him lurking around corners and merely smile.

So he grew to be a child of extreme stealth and cunning, known for his rakish grin and wild tousled looks and not at all for stealing out alone at night to go swimming in the lake, or to prowl the woods, or snatch an extra pastry from the kitchen pantries, just because he could.

And then came the Turn.

God, yes. What a catastrophe.

As he was the son of the two strongest members of the tribe, no one had any doubts about his ability to survive this particular rite of passage. Even he had assumed it would happen just as it should, perhaps when he was fourteen or fifteen, as it had with Kimber, his brother.

But the Gift hadn't come to him at fourteen. It had come to him two days after his twelfth birthday, by thin gray starlight, when he was by himself in the most ghastly place of all the shire. The rough earth of outlaws, the Field of Bones.

He'd had no business going there. Had he been caught, his parents and the Council would have reacted far more strongly than the usual confinement to rooms with bread and water. There would have been a lashing. There would have been blood, at the least.

The Field—bound from the waterfall past Blackstone Fell, to the half circle of oak and rowan woods to the west, to the bog marsh that fed small muddy streams into the River Fier—all of it was labeled *profanus*. Profane. To cross those boundaries without permission was considered one of the most grave offenses possible. And the Council of Darkfrith enjoyed a very long list of possible offenses.

Certainly there are few swifter ways to capture the interest of a pubescent boy than to tell him something is forbidden to him. For years Rhys had cherished the notion of the Field with the same awestruck, morbid wonder as all the rest of his friends. The elders would whisper tales of the *drákon* outcasts buried there, their bones scorched and scattered, no markers, no memories of them beyond what passed from lips to lips over generations. The dead strewn there no longer even had names; the remains of their lives and passions and crimes were now little more than terrible, uneven lumps beneath wild grasses. Only a very few of the living had ever even seen those lumps, and then only for the most dire of reasons.

A tribe member went there to execute, or he went there to be executed. A handful of witnesses were allowed for the burning. That was all.

Rhys had slipped past that particular law just once, and never again. Once was enough.

He'd gone on a moonless night, of course, because there would be legions of dragons overhead, no matter the light or the weather. At nightfall, the tribe's true nature reigned. His kind always flew if they could.

So it had been dark. And it had been easy. His heart had kept up a hard, sick hammer in his chest, but he had managed to breathe through it, finding his way out of the manor house, following all the secret paths he knew, easing from cover to cover. He had a story prepared in the event he was discovered: He was out because

Thomas Hawkins from the village had told him there was a pair of red foxes that ventured into the Fell deep at night, and Rhys had never before seen a live fox. It had the virtue of being true, and he thought he'd be able to say it with credible sincerity—but he hadn't been discovered. So he'd saved the foxes for another time.

The Field appeared just as he had imagined it, a murky darkness between the trees, the path that led to it faint with sparse use. It seemed more a large open hollow than a field; the path peaked upon a hill above it and then curved downward, so that when he reached the end of the woods the shadowy depression gave the illusion of rising inexorably to meet him.

He saw no lumps. Not at first. He stood beneath the boughs of an oak and stared for a while as he chewed at his thumbnail, abruptly reluctant to take the step that would free him from the forest and lead him down into the long grasses.

Overhead were clouds and stars and his kin very distant, stealthy as reapers, gaunt streamers with wings that hissed and cut into the night. He glanced up once but no one was in sight; Rhys listened to them instead, far more preoccupied with detecting any sort of worrisome stirring below.

Yet the hollow awaited him without motion. Even the mists that had begun to lift and clump with the damp were at rest down there, dull, slaty strips of fog unrolled between the weeds.

Like skeleton fingers. Like cloudy poison.

Rhys spat out a sliver of nail, dropping his hand. He had come all this way. There was no reason not to finish the job. He'd be the only one he knew who'd ever done it. It would gain him the unmitigated envy of his brother and no doubt a buss or two from one of the more daring village girls, and there was no reason at all not to move his feet and go forward, except that he realized he'd begun to respire rather too quickly, and he was feeling light-headed, yes, definitely light-headed, and the sound of his lungs laboring for air had become much, much too loud in the leering, eager, poisonous silence—

He was no longer beneath the oak. He was on his knees on the path falling downward to the Field, scrabbling to stop himself, his hands clawing at the dirt, mist in his eyes—

The dirt broke his hands apart. He shattered, his hands and arms and chest and body—shattered into smoke, so quickly, so horrifically, he didn't even have time to squeak with shock.

He was aware of his clothing falling away. Shirt, breeches, the tie in his hair. He was aware that he no longer felt the path, or gravity, or his heart in his chest.

All he felt was pain.

As a toddler he'd once stuck his fist into a scalding pot of tea when no one could quite stop him in time, and it had been like this: an instant of nothing but surprise, then searing, shrieking agony that bubbled his skin and the world went red and raw and weeping, and there was nothing he could *do* about it—he was still breaking apart, thinner and thinner—

The stars were spinning above him, below him. The Field of Bones was a yawning dark mouth, ready to eat him, ready to swallow. A fearsome cold lightness was beginning to transmute the red-fire pain but somehow it actually felt worse, because Rhys knew it was the last of himself, dissolving.

He was the same color as the mist. He was as chill and wan as the mist...less substantial. Gossamer. The indigo sky reached down and drew him into threads.

No, he thought, from some deep, invisible place that was no longer inside him but around him, through him, lancing and connecting the very stars.

No.

He would not die like this. He would not be remembered for this, death in a field, profane, unforgiven.

He focused on the ground. He made himself *pull* with all his might, with every atom of will he could muster, *pull, pull,* until the cold began to recede into a heavier weight, and he felt the smoke that used to be hands and feet and legs and head gain density, change shape—and with one final mighty heaving effort he found himself nearly back to earth.

He reached for it with both hands. He stretched for it, pinwheeling, and finally connected at a full run.

Clots of dirt spewed around him. Moss and grass kicked up, great ropy furrows ripped through the green, because he was no longer Lord Rhys Langford, a brown-haired boy unseen and unheard.

He was Rhys the full-blooded *drákon,* and his talons were sharp and long, and his wings unfolded in bright canopies against his back, slowing his fall, then tumbling him into a roll until his head struck a rock that blanked everything into white.

That was how he came to be a dragon the first time. That was his Turn. And when he'd come groggily awake, naked in that field, it was to spend the rest of the night putting human hands upon black and rotting bones, digging and digging and spitting the taste of mold from his mouth until his tongue swelled to dry leather and his lips chapped.

It had taken hours to rebury the dead.

So there had been no kisses from fair maidens. No envy from his brother. He'd never told a soul about going to the Field; he did not dare. When his mother had inquired, he said he'd gotten the gash on his head by leaping from the dock into Fire Lake, which everyone believed. Or pretended to.

He'd always been the one who pushed his limits as far as he could; no one ever seemed to question that.

Still, he'd sobered a bit after that night. Perhaps it was the notion of rubbing so closely against a vast Nothing. Perhaps it was the secret wonder at his own inner will, the unexpected ability to scrape his hide back together when so many others—boys he knew, boys he named friends—had not.

Perhaps it was just plain fear. Twelve was damned young to be slapped in the face with the prospect of sudden annihilation. Whatever it was, from that night on Rhys found himself tempered. Not in a bad way. After all, tempered iron was strong steel, and the dragon in him appreciated the power of steel.

He began to see his life in the shire in a new light. He began to take better note of all the rules, all the regulations, not so he could trick his way around them but so that he could understand the forces that had shaped his history, his tribe. He began to appreciate the beauty and natural order surrounding him, his family, their society, the sprawling village and shady cobblestone lanes and the sparkling manor house itself. Trees and grass-swept knolls, farms and orchards and the tribe's single flock of sheep moving from hill to hill with the seasons, bunched like cotton puffs along the dales.

It was, without question, a golden world. And by and large, Rhys Langford was determined to do his part to keep it that way.

He kept only a single secret still. Save for one pretty girl he was trying to impress, his first true love, he kept the secret of his Turn—because being tempered didn't mean there weren't nights when the need to fly rolled through him in waves of sharp, throbbing desire, and he was still young enough to laugh at the thought of soaring sly and out of bounds. The girl never told, and he never told; Rhys kept that secret until he was fifteen, and it became too cumbersome a thing to carry any longer.

A golden life, aye. A charmed life.

He tried to be grateful for every minute of it.

It was a lovely condition, to be rich and lucky both. He enjoyed the luxuries of his world; he enjoyed the savage splendor of his animal self, of becoming one with the heavens. And he enjoyed the more human elements too: fine food and wine, art and conversation, boxing and fencing. Ladies.

Music.

Oh, the music. Somehow, lately, he'd learned to appreciate all the music around him so much more than he ever had. Not just the celestial melodies of the moon and sun and stars, those electric vibrations that reflected off dragon scales, that sent ripples of harmony back through the skies. Nor just the silent, delicate songs of all the jewels and stones and metals that blessed the earth. Even human music held a sudden new appeal.

Handel, Haydn, Mozart. Italian opera, romantic ballads, street girls crooning verses about lovers across flowing rivers . . . it was all so . . . engrossing.

Why, the concert he was at right now, for instance, was certainly one of the finest he'd ever experienced. He never used to enjoy the symphony so much, but frankly, the entire affair was sublime. It was almost ridiculously better than any of his previous *concerto* experiences.

The performance chamber was baroque, heavily elaborate plaster friezes done up in shades of mauve and rose and rich buttery cream. He sat not in the middle of the audience but just off to the left, in a satinwood chair far more comfortable than what he remembered. Because Rhys knew this place, knew it right down to the oiled planks of the dais the orchestra played upon. He was in the Von Zonnenburg assembly hall in Soho Square. In London. He'd been here countless times—well, perhaps not countless. A dozen times. It was a venue that suited very well his parents' notion of proper aristocratic entertainment. The Marquess and Marchioness of Langford played their human roles with expert skill, and they'd insisted that each of their children learn to do the same.

Rhys had dozed off on all the other occasions he'd come. He was fairly certain of that.

But now—

Every candle in the six dangling crystal chandeliers was lit. There were at least two hundred of them, two hundred tiny sweet flames magnified, their light chopped into prisms that cast chips of color all across the chamber. They managed a luminance he'd never discerned before, perfect white candles dripping perfect little tears into their crystal cups. Their brass polished chains shimmered like molten gold with the rising heat.

The candlelight lent a soft-shadowed clarity to the musicians before him. He admired their satin jackets and old-fashioned rolled wigs, their hands moving over bows and valves and strings in effortless agreement. Rhys didn't know the piece they were performing, but it illumed his surroundings as much as the chandeliers did. It was light and loud and complex and simple and . . . blissful. He could lounge in the satinwood chair all night, hearing it.

It wasn't particularly bothersome that he seemed to be the only member of the audience in attendance. He thought that perhaps this might be a final rehearsal, something of that sort. He was, after all, a lord; rules were bent all the time for the *ton*. And it wasn't as if he didn't appreciate the artistry, the splendor, of their work.

He leaned back, a half smile on his lips, tapping his fingers against the arm of his chair. The music thrilled on and on, and he thought he'd never been so content in his life.

Just then a movement to his right caught his eye. Rhys glanced over. A woman was taking her seat three chairs down, skirts and petticoats rustling.

Her attention was fixed upon the musicians, just as his had been. She was gentry at least, dressed in a frock of rose damask and cream ruffles to match the hall, a wrap of stiff white gauze framing her shoulders. Light pooled around her; her ringleted hair was very pale, her powdered skin was very pale; compared to the rest of the chamber she was alabaster and shimmer, actually a little too bright to behold. His eyes began to tear.

She opened her fan; he was dazzled by the flash of pink rubies on lace. She lifted it to her face and turned her head, meeting his gaze from beneath kohled lashes.

He thought she might be beautiful. It was damned hard to tell, what with all the candlelight, but of course she was beautiful. On this stupendous night, in this soaringly exquisite place, how could she be anything but?

She murmured his name. He sat up straighter and offered her a civil nod. She was young, and she was fair, and if she knew him, the last thing he'd want to do was ignore her, because who knew what the night would bring after the music ended—

Her fan lowered. She studied him with eyes of velvety black.

"It's not real," she whispered. "You do know that. It's not real. None of it."

His mouth opened. He wanted to speak and could not; no sound emerged. His hands gripped the chair but that was all he could do. He couldn't move, he couldn't breathe. For one long, horrible moment the entire world went dark. The music played on, but it was different now, it was sly and terrible and crept in tendrils through him, eating away at him like a cancer.

The woman stood. She turned to face him; the wrap slipped down her arms.

"Is this the best of you, then?" she asked in her cultured voice, cool and sensual, a blade of light surrounded by that darkness. "Is this the best I can expect of you? You lazy bastard. I'm not going to risk my neck helping you if you don't even try."

Lazy bastard. Lazy bastard—

He knew her. Her realized it just then. Her name escaped him—he'd loved her once, and he knew her—

Rhys did not wake up. He could not evade those tendrils even now, not enough. He still couldn't really move. He couldn't see, or Turn.

But he did manage a single, heaving breath. And it didn't taste like Soho, or London, or anything civilized. It tasted like cold, wormy dirt. It tasted like death.

And *that*, Rhys realized, was real.

His teeth were clenched. His jaw locked. His back and legs and entire body were a frozen spasm of rigid agony, and the symphony never ceased.

He tried to shut it out. He reached for the first clear image that flashed behind his lids—light; the bright and unforgiving face of—

"Zoe."

She jolted awake in the night, instantly, awfully, her every sense flooded with dread, her skin slick with cold sweat. She did not gasp or twitch; she didn't breathe at all. She lay in the bed with her eyes wide open and knew that whoever had crept into the suite with her would see only a mattress and gems and strangely rumpled sheets.

The wash of her Gift hummed across her body, disguising her, an instinctive defense. The power of it chilled her blood even as the man's voice she'd heard echoed back into nothing, a memory. A bad dream.

But she lay there a very long time anyway, as motionless as she could be. She listened to the sounds of the city pushing over the treetops of the park, past her walls: dogs barking. Horses sighing, plodding hooves, iron-wheeled carts being pulled over cobblestones. Men and women laughing, even at this hour, and tavern music, and the very clouds above her dissolving, particle by particle, drop by drop, with the slow building heat of the coming morning. And no one spoke her name again.

She'd dreamt it. That was all.

God, what a fright. It hadn't felt at all like a dream; when she'd opened her eyes she would have sworn there was a man standing over her, shadowed and close. But there wasn't. There was no human smell anywhere nearby.

Slowly she sat up in the bed, rubbing her hands over her face, the rings on her fingers warm and rigid against her cheeks. With her head bowed she sucked in a lungful of air, released it, and watched as the locks of her hair became once again visible, phantom-pale strands shrouding her face and shoulders.

Without meaning to, she glanced at the mirror. It was exactly where she had left it, propped against the wall. The crack down the middle became a sharp silvery thunderbolt in the dark, frozen forever against the blue.

The ghosts shifted and sighed against it. They brightened and faded, and tried so hard to speak.

Zoe slipped from the bed. She padded to the glass, her feet chilled against the floor, and knelt before its wide, clear expanse, the bangles at her wrists chiming softly as she moved.

She touched it lightly. It was cold, very cold, beneath her fingertips.

"Hayden?"

No response. In the silence of the chamber, in this dark small hour, even the beings that haunted her on the other side seemed to have grown weak.

"Hayden, are you there? Was it you?"

Something did stir then. Something did change, a new shape forming against the endless blue. It looked like the outline of a man...perhaps a man, shaded and haloed with smoke...and then nothing: The smoke and man curled up and away.

She leaned forward, staring harder, but the light was too murky, and whatever she'd seen did not appear again.

Zoe leaned back on her heels, the anklets stretched tight against her skin, then gave it up and sank all the way to the floor.

She thought of her bed back in the cottage at home, the plush feather mattress. Of the nightingales that would rouse at dusk, serenading her as she'd sit and dream by the parlor window. The silver-faced clock gently ticking upon the mantel, a wedding gift to her great-grandparents. The Wedgwood creamware on the shelves in the kitchen, the handsome rosewood chairs and table, the silk azure curtains she'd help sew herself as a child.

The dense eastern woods. The soft summer nights.

She'd imagined a hundred different lives in that cottage. She'd imagined being married in the vine-covered gazebo in back, as Cerise had done, and cutting greens for her husband's meals from her garden. She'd imagined her own children growing up there, admiring the clock, pouring the cream, stroking the curtains as they gazed at the wild woods just beyond reach. Just as she had done.

Hayden or something else, the shade in the mirror did not reappear, no matter how firmly she pressed her fingers to the glass. So Zoe went back to bed.

CHAPTER FIVE

The most prized possession of Zoe Lane's youth had not been a doll, or a blanket, or a carved toy pony, all the things her sister and friends had cherished to the point of battered oblivion. Even as a girl, Zoe privately thought that dolls were a silly waste of time, and blankets were meant for babies. Toy ponies were fine enough, but since she'd likely never own a real one, idolizing a creature that would only bolt at the sight of her seemed, well, stupid.

No. While Cerise and all the other girls would gather and giggle over their pretend games, playing house-on-the-hill, picking boys for pretend husbands, Zoe was usually alone in her room or the lush cool forest, nestled in a bed of crushed buttercups or forget-me-nots. Studying the Book.

Her Book.

She'd found it at Uncle Anton's house, dusty in his library, its spine an intriguing gleam of Gothic, silvery lettering. Young Zoe liked books and always had, their scent of ink and fine paper, the crack of their bindings, rough-edged pages. Words and words and words that sometimes made sense and sometimes did not, but that always seem to beckon to her with the answers to questions she'd never even thought to ask.

This particular book was thick and heavy and had very few words. It was mostly pictures. Engravings.

Of dragons.

They were extremely frightening. Certainly Uncle Anton would never have given it to her had he bothered to look through it; *Mr. Merick's Compleat Compendium of Dragones, Merfolk, and Other Fiendish Creatures* was stuffed chock-a-block with violence and gore, the likes of which had never before darkened the genteel doors of Myers Cottage. Until Zoe had sneaked it in under her pinafore.

By candlelight, by the dappled light of the woods, she'd examined the pictures and memorized their gruesome tales. None of the dragons looked like anyone she knew. There was no beauty to them, no lithe, ribbony elegance. They were fat-bellied and repugnant. They had fangs that dripped venom, and bulging snake eyes, and forked tongues. They terrorized villages and kidnapped virgins, and breathed fire across crops and frantic peasants waving pitchforks.

And none of them, not one, were heroes.

None of them had wives or little children waiting for them at home. None of them took tea with crumpets, or harvested wheat by the autumn moon, or played chess, or danced a jig. Zoe's own father had died a mere year after she was born, so she had no memories of his doing any of those things. But she knew how other *drákon* fathers behaved. As far as she could tell, there wasn't a stolen virgin anywhere to be found in Darkfrith.

Yet the dragons in the book were exactly how Mr. Merick's title depicted them: fiendish.

That was seven-year-old Zoe's first uncensored introduction to the human world, which was clearly a place filled with farmers bearing sharp tools who desired nothing more than to stab her straight through the heart.

For the first few weeks after discovering the Book she slept with a lamp burning all night by her bed, until Cerise had tattled and Mother made her stop.

Slowly, over time, she came to comprehend the nature of the stories, the mortal fear behind them. The Others could not or would not accept the notion of a dragon as a hero and so dragons were cast strictly as villains instead. Why else would a human hunt a dragon? The *drákon* of Darkfrith never killed without good cause, never scorched anyone else's crops, never bullied other villages. The careful surface of their lives was as placid and bucolic as a fine oil painting. No one wished for outside attention.

It had taken her years to notice what had been apparent all her life: that despite all that—or perhaps because of it—beyond the most necessary of trading and commerce, Darkfrith remained isolated from the human realm. Even the post proved irregular at best. It was as if at some undefined point in the past, the entire shire had been encased in a vast, transparent bubble that repelled all but the most persistent of visitors.

Getting in was difficult. Leaving, as it had turned out, had been as simple as taking a stroll down a moonlit lane.

It seemed nearly impossible here, beneath the china-blue autumn sky of France, with the sun warm on her shoulders and a cup of steaming *café au lait* in her hand, that any of the pampered, chattering aristocrats seated with her on the coffeehouse patio would harbor any thoughts of pitchforks and dragon hearts.

And yet . . . someone was. Someone. She knew it.

Zoe kept her nose buried in the book she'd purchased a few days ago, feigning to read. She was prim and proper-looking enough, she thought, to blend in here: Her gown was apple-green velvet, her hat was fashionably straw, and the book was small enough to be discreet.

It was entitled, in French, *A Young Person's Useful Guide to Social Modesty & Moral Certitude.* It was not nearly as interesting as the conversations around her.

The unspoken ones, of course.

She could not actually read thoughts, not like the sentences printed upon the pages before her. She could more sense them. She could choose the direction of the deep blue cloak and fling it there and see what it dragged back to her. Sometimes there were images, sometimes entire discussions. Sometimes there were only emotions, or deep quick memories that made no sense to her. But nearly every time now she flung the cloak, some manner of information came back. She was getting better and better at it.

One week ago she'd been walking by this very café near the Palais Royal when she'd first felt it: a slow-boiling malice, something thicker and heavier than the usual petty grievances she was used to brushing up against. It had stopped her in her tracks, literally—much to the annoyance of the water-carrier walking behind her—freezing her in place with a single whispery phrase that had snaked out from the mess of tables and coffee-scented confusion and transformed into a wall right in front of her:

—*over two hundred* sanf inimicus, *yes, soon enough to raze the entire*—

Her feet, her heart, her blood—all instant ice.

The *sanf* were the peasants with pitchforks made real, an ancient order whose sole purpose was to destroy her kind. The ones who, according to the Zaharen *drákon* in Transylvania, had found and killed the Darkfrith emissaries.

Hayden. Golden-haired, gentian-eyed Hayden, who smiled at her jokes and ate her cooking without complaint, no matter how abysmal it was.

She'd managed to keep walking, albeit much more slowly, shaking the water from her skirts. She'd kept her head bowed and her eyes to the paving stones and tried and tried to get the cloak to work for her again, to tell her who had conjured those words.

But she'd gotten nothing more. The fashionable galleries and restaurants around the Palais were packed with Others, everyone laughing and talking and eating and belching and getting roundly drunk. Any one of them could have been an enemy.

It didn't even occur to her until she was in bed that night that the sentence she'd caught had been in English.

She'd come back every morning since. She'd altered her hair, her frocks, her hats. She'd sipped coffee and tea and *bavaroise* all the day until her fingers trembled and her stomach rebelled, and even so she'd not slammed into that wall of thought again, not in any language. But it had been her best lead so far in all her wanderings through the city. It was her first solid link to the fate of her fiancé, and she wasn't going to give it up yet.

The *café au lait* was still fresh enough to smell enticing. A curled brown leaf from the apple tree arching above had fallen and landed at the edge of the saucer, precisely balanced. Zoe brushed it aside, watched it flutter down to the granite floor.

Hayden. Tell me where to look.

On a fine afternoon such as this the patio tables were popular; it was common custom for the lords and ladies to share. The pair of mink-bedecked matrons at her own were drinking their coffee lukewarm and sugared and discussing—in French—a play they'd heard about but hadn't yet seen. A dandy with brilliant orange heels and a rapier so long it jutted back beneath the table had claimed the final chair and turned it around so that he could join the circle of his friends nearby, agonizing loudly—also in French—over his losses at a horse race. All five of them were drinking absinthe.

Zoe set down her book. She brought the rim of her cup to her lips and let her gaze drift to the window just to her right. Behind it were slender dull flames from the wall sconces of the coffeehouse, waiters cutting back and forth, patrons seated at the inside tables. The interior was dim and the day was bright; it was far easier to see the reflections of the people outside with her, bright colors from sunlit parasols and coats, everyone white-haired, ruby-mouthed. She found her own eyes there in the glass, the arch of her brows, the ribbon of her hat and the curve of her chin—and then noticed something else, something new.

A shadow man, just over her shoulder.

She looked back, very quickly, at the empty space behind her, and then at the window again. The man continued to face her, his features dark and blurred, his posture radiating intent.

The coffee curdled in her throat.

The matrons still ignored her; the dandies were going on about the chances of a gelding against a mare; the shadow in the window took a step closer, close enough for Zoe to make out the faint, evil halo of smoke curling around him like steam rising from a hot roof.

She watched, her heart pounding, the cup a forgotten weight in her fingers, as his hand lifted, hovered ominously above her shoulder. And then—God help her, an actual chill rippled over her flesh as his dark shadow fingers glided slowly down the reflection of her arm—humid, cold, the shadows seeping down to stain her bones.

A voice spoke in her ear.

"Ma'moiselle."

Zoe snapped forward in her chair, sloshing the coffee over her hand. The two matrons made little birdlike noises of surprise, but the waiter who had approached only set down his carafe of fresh brew and offered his linen towel instead, apologizing repeatedly, mopping at her skin. The liquid had not been hot enough to burn—but she felt the tingling begin anyway, spreading up from her knuckles to her forearm.

She stood at once. She grabbed her book and shawl and nodded at the waiter, who was still apologizing, and sidestepped out of the patio into the rush of the street.

If she could get to somewhere private, somewhere where no one would see, she'd be all right. She could control it, *damn* it, she'd been able to control it for *months* now—

She couldn't help the last wild glance at the window as she rushed past, but this time Zoe saw only herself.

Quite a few of the coffeehouse patrons looked up as the young woman passed, and kept looking if they happened to catch a glimpse of her face. She'd had an entire group of admiring gentlemen quietly betting on who would introduce himself to her first not three tables distant, and the steady, silent attention of a blue-eyed, elderly woman seated inside... but it was a newspaper boy named Yves on the corner who saw the demoiselle duck into the alleyway, almost running, and who thought to follow.

When he peered past the bricks he saw her standing forlorn at the end of the way, piles of refuse and wooden pallets blocking her way out the other side. The lady was breathing heavily with her back to him, holding her hands before her face.

Just then someone called for a paper. He turned around and sold three copies before he knew it, and by the time he looked back for the lady, the alleyway was empty.

But—there was her gown, all tumbled in a heap by the refuse. And shoes. And a straw hat, and a shawl, and a real book bound in blue, just tossed on top.

71

He was able to sell it all for a tidy sum the next day to old Thérèse at the *Hôtel-Dieu* in Montpellier, except for the book, which he presented to his mother.

She thanked him very sweetly for it too.

She wasn't here.

Granted, he wasn't precisely sure where *here* was. Or even when. The one true certainty Rhys had was that although the symphony still echoed around him, he was no longer in the assembly hall in Soho. The chairs and musicians and sparkling chandeliers had all vanished. If he concentrated hard enough, he could dim the music, but it took a great deal of effort that usually ended up leaving him drained and weary.

And when he was weary, the music hall rushed back in full bloody glory. He was growing to loathe the combination of rose, mauve, and cream.

But he was getting better at fending it off. Right now, for in- stance, he stood by a road somewhere—a townish sort of road, nar- row and shadowed, one he'd never seen before. Definitely *not* Darkfrith. If this was his imagination, he supposed he deserved some credit for the details: the cobblestones were convincingly grimy; the gutters choked with garbage; the buildings were slaty and tall and streaked with damp; the people wore coats and shawls and hats and walked very quickly past him with their heads bowed or their faces turned away. A rat was picking through a mound of putrid something beneath a yellow-leafed shrub in a pot by an open door; apparently it was the only thing willing to see him, be- cause it kept throwing him beady, distrustful glances as it rum- maged. When Rhys took a step toward it, it turned and scuttled back through the darkness of the doorway.

He'd discovered rather quickly that he couldn't move much farther than that. A few steps in any direction, that was all. No matter how strongly he leaned or shoved, he was essentially fixed in this ruddy spot.

Everything was tinted blue and gray, as if it were raining, but it was not. There was nothing bright around him at all, not even the sun in the sky, which was how Rhys knew that Zoe Lane wasn't nearby.

Zoe alone shone with color.

He'd found her twice now. Just twice. And the second time had been so different from the first, he could not help but think that perhaps that first time, together with her in the hall, with the light, and the musicians—perhaps he had dreamt that one. Because the next time he'd seen her she looked different, for one thing. Not so polished, not so alabaster-perfect. She'd looked...almost human.

Which was ridiculous. Apart from the members of his family, she had to be the most absolute model example of the female *drákon* he'd ever known. She was stunning and always had been, blindingly so. She was intelligent and stubborn and completely un-afraid of convention. Had she inherited the ability to Turn into dragon, he could only imagine the terror she'd have stricken into the hearts of the men of the shire.

Not that she hadn't accomplished that anyway. He hadn't known a single boy their age who hadn't boasted of at least *trying* to kiss her. She was their unspoken grail, their adolescent hope and despair; remembering it now, he wondered if she'd even realized how many grubby fights she'd inspired. Young love was a wild and capricious creature, and Zoe, with her sparkling eyes and swift graceful step, seemed to have them all tethered to her lead without even trying.

But Rhys had loved her first. And he'd gotten that first kiss. He knew it, because she'd told him so herself when it happened. It had been in the forest, and they were all of thirteen, and he was going to prove to her that he could Turn, because at that time, there seemed to be nothing more important in the world than that she know his secret.

So he'd done it. And he'd stayed that way, an emerald dragon in the emerald woods, letting her circle him in their hidden clearing, leaves and sweet grasses ripe with summer beneath their feet. She'd held her skirts with one hand and allowed the other to trail along the ridges of his spine as she walked deliberately all the way around him.

Her touch had felt like fire. The most teeth-clenching, unbearable, and exciting fire. It ripped through him like nothing he'd ever felt before, not even his first Turn. Somehow he'd managed to follow her only with his eyes; the clearing was small and Rhys the dragon was not. She'd finished her circle and met his gaze and licked her lips and smiled, and his willpower went to ash.

He'd Turned back, very quickly, and kissed her hard on that smile before she could stop him or draw away.

She'd done neither, though. Zoe had only closed her eyes and puckered her lips in return, cool and composed against the fever in his blood.

In that instant he loved her so much he thought his heart was going to explode.

When he'd pulled away, panting, her smile grew wider and her long lashes lifted. He was drowning in exquisite dark depths.

"It was wetter than I thought it would be."

He heard himself say, faintly, "What?"

"My first kiss." Her head tipped as she gazed up at him; a lock of hair that had come free of her cap curled against peach-blossom skin. "Shorter too," she added pointedly.

So he'd kissed her again.

That was Zoe. Never shy about hitting him over the head with the truth.

He needed that now. Rhys ran his hands through his own hair, staring around him at the unknown road, baffled. He needed some truth, some clarity at least.

Hell, he must be dreaming the whole thing. Because the second time he'd seen her, she'd *also* been somewhere definitely not Darkfrith—and he could think of no reason why she wouldn't be safely cloistered in the shire. But she'd absolutely been in another place, somewhere cleaner and more stylish than his grimy little road, and the people surrounding her had been no one familiar at all.

Coffee cups, wineglasses, trees overhead. He'd heard voices but only as a slur of soft babbling sound; no words. No meaning. And again, no depth of color, but for her. Zoe, with her ivory hair and roses in her cheeks. And painted lips. And a dress this time of verdant green. A matching ribbon on her hat. She looked like springtime in the middle of drab winter, and even if he'd wanted to, he'd have been unable to tear his eyes from her.

She'd seen him too. No one else had—there had been no rodents on that crowded little patio—but Zoe had seen him. And he thought . . . he thought perhaps she'd even felt him. He'd almost felt *her*. Almost felt the warmth of her shoulder, the texture of her sleeve. Her eyes had grown round as saucers as she'd stared back at his reflection in the window glass.

But something moved behind them, and she'd started—and vanished. He'd been encased instantly in darkness again, the cursed music. After trying very, very hard, he'd appeared here, on this dismal little street. He could summon nothing else.

He couldn't Turn, either. Not to smoke. Not to dragon.

He was stuck.

Rhys sat down on the sidewalk across from the shrub and contemplated its faded yellow leaves. The dull gray human men and women brushed past him as if he were invisible. As if he were a ghost.

All those years of practicing his stealth, and now he could barely frighten a rat. The irony of it seemed almost humorous at first—and then most definitely not.

To hell with this.

Rhys narrowed his eyes at the shrub. His breathing began to slow: gently, watchfully, the whispered *whoosh whoosh whoosh* of blood through arteries and veins gradually overtaking the bright terrible music that soared at the edges of his being. If he could just relax enough, focus enough on what he knew of her—her shape and scent and colors, her eyes, her lips, that long-ago kiss burned into his soul—he was sure he could find her again. . . .

But he must be caught up in some sort of bizarrely tangled dream after all. Because when Rhys thought he finally caught a glimpse of pure, pretty color from the corner of his vision, he could have sworn it was Zoe running, quite astonishingly nude, down a busy city street. And only the horses and stray dogs seemed to notice.

CHAPTER SIX

Zoe sat on the edge of her bed wrapped in just a blanket, contemplating her feet. They were cut and cold and so dirty she was loath to put on stockings or shoes for fear of permanently mucking them up.

Paris was disgustingly filthy. Especially when one was forced to traverse it barefoot.

She had five gowns left. Three pairs of shoes. Four sets of stockings, garters, bibs. One corset and bustle.

Three of the five dresses she had purchased here. Her work as a seamstress would have meant a modest living nearly anywhere else, but Darkfrith—as ever—had evolved its own set of rules and social structures. She was no more and no less well-off than nearly anyone else in the tribe, but by the standards of the rest of the country, she was practically gentry. Certainly no one from the green hills of the shire ever starved. No one flaunted their wealth either. Barring the Alpha and his estate, the *drákon* of England lived their quiet, calm lives in the grip of secret luxury.

But only three gowns had fit into the valise. Besides, she'd needed room for her jewelry.

She lifted a foot, examined it critically. Were she able to Turn to smoke, all the dirt would fall away, the little nicks and blood would no longer matter—it was a fine Gift, smoke. She could fly with it, she could transform herself to haze and wind and survive even dire injury. Nothing would hold her back.

But no, *she* had gotten invisibility. Lovely. Especially when it manifested upon the slightest degree of stress. Or a splash of warm coffee.

Zoe lowered her foot again and wished gloomily for a bath. A real bath, with a full tub, and hot water, and lavender soap and—

The hairs on the back of her neck abruptly prickled.

She was no longer alone in the room.

Even as leapt up she was vanishing; the blanket slithered in a rumpled heap to the floor. She stood there half-crouched, frantically scanning the chamber.

Crimson walls, faded drapery. The bed and broken mirror, silent. No breathing or foreign scent. No heartbeat but her own.

Yet she was not alone.

It was close to teatime and the setting sun was trying hard to slice past the break in the curtains. A thin streak of topazed light fell against the far wall, cut downward to gloss the dark wooden floor. Slowly she backed to the gloom of the nearest corner; the grime on her feet was still quite visible.

Nothing else stirred save a tiny plume of motes, rushed to life by her ankles.

She sucked in air past her teeth and spoke, her voice coming harsh.

"Who's there?"

No one answered. Her heart thumped so loudly against her breastbone she wondered it couldn't be heard all the way across the palace.

"I *know* you're there," she snarled, "whatever you are. Show yourself and I won't—"

"Zoe?"

Despite herself she jumped a little, and the motes swirled anew.

"Hayden?" She eased a step forward, still seeing nothing. "Hayden?"

There came a new sound, softer than a sigh, low and long. She turned a circle.

"Where are you?"

"Ah..."

The mirror. Of course, the mirror. She snatched up the blanket and sank to her knees before it, but it was empty. It showed only the room, her face, the blue.

"I don't see you," she said, frustrated. Her fingers curled into a fist against the glass. "Hayden, where are you?"

"Here," he said, behind her.

But he wasn't. There was only the wall and window, and the band of sunlight that now arrowed hard across her chest.

"Here," he said again, quieter, right in front of her.

She reached out and felt the empty air, then the curtains. Velvet met her skin in a push of heat, a heavy resistance as she inched it aside with the back of her hand. She angled out of the light and the chamber warmed to flame with the sudden sun.

"Hay..." she began, but didn't finish because her throat dried up, because he was there after all. *There,* in the glass of the window, the shadow man of before, smoke and wicked darkness paled to nearly nothing against the brilliance of the sky.

"No," murmured the shadow, shimmering thin. "Sorry, love. It's Rhys. Rhys Langford."

He watched her lips part. Astonishment, he thought. Or perhaps indignation. With Zoe, it could be difficult to tell. But she'd been expecting her lover, clearly.

Too damned bad. She got him instead.

"Where are we?" he asked, and looked her up and down. "Why are you naked?"

Her mouth snapped closed. She gathered the sage wool blanket she wore—and he was fairly certain it *was* all she wore—tighter about her shoulders.

"Not that I'm complaining," he couldn't help but add.

Ah, yes. The color in her cheeks again, growing brighter. That was anger.

He was happy enough to see it, that blush. He was happy to see any part of her, all the beautiful, living, vivid parts of her, her hair shimmering gold and coral with the waning light, long silky locks caught against smooth arms and shoulders, those pillowy lips. She wore no kohl now, but her lashes and brows had never been the same pale blond as her hair, rather a darker, gentler brown; even as a boy, he'd found it endearing.

Not that he'd ever told her that. Trying to compliment Zoe was like trying to tell a rose why he liked thorns. She wouldn't believe him and he'd likely end up fumbling it anyway.

She drew up taller with the blanket. "Are you dead?" she asked flatly.

"I don't know," he replied, interested. "What do you think?"

"One would hope for a certain grace in death. But you seem just as crass as ever."

He smiled. "Excellent news for me, then."

She only shook her head, one hand knuckled into the twists of the wool. "Are you alone? Is there . . . is anyone else with you?"

"You mean your darling husband-to-be? No. I'm alone. There *was* a rat not so very long ago—as least, I think it wasn't long ago. A rat and a bush and a door—" He was beginning to babble, the joy and sharp relief of finding her peaking into something more volatile. Rhys took a breath and cut himself short. "Where did you say we are?"

"I didn't. Paris."

He looked past her to the room. It was bare, remarkably so.

"Is this a hostelry?" he asked. "I must say, your tastes have always been a bit peculiar to me, but—"

"This," she interrupted frostily, "is the Palais des Tuileries." She dropped the curtain and he lost her, just that easily. He was left to gaze at yards of pinkish velvet gradually fading to gray.

"Zoe," he called, no longer smiling. "Zoe, I'm sorry. Come back."

The curtains began to lift back into color, although he caught no glimpse of her, and they did not stir.

"Please," he said, and hated the edge of desperation in his own voice. "I just—please."

Her fingers parted the folds. She gazed back at him warily, saturated in light that was rapidly deepening to cherry dusk. He tried his best smile—*don't run; don't go; everything's fine; all of this is perfectly, perfectly normal*—and reached out to touch her.

He wanted, very much, to graze those fingertips so close to him, to *feel* her, just as he almost had before . . . but instead Rhys only met that resistance again, the unseen glue that kept him fixed. He remained vapor and shade, nothing like the fiery, firm colors of her.

He concentrated on her nails, neat little crescents, pushed harder, sensing tension like the clear skin atop water—and then

81

sudden freedom: When his fingers met hers, they stabbed straight through.

Zoe yanked back with a muffled yelp. The curtains slapped closed once more.

Ghost.

"I don't understand." It was barely a whisper. "God help me, Zee, I swear I don't understand what's happening to me. Have I gone mad?"

"It surely seems one of us must have," she muttered from the other side. Very slowly, the velvet parted. She stood a little farther back than before and looked up at him through strands of tumbled hair, pressing the hand he'd touched to her chest as if it hurt. "You don't remember?"

Rhys shook his head, unable now to stop staring at the thing that should have been his own hand, lifted between them. The peculiar dark shape of his spread fingers. For an instant they seemed malformed, too long and bent—and then they shifted back to normal.

"You were—captured. By the *sanf inimicus,* back in Darkfrith. No one else was there. We never knew really what happened."

"The *sanf . . .* what?"

"*Inimicus.* The Soft Enemy. Human hunters, Rhys, they came to the shire—all we found was your blood in a field. Truly, you don't remember?"

"No, I . . ." he started to say, but the room beyond her took on a slow, dizzying tilt, everything sweeping to the left, cherry Zoe and the bed and walls, he couldn't stop it, the colors merging and swirling into dots, into darkness—

—he'd been out walking, hot and angry about something. It was the soft ashen glow just before daybreak and he'd been pacing through a meadow. A wet meadow. Dew. There were bracken and wildflowers and he had been blind with his thoughts, careless, and they had sur-

rounded him so quickly—in the shire! in the bloody goddamned shire!—and there had been a Voice telling him not to fight them, not to Turn, although he was trying like hell to anyway, sharp pain and the taste of grass in his mouth and then—music. All that music, the symphony that had never ceased until—

He felt ill. He felt himself fading and this time let it happen, surrendering to the smooth dull gray until it was all that was left.

Zoe sat cross-legged on the floor, the mirror on one side, the window on the other. She was stiff and sore and her feet were still a mess, but she'd managed to dress and get out long enough to find food, a bottle of dry white wine, and a basin of clean water for washing.

By the flame of her single candle she ate fried hamsteak and a wedge of sharp Cantal, bread smeared with butter gone hard with the chill of the night and still delicious enough to melt on her tongue.

The candle in its holder dripped gobs of honeyed wax, puddling fat along the pewter rim. It was beeswax, not tallow. Tallow smoked too much.

She didn't quite dare to crack the curtains to see the windowpanes—it was crisply cold out there, and even by this weak light she glittered with jewels—but she supposed if he did return, she'd hear him.

She flexed her toes in her stiff buckled shoes, wincing at the ache. Outside the window the wind began an eerie moan; it was echoed by the sound of birds very far off. Owls, she thought, though she'd only heard owls a few times before in her life. They groaned to match the weather, a pair of them somewhere out there in the stone forest of the city.

She lifted a bite of cheese to her mouth and cut her eyes away from the tiny fierce sparks of the diamonds on her wrist.

"Zee."

She didn't rise or startle. "I'm here."

"I can't find you."

"The curtains have to be closed. I can't risk the light."

"Oh."

The wind caught a loose pane in the window, a hard rattle of glass against its metal seam.

"Zee, I think I . . . might be dead."

"Yes," she agreed, quiet. "I think you might be."

She heard his sigh. "I don't remember it. Dying. I don't remember that at all."

"But the *sanf*? Do you remember them?"

"Aye. *Them.* The fight. The woods. How long ago was that?"

"A few months."

"That's all?" He gave a laugh, short and bitter. "It seems like forever ago. Seems like forever I've been in this damned dark place."

She pressed a thumb into a pool of cooling wax; it smarted, but she didn't move her hand. After a moment, he spoke again.

"Why can you hear me? And see me? Why only you?"

He sounded so real, just like he had in life. There was no unearthly echo to his words, no spectral sensation at all beyond that steady wind moan rising and falling beyond him. He sounded bewildered, and hurt, and beneath that, angry. All those things, and by just the pitch of his voice she could envision the expression on his face. She didn't need to see it, green eyes troubled, chiseled lips drawn to a line. That single sly curl of chestnut hair that always seemed to flop down to his eyes no matter how often he shoved it aside.

"It's a curse," she said, and lifted her thumb free of the wax.

"What? Really?"

"Yes."

"No." He was stronger suddenly, excited. "It's a *Gift*, isn't it? You've got a Gift."

She shrugged, realized he couldn't see it, and said, "Have it your way."

"By God, Zee—that's . . . that's . . ."

She rolled a piece of wax between her index finger and thumb, waiting.

". . . lucky for me," he finished, more sober than before. "I suppose. Lucky for me, eh?"

The wax was tacky, turning gray against her skin. She flicked it across the chamber.

"Is it just me? Or can you talk to anyone dead? Are there others like me?"

"Yes. And no, not quite like you. They're here, they're around me. I can nearly hear their voices at times, a whole chorus of them . . . and then in glass, in mirrors especially, I see them, small lights. You're much clearer than the rest. With the others, it's more like . . . I feel them. I can feel them reaching for me. But they're slight and thin and distant, as if they're on the far side of a lake, perhaps." She traced the oval imprint of her thumb in the wax. "You're the only one who speaks audibly."

"Tell me about my family. What happened to them? Was anyone else hurt in the attack?"

"No one else, only you. The Princess Maricara was briefly taken, but she made it back safely. There was a girl, a young girl from the village, she was taken too. . . ."

"Honor Carlisle," he said, sounding surprised. "Yes. I remember. I was there for that. I was part of the hunt for her."

"She's still missing. I don't suppose . . . Are you certain you're alone?"

The wind rattled the pane, shifting directions, whistling a note so low and keen it almost hurt.

"I'm not alone," Rhys said. "I have you."

Zoe leaned forward and snuffed out the candle. She climbed to her feet and pulled apart the curtains, just enough illumination from beyond to discern his outline: darkness against dark, smoke and stars and charcoal clouds pushed across the sky, a pale lemon moon shining behind them. The pane of glass that held his heart shivered; it was the loose one, the one the wind took.

She could nearly see him. Standing so close, even without the candle, she thought she could nearly see his face. An acrid trail of fumes from the pinched wick rose up in loops to sting her eyes.

"I want you to know," she said, "that I will do everything in my power to avenge your death. I swear it."

Shadow Rhys shook his head. "Don't say that. What could you do?"

She gazed back at him, silent.

"Ah," he said, very soft. "Aha. Here you are, in Paris. Unaccompanied. Gifted. Did you run away?" He answered the question before she could speak. "Of course you did. They'd never let you leave." He lifted a hand, fingers curved, just like on the coffeehouse patio. "But did you honestly think these Others, these enemies of ours, would fail to notice a dragon hunting them, even in a city this size?"

"I wouldn't know," she said. "There is no dragon hunting them."

"What are *you* then?"

"I cannot Turn."

His head tipped. She could feel the speculation in his gaze.

"I'm not lying. I can't Turn."

"That's bloody bad news, love, because I don't think I'm going to be much help to you." He seemed to push against the glass. "Not from where I am."

"I don't need your help. I can do this on my own."

"You can't be ser—"

"Look around you, Rhys Langford," she hissed, struggling to

keep her voice subdued. "Look at what I've already done. Against all the council's precautions, I've escaped Darkfrith. Against all their dire predictions, I've made it single-handedly to the Continent, and I've been here for weeks. *Undetected.* If I can't find the *sanf inimicus* here, I'll keep going, all the way to Transylvania if I must. I *will* find them."

"Why?" The anger was back, full force. "I don't want your vengeance. Don't be a fool. Whatever they did to me, it's not worth your safety."

She stepped back, drew a steadying breath. "Did you really think that this was entirely about you?"

He paused as the moon was swallowed by a thick rushing cloud; trees and gardens and sky: everything pitch, a spill of ink all the way across the heavens.

"Ah," he said again. "I see. Hayden."

"Hayden."

From somewhere far below came a telltale footfall, nothing nocturnal—heavy steps across gravel. The subtle *sisss* of a phosphorus match.

"Listen." Rhys turned his head. "Do you hear it?"

She nodded, afraid to speak, scanning the grounds, straining to make out more.

"That music," the shadow whispered. "It's so damned... beautiful."

He misted away. She was left with a clear view of the emerging moon, a rime of yellow glow just beginning to devour the edge of the cloud.

CHAPTER SEVEN

My Dearest Friend,

I hope this note finds you happy and well.

I have reached the shores of France. My passage was Uneventful. I've a coach and four and a Man to take me as far as Paris, where I shall have to hire someone New for the leg to Dijon. (You will understand that I remain Inside the carriage as much as possible, away from the Horses. Yet I confess I long to be free of such confinement. The coach is ill sprung and the roads of France are choked with carts. Their condition is Quite Atrocious.)

Thus far I have witnessed Woods and Plains rolling on for many miles, with Vineyards and Cathedrals sharing space in seemingly equal measure. I have dined upon Fried Trout with cream, and beered-Beef Stew, and a Fine Onion Tart they call <u>Zewelwai</u>, none of which Compares to your Cookery, of course.

I found you a small trinket today in the Town of Amiens, a very little Stone but one I trust will Please you, and it is from here I shall Post this Message. You are in my Fondest thoughts and dreams. I pray you remember me the Same,

Yours,

H.

The morning was not quite warm enough to melt the sludge of the coach yard entirely, and the turned-up edges of mud sparkled with frost under the sun like sea glitter with Zoe's every step. There were cobblestones visible under the mud, but they appeared and disappeared like red rock islands in that dirt-and-straw sea. It had rained late last night and then dropped to freezing, and the yard still hadn't been scraped clean.

Travelers clumped back and forth along wooden planks laid in paths over the muck, a great busy swarm of men and women and children hastening from plank to plank, and stableboys not bothering with any of it, stamping in their boots straight alongside. Everyone was talking, moving, pointing. An incoming postboy blew his horn as his *berline* clattered through the brick-pillared entrance, a set of six matched grays and a crest on the door, the heavy wheels spinning so close to the path that more than a few of the people jumped from the wood to the mud on the other side, cursing.

Zoe lingered near the entrance of the yard, fingering the letter she kept in her reticule, observing the commotion.

SHANA ABÉ

Hayden had been correct: Horses were a problem. And as this particular coach yard was the busiest she'd seen so far, it held many, many horses, most of them fresh from their stalls and eager for their paces. A few were already beginning to notice the scent of predator in the air, skins twitching beneath their harnesses as they turned their heads toward her, curled back their lips.

A tabby cat with a white spot on its nose had been grooming itself atop one of the pillars; it appeared oblivious until the breeze shifted, pushing past Zoe, ruffling the edging of her coat.

The cat ceased its bath, orange eyes opening wide. With an impressive arch and a hiss it leapt away, fleeing with a bristling striped tail toward the stables just visible past the ticketing office.

There was no help for it, though. She waited, hoping the wind would shift again, but when it didn't she lifted her chin and walked rapidly into the human crowd.

The planks wobbled with every step, bouncing like a child's seesaw. A woman in a stern black bonnet with a little girl in tow shoved past without a word, her bag smacking Zoe in the hip. A man coming from the other direction touched a hand to his cocked hat as he smirked at her; she lowered her gaze and concentrated on keeping her footing.

The horses downwind began to make noises of distress. The grays in particular grew skittish, starting to kick; they'd been led too close to the path, and the postboy atop the lead had to drop his horn to hold on with both hands.

She held her breath and picked up her pace, overtaking the woman with the bag again, ignoring the woman's startled glance past the brim of her bonnet.

The ticketing office was also brick, two-thirds of it covered in a tangle of ivy that had already withered brown with the coming winter. There was a queue to get in. There was a queue to go around. She drew up as close as she could to the main doors and pulled her coat closer, shuffling along as the animals all around slowly began to work themselves into a frenzy.

The main doors to the office were open to accommodate the line. The windows were closed and paneled in glass, the old-fashioned kind, thick and round and wavy. The plank path angled away from them in such a way that she couldn't see her likeness. But she saw the shadow there anyway. The dead man watching her, distorted with the panes.

"Go away," Zoe murmured under her breath, a puff of frost rising to her nose.

No one noticed. The queue crept along.

As she drew closer the lines and shapes of him grew more distinct, the smoke a nimbus of twists and curls warped with the shape of the blown glass.

He didn't move. She felt his gaze again, felt the intensity of his look.

When she'd awoken this morning she'd been alone; even the ghosts in the mirror had shrunk down to nearly nothing, flitting back and forth like fireflies against the indigo blue. After dressing she'd dared a peek at the window, but it had been only a window again.

She'd decided to skip her daily routine at the Palais Royal. She'd return to her original plan, the one she'd been following before she'd caught that single phrase about the *sanf*. She'd consumed enough coffee to last her a lifetime, anyway.

Three feet from the rounded-glass window the shadow turned to follow her, still not speaking. Not leaving. But it was him, no doubt. She recognized that stance, relaxed and tall and proud. The span of his shoulders, the curl of his hair.

A man in a teal surtout and scuffed boots at the ticketing desk was quarreling with the clerk, flourishing a sheaf of papers and speaking with his hands in that way Zoe had noticed was particular to the French: wide, emphatic gestures that managed to be both elegant and slightly dangerous for anyone standing too near. She was inside the office now, out of the sun but too far from the fire crackling in the hearth on the other side of the room to be warmed. The chairs, the walls, the very floor: Everything stank of people and hay and stale garlic.

An enormous framed map on the wall showed the maze of Paris, circles and circles of streets with black lane spokes fanning out in every direction. It was covered in glass, smeared with fingerprints. Two small girls and an older boy stood beneath it, sharing a sweetmeat with guilty glances.

The shadow emerged like a slick from the eastern corner, even more of him than the window had revealed.

After one quick glance Zoe turned and faced ahead. She was next in the queue. Finally next.

"Yes, which province?" intoned the agent, without glancing at her. He was busy stamping the sheaf of papers the man had given him, marking whatever it was with bright red ink, one page after another after another.

"I beg your pardon. I'm here to inquire about a passenger that might have been through a few months past."

The clerk snorted a laugh, still without glancing up. He was middle-aged and potbellied, and his wig badly needed to be floured.

"We are the largest yard in the city, Madame. We have many passengers."

"Mademoiselle," Zoe corrected, and smiled when his eyes flicked to hers.

"Mademoiselle," he repeated, and set down his stamp. A frown line made a vertical crease between his eyebrows; his fingers were ink-stained, set lightly upon the book of tickets beneath his hands. "We have many passengers," he said again, with a shade more courtesy. "I'm afraid there is no way to discover who has come and gone."

"This man would have hired a coachman from you. He was English, and had a private carriage."

The clerk shook his head and spread his hands, his mouth pursed. "It is impossible, mademoiselle. There are record books, of course, but we cannot allow the public—"

"Oh, but I'm not the public," she said, lowering her voice but still smiling. "He's my brother. It's a family matter, you see. Please, monsieur. I'm ... desperate to find him."

At the edge of her vision she saw the shadow shift along the frame, sliding closer.

"I'm sorry." And the clerk truly did look sorry, the vertical frown deepening, color stealing in a hot flush up his neck. His fingers did a fretful tap across the ticket book. "It cannot be done."

"You don't have it," said the shadow in blunt English. "Give it up. It's not your Gift."

The varied skills of the *drákon* threaded through the tapestry of their bloodlines like brightly woven strands of silver and gold, stronger in some families, weaker in others. Most of the menfolk of the shire could still Turn, less than a handful of the women. But everyone heard the music of the stones and stars. Everyone knew how to hunt with talons or simply guns; how to lope through the forests unseen; how to taste the flavors of the wind; to feel the coming rain humid along their skin, or the bright full moon rising in their blood. Barring Zoe's own strange talents, it wasn't usually difficult to predict which child would grow to inherit the best of their ways; their lineage was, after all, strictly controlled. But one of the few Gifts that eluded prediction, time after time, was that of Persuasion. The ability to direct the Others to a dragon's will merely by using her voice.

And Rhys was right. It wasn't her Gift.

Damn it.

"Please, mademoiselle. I must—I must help the next customer. My most profound apologies."

"Of course. If only there was someone else I could speak to. Someone perhaps to show me the books..."

Like a trained dog responding to a cue, the man glanced swiftly over his shoulder, to a half-cracked door revealing a rectangle of wainscoting and pale blue wallpaper. The plaque on the door was speckled brass. It was etched in scrolled lettering: *M. Racine.*

"It cannot be done," the clerk said once more.

Zoe bowed her head in acquiescence, moving meekly aside. The woman in the black bonnet pressing close behind her huffed audibly and stepped up to the desk. The girl dragged behind watched Zoe with solemn chocolate eyes.

"A noble effort," said the shadow. "Well played. Now go home."

She winked at the girl and walked away, easing around the line of impatient travelers, back into the brilliance of the day. She paused to take a breath of nongarlic air, and a bay being led by a groom close by shied away with a squeal of white frost, hauling the man with him through the mud.

Time to go. Yet once back at the street Zoe did not turn left, the way to Tuileries. She went right instead, very quickly, past the tavern that had a spill of journeymen lounging menacingly upon its steps. Past the cigar shop with the broken bell over its door, leaking the bouquet of dried tobacco from the chinks in the jamb. Past the china dealer, and the stay maker, until she found just what she was looking for.

The next storefront was empty; she'd taken good note of that on her way to the coach yard. From the peeling paint on the sign she guessed it had once been the establishment of a tailor, but the windows now were covered in soot, and the few shelves that she could see inside had been cleared. It had the advantage, moreover, of a back door in the alley just around the corner and a lock that had corroded into flakes. She could smell the rust of it, even from here.

It took only a quick glance around and a squeeze of the latch for the door to give way. And she was safely inside before the journeyman who had ambled up to follow her could discover where she'd gone.

Dust coated everything. The light from the windows in the front room was positively brown; combined with the cool damp air it gave her the sensation of stepping into a cave. A very musty cave.

She crossed to a table pushed askew against the back wall and lifted her arms to remove her pins, and then her hat. When she peered aside to make sure the windows were truly out of the line of sight, her right shoe crunched against glass.

"This isn't home," said a voice nearby, very dry.

Zoe bent down to examine the glass more closely. A shattered mirror. Of course. And Rhys, the smoky darkness that shimmered from piece to piece.

"It isn't," she agreed, stepping away, beginning to pull at her gloves.

"Forgive me, I can't really tell," he said. "But isn't it a bit brisk for disrobing?"

She paused and arched a brow at the largest shard. "Not that you're complaining, my lord?"

"Not in the least. But Zoe . . . what *are* you doing?"

"Kindly don't look."

"What?"

"Don't. Look."

"*Are* you disrobing?" The shadow seemed to grow darker, thicker, agitated across the broken glass.

"I am. Fine, then. Go ahead and look. It hardly matters anyway."

She wore a chemise dress of long-sleeved lavender merino, stylish and warm and relatively simple. No hoops, no bustle to hinder her, only a tube of fitted cloth and a wide gray satin sash that tied beneath her breasts. It was dreadfully daring, but for all its modish fashion, she'd purchased it for only one reason, that it was easy to slip on and off.

She glanced down at the pieces of mirror, running her fingers along the sash.

"Are you watching?"

"Oh, yes," he said, low.

"Excellent." And she let her Gift loose, every inch of her becoming transparent.

The shadow did not move. Nor did he speak; perhaps she'd finally shaken him speechless. But she could see him still there on the floor, a flat darkening in the debris.

She worked quickly now, feeling the cold despite her bravado. The dress and cloak and petticoats, the corset, garters, stockings. Shoes. Reticule. She picked up everything, stepping carefully over the glass, folded it, and set it all upon the table by her hat.

Rhys apparently found his voice. "What are you doing?" he demanded as she began to open the door to the alley. "Zoe! You can't go out there like that!"

"Don't worry. I'll be back soon." And she closed the door gently behind her.

She was insane. She must be. It was the only explanation. Why else would a grown woman—a *drákon* woman, raised in their own wild ways, certainly, but always to modesty—go out in public without a stitch of clothing on her body?

He cast out his senses to find her again, frantically. It took him a good long moment to separate himself from the abandoned storeroom with her garments. He tried to focus on her—eyes, lips, anything—but what he kept seeing was the hem of her gown, a demure purpled fold draped carelessly over the edge of the table, trimmed with gray ribbon. Feminine. Discarded.

Then he was back in the coach yard. He was gazing out from the same place as before when he'd first caught sight of her, all the dim-faced people shoved into their lines, carriages careening through, rumpled passengers emerging from dark interiors to squint at the light of day.

And Zoe. Right there, right *there,* picking her way nude through the stiffened mud, arms out, lips compressed, every single steed she passed bucking in its traces to the shouts of the coachmen and guards.

No one human even glanced at her. A modern-day Godiva, tiptoeing through a mass of Others, sunlight bouncing off her bright hair and bare skin like a halo from heaven itself. And no one even looked.

Getting through the main doors was the most difficult part. She had to wait until the family clumped there were summoned inside en masse, father-mother-daughter-daughter-son, until there was room enough to sidle by them. Even still she'd bumped the elbow of the eldest daughter, who swatted at the air in a distracted sort of way, listening to her father argue for better seats on the stage to Limoges.

The clerk had slouched back in his chair with the weary mien of a man who'd suffered too long a day already. He certainly didn't look up as Zoe slipped around his desk, moving quickly and silently to the door of M. Racine.

It was still only barely open. She was pushing it gradually wider, wider, until a sudden gust of wind from the main doors yanked it out of her hand, banging the edge hard against the wall.

The clerk gave an irritated sigh and scraped back his chair. She just managed to dart inside before he grabbed the knob and slammed the door shut.

Well. Here she was.

Monsieur Racine was not at his desk today, it seemed. His office was cramped and crammed from floor to ceiling with books and ledgers: leather-bound, cloth-bound, stacks and stacks of them. His oil lamps were unlit; his fireplace held a mound of gray-feathered ash, the coal bucket empty beside it. Another map on the wall, and a small, crude watercolor of a church. A rug, surprisingly plush, covered most of the floor; a caped greatcoat still swayed gently from its hook on the back of the door.

She shivered, reaching for the greatcoat. The sole window was shrouded with blond lace curtains and blocked with a fern on a pedestal. No one would see, and there was no sense in freezing before she was done.

Books. She started with the shelves closest to her, but they were all just columns of accounts, sums of figures with odd abbreviations, sorted by year. Nothing about passengers. She moved on to the next shelf, and the glass face of the map of France shifted into dusk.

"Zoe?" His voice was very soft now.

"Yes," she whispered, even softer, her unseen finger tracing the years imprinted on the spines in front of her. "I can't talk now."

1777. 1778. 1779...

Approvisionnements. Chevaux. Bureaux des douanes.

"Zoe...why is it no one sees you?"

Clients.

She let out her breath in relief, pulling free the book marked *1781/janvier–juin,* flipping quickly through the pages. The cuffs of the coat sleeves were much too long; they kept catching against the paper.

"Zee."

"Yes, fine." She willed herself visible, sparing him a swift glance before going back to the book. "Invisibility. Another Gift."

"Er..."

He sounded strange, strange enough for her to pause and shoot him a longer look. The smoke defining his edges lifted into coils, nearly alive; otherwise the shade of Lord Rhys Langford was motionless against the pastel colors of the map.

"What?" she asked, losing patience.

"Nothing. Sorry." He seemed to run a hand through his hair. "Please, do carry on with your incredibly reckless behavior."

A retort was on the tip of her tongue, but just then the heavy book shifted in her hands, and she glimpsed what she needed, what she'd been searching and hoping for all these weeks. She bent her head to the page and the words died unsaid.

The entry had been scratched by a quill clearly needing fresh ink. The letters were sketchy, almost faded, but their meaning came clear as crystal:

29 mai. Henri Jones, Anglais par l'intermédiaire de Calais. Cocher à Dijon: Alain Fortin. Payé entièrement, pièces d'or.

Henry Jones, an Englishman by way of Calais, on his way to Dijon. Paid in gold.

Hayden James. He wouldn't use his real name, of course not. And he would carry coin with him instead of vouchers; it was safer. More anonymous.

The timing, the particulars. It was he. It had to be.

"Someone's coming," warned the shadow.

She had time to drop the book and shrug out of the coat, scooting far back against the wall. The porcelain knob turned and a new man entered, not the potbellied clerk. He was thin and bespectacled and bearded; his first glance was to the cold hearth. His second was to his greatcoat and the book, lying haphazard upon the floor.

He walked forward and Zoe walked back, their steps exactly matched until she hit a corner and there was nowhere else to go. She held her breath, trying to be as quiet as possible as the man bent down to scoop the coat up over his arm, then grabbed the book. He stood in place, examining the empty spot in the shelves where the book should be, all the other spines still neatly aligned, then shrugged and slipped it back into line. He rehung the greatcoat and rubbed his hands against the chill, glancing once more at the hearth. But instead of searching for more coals for his fire he busied himself with lighting the lamps, one after another, until the room fairly blazed with light.

Then he sat at his desk. He pulled papers from a drawer, a strongbox of coins and notes, leaning close over them as Zoe inched around him, actually sucking in her stomach when he raised an arm to rub at his neck.

"I fail to understand what you've gained by this," complained the shadow from his place on the wall.

A name. An actual time and date, and the name of the coachman who had carried Hayden away to silence.

"And now you're trapped," Rhys went on. He sounded aggravated, stretching to fill the boundaries of the glass. "He locked the door, I saw it. So much for clever ideas. What now, Lady Godiva?"

She threw a quelling look to the glass, even knowing he couldn't see it. In three steps she was back at the door. Zoe lifted her hand and rapped the wood twice, imperious.

The man glanced up. He placed the box back inside the desk, removed his spectacles, and walked to the door—she squeezed out of his way by pressing flat against the wall—then opened it wide.

Before he'd even finished peering around at the empty space she was filling it, half-hopping in her haste to get by.

She smacked into a woman clutching a wicker cage crammed with chickens. *Chickens.* Feathers and screams followed her all the way back out to the yard.

CHAPTER EIGHT

He remained with her through the city streets, stealing along from window to window, and at times—once the sun grew higher and the day began to warm—following her through the flat smooth puddles dotting the roads. She was easy to find. It was growing easier and easier to find her, to think of her colors, her light. And there she'd be.

Right now she was crossing a busy intersection with a hand pressed to her hat, her skirts lifted to show a flash of ankles and silver-buckled shoes as she hurried along, dodging mules and carts and another carriage, this one drawn by a team in blinders that snorted and scrambled by her with only inches to spare. Her purple dress was pulled nearly sideways with their passage.

It about stopped his heart. If he'd still had one, that is. Bloody foreigners. He'd never seen such abominable driving, and he

SHANA ABÉ

himself had come to his skills strictly by way of the inebriated mercies of the ostlers at Cambridge, none of whom had proven amiss to a bribe of guineas, no matter how the cattle protested.

She'd reached the other side of the intersection. He found a new set of windows fronting a tooth-puller's shop scribbled in florid red paint—*Monsieur Béland! Le Dentiste Célèbre!*—and kept by her side.

The symphony hounded him much as he hounded Zoe, slinking ever closer to his heels with its alluring siren call. The best he could do was to outrun it, or push it to the edges of his awareness. When he stilled it hovered, sometimes softer, sometimes aggressively forte, and always so spellbinding that if he devoted even a thread of himself to the flow of the notes, he was lost.

He was back in the assembly hall in Soho, or stranded on that gray little street.

But Zoe helped keep it at bay. Naked or dressed, she was his beacon. He didn't know why, and he didn't care. She kept the music away. That was enough.

It was a strange sort of death. There was no pain, no joy, no bright pleasure but what she brought him, and even that was more Rhys savoring her than Zoe attempting to bring him any manner of relief.

It had been so long since he had allowed himself truly to look at her. It was odd to realize that. They'd known each other forever, had been friends once, and then a little more than that. He imagined he knew her face and figure nearly like he knew his own. He knew her walk—gads, how many times had he watched her walk away from him back home? That sultry sashay, that swish of her skirts with her heels clicking like Spanish castanets against paving stones.

How many times had he spotted the radiance of her hair in a

crowd of darker blondes, heard her laughter in the village tavern above all others, silvery and bright? How many times had he caught himself staring at her from across a room—common places, amicable places, the library or the tea shop or confectionary—simply absorbed in the complexity of her expressions? The way her lashes lowered when she was pensive and thinking. The pink curve of her lips when she was pleased, or pretending to be pleased. The flex of her fingers when a suitor bowed over them: ladylike, relaxed, not quite bent enough to be a true grasp in return. Not quite stiff enough to dash all hopes, either.

He'd grown up watching her yet keeping apart. In a way, this was no different. And so Rhys supposed if this was to be his eternity, he could have done far worse.

Except for the nudity. That bit was rather more hellish than not.

It seemed she truly was invisible, at least to human eyes. He couldn't imagine any other reason for a gorgeous, unclad woman to be publicly ignored, even in France. And it made sense that if she wished to remain unseen, she would have to undress. Indeed, now that he thought about it, it reflected a certain lovely symmetry with the whole notion of the Turn, that to fully accept the wonders of this Gift, human things would be perforce left behind.

But she was not invisible to him. She was gloriously, achingly in sight.

He could not count the number of dreams he'd had about her over the years. Certainly he couldn't count the daydreams, the hot fevered adolescent fantasies of her. They usually involved him and her and Fire Lake at home, the cool shady part of the lake. Swimming. The blue-green waters and the two of them splashing, and then there would be sun between them on the waves, a little blinding, and she would magically be without clothes, without the grave and unsmiling inhibitions that had kept him at arm's length for so long... and they would come together with slippery arms and legs, and kiss....

Never in those dreams had he seen her as he did today. Unabashed. And—ah, God, his throat closed just evoking the details—*running*. Naked.

It aroused him. It frightened him. It left him nearly dizzy with agitation.

Invisibility. Of all the damned Gifts... It figured that Zoe Lane would get the one that left her unclothed and vulnerable, without even the ability to lift from the earth as smoke to escape their enemies.

Invisibility—and him: a ghost without freedom, the memory of a man. So not just one Gift, he realized, but two. With all the simmering power of their sires and dams, with all their generations of deliberate breeding to hone their skills, Zoe had these two.

Something had to be her shield, then. Something had to protect her.

Somehow.

He was tied to her for a reason. He could feel it.

Hell, it wasn't as if he had anything more pressing to do.

Slipping into Tuileries by day was slightly more tricky than at night. Usually she managed it by waiting until the streets were a little more clear, and the shadows of the trees sent a pattern of dark confusion across the walk and walls. But the day was warming rapidly, without a cloud across the scrubbed blue sky. She simply had to brazen it out; the fact was, she wanted back in her rooms. She needed peace and calm, far from people and trembling animals, to think about what to do next.

If anyone saw her slip through the gate with the broken lock, no one said anything. Metal met metal with only small, musical chimes, and then she was gone to the trees.

She knew this place by now. She knew where to find the walks without gravel, when to remain behind tree trunks or overgrown hedges. The gardens themselves were vast and eerily haunting; it was easy to imagine kings and queens taking their leisure here, once upon a time. There were massive Egyptian statues of black basalt tucked away in overgrown arbors, ponds with lily pads and algae spreading green across once-polished pink alabaster. The lawns were still weeded but the fountains and jets bubbled with water no more; their pumps were frozen shut.

There was even a labyrinth of hawthorn hedges with shoots that had poked out and blossomed untrimmed. She'd memorized the path from her room, then tried it one night, just because. In its center she'd discovered a bronze sculpture of Venus, a magnificent web of moonlight and dew fanning from her ear to her shoulder, the spider a dark round dot by the loop of her earring.

Barring the occasional bored soldier walking about, the royal gardens of Tuileries remained deserted. But for today.

Far off in the distance she could make out the blue-and-gold coats of an army company, a huge group clustered by the central entrance to the palace. It startled her enough that she withdrew behind a chestnut and remained there, watching.

One of the soldiers was standing on a box and speaking to the rest, his words nearly loud enough to make out. At a barked command the mass of men fell into order, their stamped boots echoing across the air.

Zoe sighed and began once again to remove her coat and the lavender gown. At least it wasn't as chilly as this morning.

When she stepped out of the trees the sunlight felt like welcome on her back. She'd tucked her clothing beneath a bench so forgotten by the groundskeepers it was more moss and lichen than iron filigree.

Her feet had picked up more filth. It was the only sure way to follow her, the strangely inverted soles of grime that pressed into the grass and rocks. Perhaps no one would notice.

Or perhaps they would.

Zut.

She was seated invisible at the edge of a reflecting pool that held the rainfall from last night, rubbing her feet together beneath the chilled water, her skin goose-pimpled, when he spoke.

"What *did* we learn this morning?"

She took a good look around before answering him, but the soldiers were still acres away.

"I have the name of the man who drove Hayden to Dijon. Later on today..." She paused, thinking about it. "Later today I'll go back. If he's in town, I'll find him."

"Back to the stables."

"Yes."

"With all those quiet, peaceful horses, which aren't at all horrified by the mere hint of your presence."

Rhys was a dark ripple across the surface of the pool, a handsome silhouette just visible, gray smoke writhing like tendrils, overlapping where her own image should be.

"The coachmen can't spend all their time in the stables," she mused. "If he's here, he'll want to go out at night at least. Men like to gamble. Men like to drink. Cards. Women."

"Yes," drawled Rhys. "We men are funny like that."

"Well, then. I'll simply go out with them."

"Splendid."

"I *am* female. I'll be where they are, happy to engage with them. What could be more natural?"

"Great God," said the shadow, faint. "And then what? An interrogation over whist and port? You'll *charm* the truth out of him?"

She leaned forward to see him better, and the water sloshed around her ankles. "You think I'm a child still, don't you? You think I'm weak."

"I think," he said carefully, "that you have a somewhat elevated sense of your own ruthlessness. Zoe, consider it. Until the *sanf* arrived, you'd never even left the shire. You have spent your entire life cocooned in a place designed strictly to enforce your own sense of security, to remind you of your matchlessness. This"—he lifted a shadow arm, a dark stabbing slash across the shining blue sky—"all *this* is the human world. It's rough and raw and it stinks and it cheats. And their rules are not like ours."

"No," she murmured, watching the soldiers march smartly in place, bayonets flashing in the distance. "Their rules are more honest."

She actually felt his anger. It rolled over her like a winter storm, prickling her skin worse. "Damn it, Zee, why do you have to be so stubborn? What do you honestly think you can do against them?"

"A great many things," she answered calmly. "Invisible, remember?"

He seemed to grow thicker upon the water, more opaque. "Have you even thought this through? What were you planning to do after?"

"After what?"

"After everything." He waved a hand. "All this. Your search. Your vengeance. Death to the *sanf inimicus,* all glory to the *drákon.*"

She stared at the smear of him upon the pool.

"Don't you ever want to go home?" the shadow asked, more gently. "Doesn't home matter to you?"

He saw her look away, her jetty gaze searching the horizon, then dropping down to her hands flat upon her thighs. She hadn't even realized yet how he had found her. That she was supposedly unseen, and yet he was here.

"If Hayden is dead..." she began, and swallowed, and for some unknown reason Rhys's heart clenched. She took a breath and went on. "If he's dead, then I don't really know what home is left for me anywhere."

"Zee. The shire is your birthright. Your family's still there. You're young and beautiful. You're Gifted, Gifts like no one else's. There's not a chance in Hades you'd be left..."

Alone, he almost said. *Unwed.* And then he realized what it meant.

She was Gifted, extraordinarily so. She would belong to the Alpha. But not to Rhys's father—wed—and not to his brother—engaged.

To him. The sole male of his line yet single, yet unattached. To *him.*

She was still staring down at her hands. He saw the corners of her lips quirk, a cynical little smile that managed to reveal a flash of dimples.

Oh, God. Oh, God, she was pretty.

"Yes," she murmured, as if she'd read his mind. "I know. In some ways, we're less enlightened than the Others, no matter how you protest otherwise. By a twist of chance, I can do this." She lifted straight a lovely long leg that dripped water but cast no shadow, left no reflection upon the pool beyond the diminutive, spreading circles of falling drops. "And so in the eyes of the tribe I become less than a person. Less than even a female. I become a belonging. Chattel."

"No," he whispered. "You're precious, don't you see? Like a diamond. Like treasure."

108

"Or like a well-bred sow." She came to her feet, stepping delicately from the pool.

Sunlight blazed across her, every naked inch of her. She stood still and held a hand to her eyes to shield them—would that even help?—staring hard at the men now marching in an infinite square around the front of the park to the shouted orders of their leader.

Her breasts. Rosy nipples tight with cold. The enticing curve of her waist. Her legs slightly apart, her hair flowing and stirring against her hips, that sweet patch of curls lower down, brown like her lashes. She was a stern Diana gazing out at her domain, preparing for the hunt.

Holy hell. If only he were still alive.

"I'm going in now," she said.

He nodded, then cleared his throat. "Yes. All right."

She walked away. He watched her, slipping from pool to pool, then to the windows of the palace, until she was past the soldiers, all the way inside.

The girl was different from all the others.

She wasn't wearing white, for one thing, the standard style of dress for young women inclined to dance. Her frock was instead a sober dark gray shot with some sort of glisteny blue thread; every time she moved the dress changed colors, shifting from gray to sapphire beneath the light of the sconces set high along the walls. And although she sat at a table with a group of other laughing, sweating girls and quite a few beaux, she didn't speak to them. She barely glanced at them.

She did wear the same colorful coronet of paper flowers across her brow that nearly all the girls here did; they were handed out at the door, so that wasn't too surprising. But on her the stiff orange and violet blooms seemed more vivid, more like real flowers than not.

Yet what set her apart most of all from all the other bright-eyed *jeunes femmes* in the dance hall tonight was simply her looks.

She was the most beautiful woman around, by far. Beneath the flowers, beneath her loosely pinned and powdered hair was a face unmatched by any he'd seen in years. And he'd seen quite a few faces. No sweat, no wine-flushed cheeks. Just pure...ice.

He was a man from the countryside, not the putrid city. He'd grown up amid fields of wheat and poppies and placid cows. He was still most comfortable there, out there on those endless roads that rambled through the seasons, and to him, this girl had a winter kind of beauty, like snow falling thick and hushed in the woods. Or stars twinkling against an ebony sky.

She'd been asked to dance at least five times since he'd first noticed her, and she'd refused them all with a dazzling smile, gathering men around her as easily as if she'd beckoned them with the crook of her finger.

He took a swig of his beer. The beauty leaned back in her chair and threw him a sidelong look; he caught a glimpse of that smile again, this time aimed straight at him.

One of his fellows gave him an encouraging kick under the table. Alain dropped his eyes and scratched at a sudden itch beneath his hat.

Très bien.

The dance hall was in what appeared to be the shell of a medieval chapel. The pews had been torn out to make way for the tables, but the floor still revealed traces of their anchors, the uneven edges of stone tripping up the unwary. There was a rose window above the musicians, a stained-glass medallion still blossoming with color, blood-red and cobalt and goldenrod, a weeping saint in the very middle gazing down at the merrymakers below.

The ceiling was arched and hazed with pipe smoke. A woman in a citron gown and spangled wrap was singing up on the dais, her palms spread, her throat arched; the beads and feathers decorating her wig swayed impressively every time she moved her head. Zoe couldn't really tell if she was any good. The woman sang and the people clapped and stomped and prattled; the limestone walls and floors muddled everything into a constant roar. She imagined the couples dancing in their lines managed it by the rhythm of the violoncello alone.

The barkeep behind the counter set up in the vestry never stopped moving. Mugs and glasses clattered against wood, beer and wine from the casks behind him leaving a wet sticky mess across every surface.

She'd never been to a dance hall before. The closest thing Darkfrith had to one was Cerise's tavern, which on special occasions would accommodate a revelry if all the tables and benches were pushed back. Zoe was comfortable enough amid the smoke and shouting and noise; at least she wasn't having to serve the crowd.

It was largely working-class, a sprinkling of young noblemen here and there, their shiny coats and waistcoats more garish than the plain tans and browns of the woolens most of the men wore. For the price of five *sous* she'd slipped easily into the chaos, sipping at her glass of watered red wine, watching the coachman and his friends across the chamber.

All the narrow windows to the chapel were shuttered. If Rhys lurked somewhere in the stained glass above her, she couldn't see him.

There were five men from the yard. She'd stolen enough of their thoughts to follow them here; by the time she was certain of the address, they were on their third or fourth beers, which made their minds brightly sloppy but surprisingly easy to perceive. The one named Alain, the one from the book entry, was the most subdued of the group, hardly speaking. He had a plait wrapped in a brown ribbon, pocked skin, eyes as black as her own. And he'd been stealing glances at her from behind his mug for nearly half an hour now.

If she glanced up, straight up, she could see the cloak of blue darkness hovering over her like the spread wings of a hawk. She could feel it, the silence of it, the hunger. The spirits trapped inside. To the people jammed around her it was as invisible as Zoe herself could be. Yet to her it hung opaque, sharpened to life by the strength of her own nerves and ire.

"I never knew you to dance," said a familiar voice.

Her gaze returned to the rose window, but the only shadows there were still thrown from the sconces.

"Doesn't seem your style," Rhys continued. "All that frolicking about. All that fun. Where's that dour little bluestocking who'd rather read Sophocles than flirt?"

The wineglass. He was there, small and curved, just beneath her fingers.

"I doubt most sincerely you fathom anything about my *style*," she muttered under her breath, although there was little chance of being overheard.

"Zee," said the shadow against her wine. "Truly. I have an odd feeling about all this. I think you should leave. We can—we'll make a better plan tomorrow."

She set down the glass and smiled at the black-eyed coachman who'd finally walked up, bowing low before her.

She lifted her hand to him and allowed him to lead her out to the floor, the indigo cloak trailing in a long arcing scythe behind.

CHAPTER NINE

She was a passable dancer. It wasn't due to the fact that she'd had a great many public opportunities in the past; she could count on one hand the number of *drákon* balls thrown by the Marquess and Marchioness of Langford at Chasen Manor, and certainly she'd never been invited outside the shire for any others.

No, she could dance strictly because Cerise loved to dance, and together they had practiced many a long, silly night as girls, drawing straws to see who would be the gentleman to lead. Mother had done her duty at the pianoforte, laughing almost as hard as they.

Granted, Zoe was rather better at the slower steps, but there was nothing like that being played in this packed smoky hall. Most of the sets were simple jigs, with everyone bobbing up and down and bowing and turning; even in the confusion of bodies and slapping skirts, she had the way of it nearly at once.

The coachman gave her a grin, revealing a missing front tooth. She grinned back, letting their hands remain clasped a little longer than was proper before twirling to her right to hook arms with another man.

Painted faces; bellowing voices. The frantic melodies from the fiddles and horns.

She allowed the cloak slowly to descend, slowly, slowly, enveloping her in those wings. It took concentration to hold it so firmly at bay, to keep it chained to her will. She missed two steps in a row and managed to laugh about it. The coachman laughed too.

The cloak settled over them soft as silence, wrapped them together. The man faltered a little, his smile fading, but Zoe had mastered the dance by now and moved smoothly to his side.

They clasped hands again.

She thought, *Show me.*

She saw the countryside in winter. She saw fields of snow glimmering under white-bone moonlight. Horses in front of her pulling a rig. Bitter wind in her face carrying the scent of plowed earth and seed. Manure.

No, not any of this. Hayden.

The coach yard and the stables. The other drivers smoking and drinking, a circle of cards and a lamp burning whale oil on an overturned crate.

A dun-haired man, a lean face darkened by the sun. Neither plain nor handsome. A scar across one eyebrow. Probing gray eyes, his mouth lifted into an expression of sardonic query over the splay of his cards. By the capes of his coat, likely another driver.

Hayden, she thought, ferocious.

But the same man came again, regarding her now by the deep ginger glow of firelight, speaking words she could not hear but could almost feel, syllables shaping themselves into meaning inside her ears.

...you'll like the recompense....you won't make more anywhere else, i promise you that, and for such a small thing, after all. they're criminals of a sort, you understand, a gang of them. our comrades assured me you can be discreet. and no one's complained yet about getting a few extra livres *a month for doing almost nothing....*

It came upon her in a sudden wave: nausea, rolling up from her stomach into her throat, stilling her feet. In a rush of noise the dance hall came back to her, the couples and the fiddles and the echo of drunken laughter, the residue of burning tobacco curling across her face. She stumbled to a halt and pressed a hand to her lips.

They stood there, she and the coachman in the middle of the dance floor, staring at each other through the haze. The people around them shouted in a good-natured way, jostling, trying to get them to move.

Zoe lowered her hand. "It's too warm, isn't it?" She didn't wait for his reply, instead weaving her fingers through his and pulling him along. The coachman followed, docile as a child.

The air outside the hall was hardly fresher than indoors; it left a sour wooden flavor in her mouth and still couldn't banish the aroma of pipe and beer that billowed up and around her in clouds. Groups of Others lingered outside in the pools of amber light shed from the torches, men speaking sotto voce to wet-lipped girls, couples in the shadows groping, no longer speaking at all.

She looked around quickly, searching for an isolated spot.

There was a path of flagstones winding around to the unlit side of the chapel. She followed it, still pulling the man along.

It ended in a small courtyard, dusty and rolling with debris; no one else had ventured here yet. An ancient well loomed by the stump of some long-rotted tree. Its bucket hung askew by a rope, giving an occasional mellow thump against the metal framework.

Something rustled above them. A flock of pigeons atop the roof took flight in a flurry of wings, sailing off with burbling cries.

Zoe turned and pulled the coachman closer with a coquettish tug. From beyond the turn in the path, a woman giggled and then murmured something husky and welcoming.

"I don't..." the coachman began, sounding perplexed.

She stroked the backs of her fingers to his cheek, felt the heated scruff of his beard, the pox scars beneath. "Alain, yes? Alain Fortin?"

"Yes," he whispered, staring down at her fixed as a statue, as if he'd never move again. "But how..."

The cloak dropped about them in ripples of endless blue.

...and it'll be easy. you just keep your eyes open. you contact me if you ever see anything like what i've described. the horses spooking. a fine-looking englishman or one from central europe. moneyed. inclined to remain apart from you and the beasts. it's very simple, isn't it?

and then what? zoe felt her lips ask.

nothing, my friend. and then nothing. a nice fat reward for you, that's all. better not to ask anything beyond that, eh?

The breeze stirred, redolent now of coal and oil and unwashed animals, pushing at the weight of her hair against her shoulders. She let it flow over her, through her, let it tear little holes through the veil of the cloak, larger and larger.

The coachman blinked as if coming out of a reverie. He still grasped her hand.

"Tell me his name," Zoe said to him.

Alain's eyes cut to hers. He gave a short shake of his head.

"His name," she urged softly, curling her fingers around his just a little tighter. "The name of the other driver who bribed you."

"Wha—what *are* you?" the coachman gasped.

"Drákon," came the answer, just behind her.

The cloak broke instantly into mist, voices and memories and souls twisting upward to heaven in a rising thin shriek. Gone.

She didn't flinch or jerk; she merely turned her face to address the flagstones.

"What a peculiar word. Whatever could you mean?"

"Exactly what you think," replied the man standing behind her. "I've a pistol primed and a very sharp blade, mademoiselle. Don't you smell the gunpowder? And since you're female, I doubt there's much you can do about any of it."

Zoe looked back at Alain, who was squinting at the man surely visible over her shoulder.

She freed his hand. *"Run."*

"No, don't," said the newcomer easily, and before she could react there was a blur and a *thunk* and a knife in Alain Fortin's chest, a hilt of blond wood with blood bubbling all around it.

Without any noise, without even a whimper, the coachman dropped to his knees.

From the high, bronzed lip of the chapel bell in its belfry, he watched the scene unfold.

Zoe, fair and alone with flowers in her hair, her skirts a sweep of blue shimmer, standing with her back to the man with the gun.

The bloke she'd been dancing with, bleeding a great shiny pool that was spreading in tentacles between the grooves of the flagstones.

"No," Rhys groaned, but of course it made no difference. No one even heard him.

"No," he said again as Zoe took a step toward the dying man, who had lifted one shaking hand to the blade protruding from his waistcoat, his fingers and cuffs and coat smeared with red.

Zoe, Zoe—in danger, drawn up short by the curt command of the bastard behind her.

She was small as a doll from Rhys's vantage point. He was

trapped, he couldn't leave, and the man with the gun was sure as hell going to shoot her, because there was no way she wouldn't fight him. She'd never go quietly. She'd come all the way to bloody *Paris* to fight him—the son of a bitch had to be *sanf inimicus*—and the panic and horror that pounded through Rhys felt as real as anything he'd ever known in his mortal body—how the hell was he going to save her now—

And then he was on the ground with them. With the bleeding man. He was on his knees beside him—on his goddamned knees, with hard stone beneath—and Zoe was staring down at him with a white and startled face.

"That's better," the *sanf* was saying. "Less distraction. No, no. Kindly don't move, mademoiselle. Or is it madame?" He gave a little laugh. "Do monsters even bother with our human distinctions?"

"If you know what I am," murmured Zoe, still watching Rhys, "then surely you know I'm powerless against you. I have no Gifts."

Rhys leapt to his feet. He rushed past Zoe and took a swing at the man, but his fist only passed through him. For all his freedom he was still a ghost, still smoke. The *sanf* gave no indication he knew Rhys was there; a small, pinched smile began to twist his lips as he regarded the back of her head. Rhys tried to hit him again, and again, again. He wanted to roar in frustration, and the smug bastard only stood there posed as for a portrait with his chin up and shoulders relaxed, the pistol held lazily in his hand.

"I wasn't expecting a woman, I must admit," said the man. "But then again, it does hold a certain pretty logic. Where are the rest of you? How many are there?"

"There are no others. Not here."

The man clicked his tongue. "It's not a good idea to lie to me. I'll put a bullet through you one way or another, but I can make it less painful or more."

Zoe cocked her head. "Tell me, sir. Are your eyes perchance gray?"

"I can't stop him," Rhys bit out. "I can't. I've tried. Don't antagonize him, Zee. The longer you can keep him talking, the better the odds someone else will come."

He tugged his hands through his hair, spun back to the man on the ground. If only he could rouse him—

"I'll ask you just once more, *drákon*." He spat the word. "Where are your others?"

"No others," she insisted; Rhys glanced up and she held him in a look of serene liquid black. Slowly she lifted an arm and removed the crown of flowers nestled in her coiffure. "Only me. So if you're going to shoot me, I suggest you do it now..."

"*Shit,*" said Rhys, watching her eyes grow blacker and blacker.

"...you murderous, cowardly, contemptible little prick of a human," she added pleasantly, as if she'd just made a comment upon the fine weather.

He was so cold. He was cold and yet he was not, because the only parts of his body he could feel were his chest and head. Those were cold. The rest of him... the rest of him didn't seem to exist any longer.

Alain rolled his eyes toward the woman in blue, the man—*driver, fresh to the job, came late tonight, what was his name?*—beyond her standing in the dark. They were carrying on a conversation as if he wasn't there at all, sprawled upon the ground. He remembered them both, walking here with her, lost in the winter stars of her eyes, adrift in her wake. And then the man had come.

It seemed unimportant now. His head dropped back and he was granted a view of the sky, a few pearly clouds spun out against the vault of night, straight and wispy thin like the furrows of a field. He was feeling warmer already.

119

"Get up," someone was saying in his ear. "Get up, damn you, get up!"

Alain dragged his gaze toward the voice. There was a man there beside him, a new man, brighter than all their surroundings, with wild twisting hair and eyes of wolf-shining green.

"Up!" shouted the man. "You've got to help her! Get up, *get up, get up!*"

But Alain did not think he'd be getting to his feet anytime soon. He thought, with a distant sort of amazement, that in all likelihood he'd never find his feet again.

The green-eyed man pounded his fists against Alain's chest. Surprisingly, it didn't hurt. It felt, actually—

Rhys made contact with Zoe's beau, real contact, and then there was that tug of resistance, and his hands and forearms sank into the stabbed man's chest.

He felt him breathe. He felt the blood in his lungs, the bubbly rasping ache.

He felt it.

Later on Rhys would never be able to fully explain what manic thing seized him then; divine inspiration or the devil's own hand, it hardly mattered. All that mattered was that he realized what it meant. What he could do.

And so he did it.

A few things happened at once.

Her fingers released the paper flowers to the ground.

The *sanf* with the gun stepped forward, the soles of his shoes grinding against the minute grains of dust and grit that sprinkled the courtyard with a sound in her ears that was as loud as the ocean thundering to shore. His breath hissed out; the air in front of him pushed forward, parted with measurable friction against the surface of her back.

All her muscles grew taut, every inch of her flow and movement. As she was pivoting around she was Turning invisible, a gown that stood alone, hairpins suspended midair.

He wasn't expecting it, clearly. He pulled back, his eyes widening. The barrel of the pistol wavered, stealing the pallid light in a long, silvery dart.

One shot. That's all he'd have. One shot before she reached him.

The gown floated over the stones. She herself floated, dreamlike in her state of fury and fright, dodging the hollow black dot of the barrel trying to follow her, moving closer, and closer, until the man who was the filthy hand of the *sanf inimicus* peeled his lips back into a sneer and took a quick and steady aim at her dress.

Something flashed. She heard no noise from the gun, no retort. Felt no pain.

But she froze anyway, an instinctive reaction, waiting for it, for the blood at least.

The *sanf* still stared at her, the same sneer distorting his face. And there was the blood, gurgling down his jabot, staining the dull white ruffles with dark, dark liquid, because there was a knife in his throat. He pulled it out, lurching backward, his mouth opening and closing like a fish flopped to air.

Something heavy collapsed behind her. She whirled about and saw it was the other man, Hayden's driver. He'd gotten up somehow. He'd taken the knife and *thrown* it and saved her—

Zoe flung herself to her knees, pressing both palms to his chest. Alain Fortin stared up at her with wondering eyes.

"No, no." She pushed more firmly against his wound, blood leaking through her fingers; it smelled of hot metal and salt. His heartbeat thudded in slow, hard clouts, uneven against his breast-bone. "I'm so sorry. I'm sorry."

One breath. Another.

He seemed about to speak, but instead took one last, rattling breath that squeezed away into silence.

"Thank you," she whispered, and realized she'd said it in English. *"Merci. Merci beaucoup."*

She sat back with her wet dripping hands, dazed. As soon as she did, a curious mirage seemed to take the coachman's body, a blurred swirling darkness that rose from inside him to envelop his features, his face and clothing like he was sinking into a pool—but he wasn't. The thing was rising *out* of him.

"You're welcome," said Rhys, pulling all the way free. "Damned good thing I pitched cricket at school."

She only just managed not to scream. She scrambled backward in surprise instead, her skirts caught beneath her, palms scraping against the flagstones.

"Is the other one dead?" the ghost of Rhys continued, stepping free from the body as easily as if he stepped over the raised entrance to a room. When she didn't respond he glanced down at her, brows lifted.

She could nearly *see* him—no reflection; there were no windows or glass nearby, only Rhys Langford standing there with all the depth and height and presence he'd always had in life, like a real person—perhaps one standing deep in the shade. The contours of his face, almost visible. The cut of his jaw. The gleam of his eyes.

He made a brisk motion with his hand.

"Zoe, quickly. You've got to check."

She rolled to her feet. The *sanf* lay splayed across the courtyard still clutching the knife. The pistol had dropped a few feet away. Blood had sprayed everywhere, matting his hair, a sharp arc across his cheek. The scar across his eyebrow had blanched white. He looked very dead.

A loop of something red and orange and purple lay crushed beside his elbow. She realized it was the gay circlet she'd been given for the dance, the paper flowers soaking up blood.

She couldn't take another step. She tried to and could not. It was so odd, like her feet had sunk roots all the way to the center of the earth. A strange cold shiver began crawling from her fingers to her arms to the column of her spine. To fight it she shook out her hands, hard, and heard the tiny spatter of Alain Fortin's blood hit the stones.

Rhys took the step that she did not.

"I know him," he said, his voice tight with excitement. "I know this man. I've seen him before."

She forced herself to speak. "Where?"

He shook his head, his long hair curling with smoke, then crouched down to his heels, examining the body. "I don't think he's dead yet. You'll have to finish it."

Her voice came as a strangled whisper. "No."

"You don't have a choice. Hurry. Don't worry, I'll—I'll tell you how."

"No!"

He stood, green eyes flashing. "Goddamn it. This is *exactly* what I was talking about before. You cannot let him live. He knows what you look like, that you're here in the city. He will hunt you. He will *kill* you, just as easily as he did that chap over there. These humans have no remorse. We're nothing but animals to them. Do you understand?"

She was panting, knowing he was right, that she had to do it. Their eyes clashed; she gave a short, affirmative jerk of her head. From the ground came a harsh, wet sound; they both glanced back at the man. The *sanf* twitched once and was still.

"All right," said the shadow, pushing back his hair. "Fine. Good. It's done. Do you think you can search his pockets?"

Move. Do it.

She bent and ran her hands over the *sanf*'s coat, his breeches. She found the bulge of a wallet and a fob watch on a silver chain. A holster for the gun. That was all.

"Now go." Rhys was speaking more quickly now, his words soft and rushed, though of course no one else would overhear. "The other way, not the way you came in. Get out of here before another couple wanders through. I doubt anyone's drunk enough to misinterpret this."

Zoe blinked and gestured to the coachman. "I have to—"

"No," the shadow interrupted. "Half the dance hall saw you lead him back here. Believe me, your face is unforgettable. You need to get away now.

"Please," he said, when she still only stood there, clutching the wallet in her hands. He sounded tired suddenly, nearly exhausted. "For God's sake, Zoe. Just listen to me. Please."

She did not look at the two dead men again. She picked up the crushed circlet, pitched it down the well, turned on her heel, and went.

She was sick only once on the way back to the palace, finding an alley and then a wall as she lost the contents of her stomach, a beggar lolling unconscious at the other end, the shadow standing silently beside her.

CHAPTER TEN

The Order of the Noble *Sanf Inimicus* has created a Practical Guide for the Detection and Observation of *Drákon*.

I've seen it myself. It's a little bound book, scarcely more than a brochure, stitched at the spine and stamped in black letters over lurid red leather. The print is very tiny, because it is compiled and divided into no fewer than seven different languages.

Seven. There are so many of them, I must suppose. Or perhaps that's only what they want us to believe.

French, Hungarian, German, Italian, Spanish, Romanian, and the King's good English.

(Honestly, are there even any dragons in Spain? We are creatures of the alps and the ice-crystaled sky, not the salty, sultry earth.)

So that you should know their primary list, the manner in which they have dissected us and rendered us small enough for their minds to comprehend, I shall reproduce it here for you. Memorize their words, their canny ideas. You know *they* already have.

1. A Bodily Aspect of either Great Charisma or Marvelous Beauty.
2. Skin without Blemish, and Pale as Whey.
3. Speed of Movement, such as the Eye hardly may Follow.
4. A Voice that may Command you; you know not why.
5. Sleekness of Frame: Upon the Males, a hardness of Cheekbones. Upon the Females, an impression of Fragility.
6. An Unnatural Brightness of the Eyes, betimes a Glow.
7. Straight Teeth, strong ivory, none missing.
8. An Unnatural Physical Vigor, such as may Bend a Rod of thick Steel without Effort.
9. The Ability to Frighten all other Animals in any Form, no matter how Stout.
10. An Immense Fondness of Metals and Stones. They will nearly always wear Jewels.
11. The Ability to Transform into Smoke.
12. The Ability to Transform into a Dragon.
13. A Terrible fear of Blindness. The Monsters are near helpless without Sight.

Have you noticed yet the singular peculiarity in this catalog of our attributes? Certainly there are a few traits missing, but it may take you a brief moment to realize that every single item that *is* listed . . . is true.

That doesn't seem very likely, does it? Legends of earlier times slap us with all manner of gross exaggerations: green blood, poisoned claws, hellfire shooting from our throats. Yet this little list from our most deadly enemies contains no exaggerations whatsoever. Only facts.

One might wonder how that came about. One might indeed be excused for suspecting the unthinkable. That perhaps the *Sanf Inimicus* had assistance in creating it.

From a *drákon*.

CHAPTER ELEVEN

She did not return to her apartment at the palace. She had no desire even to glimpse the mirror waiting for her there; if there were human souls caught in the blue along with the *drákon*, she didn't know. She did not want to know.

But Tuileries was home now, as close to home as Zoe was going to get, and she was familiar with it enough to anticipate which of the corridors was most deserted. Which chambers had not had human visitors in years. Which places were more redolent of cobwebs and memories than anything alive.

She sat on the floor of an empty ballroom. There were at least five ballrooms she had discovered so far, but this was the first one she'd come to, and so it was here that she sat.

Her back was pressed against an extravagant silk-papered wall. She faced the same paper across the empty chamber, burnished gold and turquoise peacocks prancing in columns, feathers out-lined with mint green and purple trim. A tiled floor of black-and-amber marble, and enormous glassed windows all along two walls that framed the unquiet night beyond. Barring the ballroom of Chasen Manor, it was the biggest chamber she'd ever seen. It might have been made for the dancing of dragons instead of the humans who walked among them.

She was a small dim blotch amid all this glory. She sat with her knees to her chest and let herself feel small. It was better than thinking about . . . anything else.

Rhys was there too. An even dimmer blotch, seated cross-legged at her side.

How humiliating to realize that he had been right about her. That she wasn't the fine, shining weapon of vengeance she had imagined she'd be.

She was someone who had gotten an innocent man—nearly in-nocent—killed. Who had clutched at the siltstone wall of an anonymous building and vomited from the stench of blood cling-ing to her fingers, and from the ricochet reaction of her own fears.

"Is it safe here?" shadow Rhys asked.

She lifted a shoulder in a shrug, disinclined to reply. She'd made it through the city and the gardens to the palace with him gliding ever beside her, had scrubbed herself as clean as she could in one of the fountains and found the ballroom and now she wished he'd just go away. She'd asked him twice, and both times he'd refused.

"It's too open," he noted, looking around. "There's only one way in or out. And I can hear people snoring below."

Zoe clutched at her knees. "It's safe enough."

He subsided. The moon had set already and so the ballroom was bathed in a murky, faded grandeur. The wires and chains that had once managed the chandeliers still hung from their bolts in the ceiling, clipped carelessly, uneven inky lines dangling straight down from the frescoes to halfway above the floor.

"You're doing me no favors by staying here," she said to her knees. "I'd like some time alone."

"What makes you suppose I'm here to please you?"

She angled him a glance from beneath her lashes.

"You are not the sum of my existence," he said casually. "Good gracious. You never used to be so vain."

"It's hardly vanity if—"

"Perhaps I've developed an interest in your stated objective of before." He met her blank stare with a hint of smile. "Revenge," he said.

"Revenge, yes." She gave a hollow laugh and leaned her head against the wall. One of the pins in her hair dug into her scalp. "Isn't it lovely?"

"No. It seldom is."

"I never wanted . . . I never desired his death. That man, Fortin. I wanted justice. Information. I didn't want him dead."

Rhys said nothing.

She heard herself whisper, "Do you believe me?"

"It doesn't matter what I believe, love. What's done is done. All that matters is what we do next."

She closed her eyes and shook her head, and Rhys's voice took on a brisker note.

"What I do believe is that our goals are essentially identical. Death or justice, however you like it, we both want to see the end of the *sanf inimicus,* although I imagine we might disagree a bit on how that comes about. And that reminds me. How, precisely, did you discover the identity of the coachman in the dance hall?"

She did not answer.

"Because there were five of them. I was able to count that many. And since I was there when you followed them from the yard to the hall, and I never once heard anyone say anything like, 'Oy, you, the bloke who drove the rig of the dragon-man, care to go dancing tonight,' I admit my curiosity is quite aflame."

Zoe shrugged again, and the shadow leaned forward with his hands loosely clasped, his elbows to his knees. "You didn't use Persuasion to get him to tell you, or to follow you outside, for that matter. So what was it?"

She met his eyes without turning her head. They were green, ghost green, against heavy black lashes. His lips lifted into that faint smile again.

"Oh, come. I'm dead anyway. Why keep secrets?"

"I have ... another Gift. I suppose it's a Gift. It's tied in a way to why I see you, I think. I have the ability sometimes to ... gather thoughts. Other people's thoughts. It doesn't always work, but tonight it did. It's how I knew for certain he was the driver for Hayden. How I knew he was also in the employ of the *sanf*."

"You read his mind," said Rhys. He didn't sound surprised or thrilled or even doubting. He sounded very, very thoughtful.

She pursed her lips and looked away. A long moment passed. The thrum of the city began to intrude upon their silence: the carriages and livestock and people along the Quai, and coffee and river water and baking bread from the early-morning cafés in St.-Honoré nearby.

"Well," the ghost said at last. "You are one sweet delight after another, Zoe Lane. I don't recall your demonstrating any of these Gifts back at home. Did they all descend in a great big lump a few months ago, or is it that you're merely more cunning than that?"

Her fingers began a quick nervous tattoo against her knees; she stilled them by knotting them together.

"Does *anyone* at home know any of this?"

"My sister."

"The council?"

"Of course not," she flashed, then lowered her voice. "Don't be an idiot. You were *on* the council, as I recall."

"Yes, but—"

"Do you think I *ever* desired to be handed over to you on a wedding platter? A nice virginal sacrifice to your esteemed bloodline?"

"Zoe." He stared at her, brows furrowed. "How long have you been Gifted?"

She tried a third shrug, as nonchalant as she could make it. "Years."

His mouth dropped open. *"Years?"*

At last she'd managed to surprise him. She felt a small, mean glow of satisfaction at that.

It had been so long since she'd seen him in any way other than that of adversary. Handsome Lord Rhys, sensual Lord Rhys, who'd wooed her with such persistence as a boy and delivered her first, scorching real kiss. The notion of marriage to him—actual marriage, forced or not—brought an unwelcome heat to her face, even now.

He began to laugh. It was small at first, growing deeper and softer, gradually shaking his entire body until he lifted a hand to pinch the bridge of his nose; finally he looked up at her from over his cupped fingers. "You *truly* don't like me, do you?"

"You have made it remarkably easy."

"I suppose so." He swiped at his eyes. "You know I always . . ."

"What," she said, sarcastic. She felt flushed now, embarrassed, and spoke swiftly to cover it. "You always admired me? Adored me from afar? Burned with unspoken passion in the depths of your black heart? That must have been quite a burden. No wonder you masked your pain with all those other girls."

"I liked you," he said simply. And smiled. "That's all. I always liked you so much."

Ah yes, there it was. His full smile, as bright and warm and open as the sun. That heartfelt, laughing allure of his that tempted her to wicked thoughts, that implied all manner of deliciously exciting secrets to share. It was the first thing about him that had attracted her as a girl. It was the last thing she recalled of him as a woman; over the years, that quick comely smile had never changed. And no matter how hard she resisted, it always made her feel the same: like she was special. Like he saved it only for her.

A donkey somewhere outside released a loud bray. It was answered by another, even louder. She began to rub absently at the hairpin stinging her scalp.

Rhys lowered his gaze and gave a nod, as if she'd asked him a question, then straightened, brisk once more. "You're going to have to go through that wallet. I'd do it myself, but..." He spread his palms.

She'd nearly forgotten; she'd stuck the wallet in her pocket. It made a heavy weight beneath her skirts.

"No time like the present," he prompted, when she didn't move.

She unbent her legs and fished it out, her fingers sticking to the leather, smeared with dried blood.

Zoe set her teeth against the smell and opened it up.

Money, a great deal of it, *louis* and *livres* and two *deniers*. A silver toothpick. A golden ring, a signet perhaps; the face had been twisted and mashed. A few folded sheets of rice paper. A small tarnished key.

Rhys reached for the papers. She noticed for the first time that he was dressed as if he was still living—real English clothing, a laced shirt with ruffled cuffs, an embroidered waistcoat of silver-gray with leaves of holly, brown breeches. Walking boots. All of them darkened as he was. Transparent but there. She'd seen him like this all along, from the very beginning, and had only now noticed. Even that wayward lock of hair still fell down his forehead, catching against his eyelashes.

"What's this?" One shadow finger trailing smoke tapped the paper, or would have; the pieces didn't rustle beneath his touch.

She lifted them, unfolded them, and narrowed her eyes at the minuscule print. They appeared to be pages torn from a book.

"It's in a language I don't recognize," she said, scanning it. "It almost looks like gibberish, but..."

"Yes?"

"It changes right here. See? It segues from gibberish into French. 'A guide for the detection and recognition of...'" Her gaze lifted to his. "'...of the *Drákon*,'" she finished, sober.

They read it in silence. When she finished she let her hand fall to her lap, the pages loose between her fingers, staring out at the rows of strutting peacocks decorating the far wall.

"Would you say my cheekbones appear 'hard'?" he asked, leaning over her, still reading. "I mean, sculpted, certainly. Angular, I would accept. But *hard*. It sounds so coarse."

"I don't think the situation calls for levity."

"I am in all seriousness, I assure you. My good confidence rides upon your answer."

"Your confidence has never needed any help from me," she snapped. "Don't you realize what this means?" She spread the papers across her skirts. "What this is?"

"It's a death list," he replied, very calm. "Of course I realize. And it's a ruddy good one too, I regret to say." He stroked his hand over hers, very brief contact; it felt like arctic fire, like needles of ice brushing her skin. "Zee. Have you taken a close look at that ring?"

She had not. But he had dropped any trace of humor; he spoke gently now, and he did not move or reach for her again. And so by his very stillness she realized what it was, the ring. Even as she picked it up carefully and turned the face to reflect the sullen night beyond the windows, she knew what she was going to see.

A dragon. It was there, frozen in the mangled gold with wings outstretched, the letter D stamped deep into the metal behind it. It was the official seal of the Shire of Darkfrith, and the unofficial insignia of the tribe itself. Every male *drákon* received one upon the completion of his first Turn. Even ghost Rhys had a ghost signet upon the smallest finger of his right hand.

All three emissaries had worn one when they'd left the shire. The Princess Maricara, along with her news of two *drákon* slain, had brought their rings back with her.

Here, then, was the third.

She turned it over, lifted it higher, but if there were initials engraved upon the inside, they had been obscured when the ring was damaged. But three Darkfrith signets missing from their owners still meant the same thing: All three owners were likely perished.

"I'm going to sleep now." Her voice sounded tiny, insignificant against the cavernous stretch of the open ballroom. She gathered the contents of the wallet and climbed to her feet.

"We don't know for certain—"

"No," she said. "Don't say it. Don't say anything. And don't follow me. I'm going to my room, and I'm—I'm going to sleep."

She realized she could hear her footsteps as she crossed the floor and modified her gait, so that by the time she reached the threshold to the antechamber beyond, she made no noise at all. It was only then that she turned, found the shadow standing with his hands at his sides in the middle of the chamber.

"I was lying before," she said quietly. "I did want the coachman dead. He betrayed Hayden, just for a handful of money. And in that instant, as soon I realized it, I wanted him dead."

Then she left.

He was back at his bleak little road. He found himself too fatigued to stand and so sat upon the curb with a fist propped to his cheek, contemplating the deserted sidewalk, the drooping yellow shrub across the street from him. The pile of leaves beneath it.

The constant music that haunted him had shifted into a slower, drowsier tune. Rhys realized it was a lullaby, one his mother used to sing, especially when his younger sisters were fussing. He could almost hear her humming the notes, that soft dusky contralto that had soothed him to sleep so many nights as a child.

No. It's not real. Rue is not here. None of this is real.

It was nighttime in this place as well, with no moon to lighten the shadows. That might be a good sign. It could mean he was still in Paris, like Zoe. Or it could just mean that because her world was night, so was his.

He'd tried to stay with her, despite her insistence that he not. She had no authority over him, after all, and a great deal of reckless abandon when it came to her own safety. So he'd tried. But it seemed his efforts with the dying coachman had sapped more of his strength than he'd imagined. As soon as Zee had left the ballroom, he'd watched the walls and gilded doors fade into this gray place.

At least there were no Others about to ignore him. Even the rat was missing.

That coachman. His mortal body, his mortal pain. Leaping into him had been the strangest sensation, like drowning, an instant iron weight submerging every particle of his being, a sliding descent without end and oh—that agony. The knife wound. The slit lung. He'd felt that a thousand times over.

Poor bastard. It was a hell of a way to die. Rhys knew that now for certain.

But for all the pain, it had been worth it. He'd managed to lift the man's arm and even to throw the knife—it had been one of the hardest things he'd ever done, but he'd managed to throw. Now that he had time to mull it over, Rhys realized it was sheer blessed luck that it'd worked, any of it. Luck, and a desperation that had sent *drákon* strength through a human arm and granted *drákon* aim through fading vision.

As soon as it was done he'd found himself unable to attempt anything else; the iron weight sank him like a ship failing at sea. He'd crumpled as the man had crumpled, and perhaps the only thing that kept him bound to the body for the moments after that was the unexpected joy of seeing Zoe again with living eyes, flawed and human as they were.

Feeling her hands upon his chest.

From someplace to his left—west? north?—bells began to toll, shattering the night. He'd never noticed them before, cathedral bells by the sound of them, pure and piercing. Rhys counted the peals to three, which made sense . . . well, at least as much sense as anything else did.

Three in the morning: too late for honest folk to gad about, too early for the libertines to trickle back home. It was the perfect hour of the dead.

The black humor of it struck him, nearly made him laugh, but instead he lay on his back to stare up at the sky.

He drew a breath, closed his eyes, and summoned Zoe once more.

For an instant he was with her. She was in bed, in that great ugly bed in her chamber, curled on her side into a ball beneath her blankets. Her hair was a spill of pale shimmer over her pillow. She'd pulled the blankets up to her nose; her brow looked peaceful enough in her slumber. One hand poked out from the covers by her face. Rings of gold shone from every finger. A cabochon ruby gleamed like a ripe strawberry on her thumb.

He stood beside her. He turned a slow circle about the room, examining the walls, the windows, the curtains. The giant cracked mirror. The floating faces within it, gazing back at him.

They were masks atop vapor, every one of them the same, sallow and ghoulish with shadowed eyes and moving lips. He couldn't hear them; the lullaby was growing stronger and stronger and if they had speech that might have reached him, he could not hear them now. If one of them was Hayden James, Rhys could not tell.

One of the beings lifted an arm and pointed mutely at Zoe in the bed. He glanced back at her and had the dizzy confusion of seeing two images at once: one the Zoe he knew, with her ivory hair and brown crescent lashes and that single lax hand aglimmer against the sheets.

But the other was a dragon, the most delicate and exquisite dragon he'd ever seen, silver and gold and edged in pink, also sleeping peacefully beneath the covers.

A terrible weakness took his legs. He staggered and was back on the gray sidewalk of the gray street, flat against the ground. When he tried to stand he couldn't; the best he could do was crawl along to a smoother stretch of stone and collapse again, utterly spent.

His mother's voice sang the words to the lullaby, verses that seemed to sift down around him and settle like stardust, straight from the heavens.

Sleep and dream, true heart, and cease to weep,
Sleep and dream, true heart, all sweet relief....

CHAPTER TWELVE

For the first time in all her long and twisting flight to Paris, Zoe was uncertain of what to do next, or even where to go.

Hayden was actually dead. Her quest, her hope—all the meaning behind her risks, all the rewards worth the possible punishment awaiting her back in the shire—all to ash.

She didn't want to return to the Palais Royal to continue her hunt. She didn't want to stay in the cold, marbled mausoleum that was Tuileries. And she would never willingly visit a dance hall ever again.

Because the city now seemed a drab and dismal place, she wandered to the flower market banking the edge of the Seine. She found a seat on a bench between a stall of nodding tulips and one of orange blossoms on cut twigs and simply watched the passersby, shoppers and vendors, giggly girls in lace caps and crinoline picking out posies, sharp-eyed women with dirt on their aprons and wide-brimmed hats that flapped with the wind, the scent of soil and pollen and bulbs nearly overpowering the stink of sewage wafting from the river below.

Rhys had apparently taken her at her word last night and left her alone. She'd seen nothing of him so far today, not even a shimmer in window glass.

Fine. It was better this way. She wanted to mourn alone.

Between Zoe's fingers was the key she'd found in the wallet of the *sanf*. It seemed too small to be a house key. Too large to be the key to a diary, or even a jewelry box. When she rubbed it hard enough, the tarnish smudged her fingers, showing brass beneath.

There was a crude letter R scratched across the surface. She traced it with her nail, over and over, without even caring what it meant.

An elderly man eased down to the other end of the bench. He sat with his legs spread, holding a box of cut tulips and piles of small sackcloth bags, one atop another, his walking stick propped aslant against the arm of the bench. His skin was parchment pale and so thin she could see the fine spidering of veins across his cheeks, the thicker blue ropes along the backs of his hands.

He withdrew a handkerchief from his greatcoat and began to mop his face; beneath his bicorne and iron-gray toupee, he was sweating profusely. Someone called a question from behind another stall and the man flapped his handkerchief in response, not bothering to shout back.

Zoe returned to her contemplation of the key.

"A young lady so fetching should not be so sad."

She lifted her head to view the man. He wasn't looking at her.

"To be young," he said. "To be alive. Flowers and the cerulean sky. These things don't last forever. Best to..." He seemed to fumble for his words a moment. "Best to appreciate them while you can."

She sat up. The man still stared straight ahead, clutching his box. "You have life," said the man. "You still have that."

She blinked a little, glanced around. No one else paid them any mind. A liveried footman and a rose dealer were bickering over the price of his garlands; the candied perfume from the orange blossoms swirled around her like nectar in the air.

And because the day was clouded and not clear, because Hayden was dead and the *sanf* were miserably, enragingly real, Zoe cast the blue cloak at the old man.

Nothing.

She tried again, frowning at him, *seeing* the indigo depths of it, *feeling* it fall about him, envelop him, his unadorned black coat and felt hat and buckled shoes. . . .

But there was nothing there. The man was a field of blue upon blue, a blank spot in the eternity of its depths.

He turned his face and looked at her, empty hazel eyes that sent a chill skittering along her skin.

"Excuse me," she managed, and stood, clutching the key in her fist.

"Will you take a flower?" asked the man, and raised a tulip to her, the petals streaked pink and red. But he held it too hard; the stem bent in his hand, and the flower fell sideways to tap his vest. "A small token to your beauty."

She walked off. She moved stiffly, her heartbeat in her ears, her feet crunching across the pea-stone gravel, and had gotten at least six feet away before she heard the man calling after her.

"Zee. Zee!"

She stopped, swiveled slowly about. He was still sitting on the bench, holding out the tulip.

She scanned the surroundings very quickly, saw no ghost nearby, no shadow or smoke beyond the white drifting spire of a nut roaster down the lane, searing chestnuts over charred wood.

"Here," said the old man. His arm gradually lowered. "I'm here, Zoe Lane."

Sweet heavens. She crossed back to him warily, clutching at her elbows beneath her shawl. The *sanf* key pressed unbending against her palm.

"I wanted to see if I could do it," said the elderly man quickly, tonelessly. "Do it again, I mean." He switched to English. "And I can. It's not as difficult as last night. This fellow's not in the best of health, but he's mobile, and he can breathe. I can *breathe*, Zoe. God, I can breathe and smell flowers. I can see you."

"Get out of him," she said, flat.

"Not yet. I still feel strong enough to—"

"Get out of him. Leave him be."

"But—"

"Have some respect for the living, Rhys Langford." Her voice was throbbing; a knot of hot fury had lodged beneath her breastbone and she didn't even know why. "He has friends here. I saw them. You don't know who he is, if he's married, who loves him. You don't know what you're doing to him. Get out."

The man fell quiet. He released the bent tulip; it flopped to the bench by his leg, then to the dirt. He took a shuddering breath and brought a hand to his face.

Zoe moved before him, sending out the cloak again. "Sir. Are you well? You seem quite pale."

...for geneviève's garden, she'll like them best. these are her favorites, yes, and then the moorish yellows to maurice, he'll be fine with those, good bulbs, good roots, exactly as i'd hoped...

"Yes," said the man, and groped until he located his handkerchief again. He dabbed at his forehead. "Thank you, mademoiselle, I'm quite well. I fear the sun off the water gave me something of a turn, but I'm better now." He peered up at her, and his eyes were watery and bright. "An old man, you know. We move in fits and starts, but we get where we're going. All in good time, yes?"

She smiled and nodded and moved on.

"There." The shadow was beside her, gliding in his graceful, smoky way. "No harm done."

She spoke without moving her lips. "You didn't know."

"I did, though. I did, in a way. I could feel his heart. I could control his respiration. I felt everything just as he did. The bench. The sun. He's hungry. He was slightly out of breath. There's a problem with his left leg, I think it's gout. But he wasn't frail." Rhys took a few longer steps and moved in front of her, his expression serious: straight dark brows, intent green eyes. "I would not have hurt him on purpose. You should know that. He was innocent, and I would not have hurt him."

She had to stop in the middle of the path so as not to walk through him. A trio of young boys knotting twine around bundles of dried lavender watched her curiously from their booth, tiny purple buds clinging to their arms and shirts, all three knives paused in midair.

Rhys inclined his head and offered her a bow, edging out of her way. She resumed walking. He kept pace.

"It is a wonder to me," he said, low. "Life. Just for those few minutes. Just that short slice of time, to feel alive again, even in pain. I—I would give anything."

She cut her eyes to him. His head was bowed; his profile was sharp and clean and as handsome as ever, and she could see right through him, past flower stalls and masted boats, all the way across the Seine. When he shook his head, the smoke that defined him bloomed up and away.

"Anything to have my life back."

"I'm sorry," she whispered, because she couldn't think of any other response.

"Are you indeed?" He smiled grimly to the ground. "So am I."

"It is the key to a door," announced the locksmith. He turned the key over and around between his blackened fingers, squinting at the shape.

Zoe set her reticule upon the counter before her. The locksmith shop was small and crammed with bits of jagged metal and machinery, shavings of brass and pewter and lead fallen into little drifts upon the floor. An apprentice with shaggy red hair worked in a corner by a window, meticulously folding crimps into a strip of copper fixed between two vises. He was seventeen or eighteen, and kept darting looks at her through his hair with every few turns of his wrist.

The locksmith, however, was easily in his eighties and had barely managed a civil greeting from over his magnified spectacles. He slapped the key from the *sanf* upon his counter with an emphatic *clink.*

"What manner of door?" Zoe asked.

The smith's face wrinkled into a grimace. "One with a lock that will fit this key."

"Dee-lightful," said Rhys, lounging with his arms crossed against the store's doorway. He had not ventured more than two steps inside. Zoe wondered if he heard what she did, all the strange and clashing songs of the metals here, groaning and sighing and frenetic singing, a near cacophony in her head.

She tried to smile past her growing headache. "Your indulgence, sir. Is it possible to be more specific?"

"It is ordinary," said the man, impatient, jabbing a finger at the key. "Do you see this shank? This rounded bow for the hand? Ordinary. It's not even a passkey. This might fit a dozen different warded locks, mademoiselle. One to a salon. To a linen closet. A butler's pantry. Do you see? There are likely ten thousand such keys in St. Germain alone."

She pressed a hand to her temple. "Yes. Thank you. I see."

"Six sous," grunted the smith.

From his place by the door, Rhys gave a snort. "Thief."

She was inclined to agree. The smith pocketed the money and turned away without another word, hobbling to a workbench crowded with tools, squatting down to his seat with an audible popping from his knees. When his fingers found and curled about a solitary pick, it shrilled a sound like a flute: a series of high, reedy notes overpowering all the rest.

The apprentice watched her leave. She felt his eyes, at least, on her back as she closed the door carefully behind her.

"What's amiss?" asked the shadow, ever alert.

She swallowed and looked around the little street, taking in the rows of tall scarlet-leafed trees with their roots growing over the curbs and the sky flashing patches of blue between the clouds. The air, not so thick now with the aroma of metal that it felt like a coating down her throat.

"Nothing. My head pains me a little. That's all."

"Are you ill?"

"No." She began walking. "It was that place. Didn't you hear it? All that noise?"

"What, from the boy in the corner there? He was quiet as a mouse."

"From the metal, Rhys." She shot him a quick look. "All the songs from the metals."

He was silent, matching her steps. A woman in a plum-colored shawl and striped skirts marching from the other direction barreled straight through him without hesitation, carrying a basket of eggs over one arm. She didn't even blink as her face broke through his chest.

The shadow puffed and dissolved and re-formed. It didn't seem like he missed a step. Zoe looked again: yes, dark and still perfect, smoke and haze.

"You didn't hear it?" she asked softly.

"Not really. I suppose I did, somewhat. But mostly what I hear . . ."

"Yes?"

"I hear another song. Something constant. Compelling." Rhys stopped in the middle of the sidewalk and so she did too, facing him, then backing up to stand against the building behind her as more people bustled by.

She pretended to adjust the ribbon of her hat, using her hand to shield her lips as she spoke.

"Is it from a stone?"

"No. I don't know. It's not like anything I've ever heard before. It changes. It's—look, I can't talk about it. I can't think about it too much. If I think on it, it grows stronger."

Zoe hesitated. "Is it . . . celestial?"

The shadow paused, then threw back his head and laughed. "Do you mean, are the heavens calling? No. I doubt that very much."

The street had cleared for the moment; there was only a caped rider on a cob coming slowly down the way, and he was still a block off. She turned to face Rhys squarely, abandoning her pretense with the hat. She remembered him speaking of music the other night, with the yellow moon and the cloud. How completely he had vanished after, as if he'd never been.

He gazed back at her from that lean and darkened face.

"You know, you should consider the possibility—"

"No."

"Rhys—"

"No," he said again, louder. The halo of smoke around him seemed to contort, grow more dense. "It's not like that. It's not heavenly music. It's . . . something more aggressive than that. I don't feel happy when I hear it. I feel absorbed. As if it wants to devour me. And it is succeeding."

The breeze took the loosened ribbons from her hat and tugged at them by her chin, strips of dancing satin. Rhys tipped his head and raised a hand as if to catch one, and the ends fluttered through his closed fingers.

"What is it now?" she asked. "The song?"

"It's a ballad. Slow. Tender. You can't hear it?" He was watching the ribbons with half-lidded eyes, sounding strangely distant.

She shook her head.

His lashes lifted, and his hand fell away. "Good. It's sentimental rubbish."

The rider and cob were nearly upon them; she captured the ribbons and tied them in a firm bow beneath her chin, beginning to walk on.

The cloak swooped over her. That quickly, she lost the street and Rhys and the trees and sky; she was suspended in the blue, weightless, voiceless, caught with all the sudden bright faces and spirits rushing toward her, eager hands reaching for her—

Hayden. She saw him. But he wasn't like the rest, not pale or glowing. He was vivid and alive and smiling at her, saying something she couldn't hear. His hair was mussed and he hadn't shaved, and she could see the sun glinting off his whiskers as he ran a hand down his cravat—

She was released back to the Paris sidewalk. She stumbled at once across a pebble and felt it as Rhys automatically reached for her, his hand pushing against, then sliding through her arm, the cold biting into her so fiercely that she yanked back, gasping.

"What is it? What's wrong?" He nearly reached for her again and only just caught himself in time, his hands clenching into fists. "Zee, what happened?"

But she had whirled about to see the rider on the horse. And the rider on the horse had twisted in his saddle to see her.

It was a boy. A young man, rather. He was ivory-skinned and black-haired and had eyes of absolute crystalline gray, nearly without color.

The boy was *drákon*.

And she had plucked the image of Hayden from his memory, she was sure of it.

She lifted her skirts and stepped straight out into the street, forgetting Rhys, forgetting the horse, which rolled its eyes at her and reared, backing away across the cobblestones in a great clatter of iron-shod hooves. The young *drákon* struggled with the reins; his hat tumbled to the ground and was trampled and still the cob wouldn't calm. Zoe stopped walking. She stood still in the street as faces began to appear in shop windows, and the horse let out a squealing protest when the boy tried to wheel it about.

He gave up, apparently. With the grace of an acrobat, he flipped his right leg over the saddle and dismounted, still holding the reins, moving swiftly to stand in front of the beast, both hands lifted to its face, his voice a soft cadence of sound.

She watched him, waiting. Shadow Rhys had appeared at her side, also watching. The Others at the windows, and on the sidewalks, moving like ants up and down the street.

"He's one of us," Rhys said. She felt his tension, the quiver of agitation ripping through him.

"I know."

The horse was settling, and the young man was running a hand down its neck. He dared a glance over his shoulder at Zoe again, and Rhys began, very quickly, to speak. "Do you remember hearing back in the shire about the *sanf inimicus,* about how they would sometimes use *drákon* of diluted blood to help in their hunt, dragons they'd either kidnapped or coerced? This can't be a coincidence.

I don't know who the hell this is, but you've got to get out of here. Now."

"His blood is not diluted," she muttered. She felt the animal in this boy as strongly as any of the strongest of the shire. As strong as Rhys himself, back in life: waves of power, tightly leashed.

"Fine! It's not! But he could still be one of them!"

A carriage rattled around a curb, hurling right toward her. She began a clipped walk toward the gray-eyed *drákon,* who had shifted with his mount to the side of the road. "I saw Hayden through him. I saw a memory of Hayden in his mind."

"Zoe—don't be stupid, I know you're not this stupid—"

"I'm not stupid at all," she said out loud, and went up to the boy.

The cob jerked its head but the *drákon* didn't loosen the reins, and it stopped after that. She stood with her arms folded to her chest to better contain her scent, and regarded the dragon-boy.

He was, of course, quite handsome, rawboned and thin in that way that the youngsters of the tribe sometimes were before finishing their final spurt of growth. He was dressed simply but well, in black buckskin and garnet velvet, a bandanna of crisp bleached linen tied about his neck. His hair had been pulled back with a leather tie, but perhaps the ride had loosened it; strands of ebony brightened and faded beneath the shifting autumn clouds.

She saw him reach for his hat, realize it was back in the street, and then grant her a formal bow anyway, one leg outstretched.

"Who are you?" she demanded in French.

"Sandu, Noble One, your servant," he replied, courteous, rising from his bow. "You must be English. Are you from the shire?"

Zoe took a step toward him, nearly as tall, certainly more deadly, at least in these slow-ticking seconds. She felt the fury of a tempest whirling through her; she felt she could destroy him with a single focused thought. From the corner of her eye, the shadow loomed larger and larger, a rising darkness just at her hand.

"I'm going to ask you a question, Sandu. Consider your answer to me with extreme care. What have you done with the yellow-haired *drákon* who came to Paris last May? The one with the whiskers and the cravat." Her voice began to shake. "What have you done with Hayden James?"

The boy raised pointed brows. "Done with him? Why, nothing, mademoiselle. I left him back at the maison, not an hour past. He said he had a letter to write."

And just then the sun came out, a beam of luminous light that splashed all across them, and lit his hair to midnight blue and the pale crystal of his eyes to summer gold.

He smiled at her, and it was breathtaking.

The *maison* was modest by Sandu's standards. He hailed from a castle, after all, the finest castle upon earth, and there would never be a human structure to compare to it.

But the Parisian house they had rented was located in a safely residential section of the city, which he knew was important. Artisans and merchants and the better sort of tradesmen had bought their homes here, solid and skinny tall brick homes with shared stables and narrow long yards, one after another after another, street after street. The same families walking about. The same screeching children playing in the lanes. The same public fountains with women gathered about them, filling pails, gossip. The same wine shops and taverns and fruit markets. Nothing in this part of St. Antoine stood out in any way, which was good.

He had memorized the way there and back to their own place, of course. He knew a score of different routes for it, and varied them day by day, just in case.

Today he took one of the longer routes, although he could not say exactly why. Perhaps it had to do with the *drákon* woman walking silently beside him.

She was spectacular. Zoe, she'd said her name was, her accent giving the syllables that frank English twist he was gradually becoming used to. Zo-eey Lane. And because Sandu recognized that name, because there could really be no question that she was at least *what* she said she was, he was taking her home.

The long way. Down the back streets. The mare clip-clopped at his other side; he would not ride while a lady was forced to walk. Although the mare had proved her patience with him until today, it was clear she would not abide this particular lady to ride.

So they walked. And it was slow. And yes, Zoe Lane was dazzling to look upon. It was no terrible inconvenience to be forced to spend more time surreptitiously studying her. Sandu would guess he was a good ten years younger than she, but that didn't mean he couldn't let loose his imagination to some slight degree. She had, after all, all that amazing silvery-white hair, more or less half-coiled and half-loose down her back, just as the Frenchwomen styled it. It was the kind of hair he imagined he could slip his fingers through, and it would feel like—like ermine. He was certain of it. And she had those lips—lips so full and rosy soft, like she'd just been kissed, like she was made to be kissed. She probably tasted like something wonderful too. Apples, or sweet cider, or lilacs.

She glanced aside and caught him staring. Sandu faced forward again quickly, pulling the mare along, feeling his cheeks begin to color.

From somewhere behind him, he could have sworn he heard a huff, like someone releasing a breath too close to his neck.

And that brought him abruptly back to the real reason he was guiding them so slowly back to the *maison:* he could not quite rid himself of the feeling that they were being followed.

He'd checked and checked, and never saw the same face twice behind them for more than a few streets in a row. If they *were* being followed, it was by someone better at tracking than he, and that really wasn't possible.

Still. He wished the skin between his shoulder blades would cease to crawl.

Finally they reached the painted brick house. He took her around the back way so he could stable the horse—Zoe Lane lingered at a distance, which he thought was a good idea—then led her step by serpentine step to the stairs of the rear entrance, not bothering to point out the hidden wires they'd strung around the perimeter of the garden, the bells that would ring when tripped, the diamonds buried in the sod that would cry out with the pressure of a foot. The red jasper they'd wedged into the wood of the doorjambs and windowsills that would rumble and hum should anyone pass through.

She was a dragon. She would smell the wires and the bells. She would hear the soft murmurs of the diamonds, the resonance of the jasper anyway.

Sandu found his key, unlocked the back door, and like the gentleman he was, allowed her to enter first.

CHAPTER THIRTEEN

The house was wreathed in the aftermath of his cologne.

She noticed it right off, that essence of sandalwood Hayden preferred, understated but always a trifle sharp for her taste—right now the most amazing perfume in the world.

She stood in a small back room, with cocked hats on pegs and wooden clogs lined up neatly beside the door. A *redingote à la lévite* hung in heavy folds from a coat stand in the corner—she knew it, every bit of it. She'd seen that coat countless times, the enameled steel buttons and wide, fashionable lapels, the slate-blue oilskin she herself had picked out because it looked so good with his hair. It was the riding coat she herself had made for him, for this journey, hours and hours of stitching by lamplight, all for the reward of his smile and a kiss.

Zoe stroked her fingers over the fabric as she walked by, taking in everything around her. Wainscoted walls painted eggshell white, chipped edges. Pale apricot plastered ceiling. The long planks of the hallway ahead of her, showing a corridor unlit, and doors open to cast rectangles of daylight all along the southern side. A runner of royal blue and rust and cream, stretching all the way to the front door.

She entered the hall. The dragon-boy remained behind her, his steps slowed to match her own. It was narrow enough so that he could not pass her without either crowding her to a wall or darting around her at the next open doorway; perhaps that mattered to him. In any case, he did not pass.

The ghost of Rhys had no such qualms. He floated beside her, then ahead, bristling with danger.

"...can't believe you're just blindly walking into this," he was saying, a shadow so dark and thick now he became almost black. Smoke coiled all the way up to the ceiling. "Anything could be lurking here, Zoe. Any manner of men. They could be using him, using what you know of him to mask their presence—"

"No," she murmured. "It's not a mask."

The dragon-boy bobbed closer to her heels. "Pardon, mademoiselle?"

"Nothing."

She didn't need to say more. She did not need to explain. Because she'd reached the front parlor, the place where Hayden's scent lingered strongest, and there he was.

There he was.

He'd swiveled in his chair to face the door, a quill still gripped between his fingers, his eyes wide, his brows lifted. His wig was powdered and tied. His banyan was forest green. There was a davenport behind him of burr walnut, and a window draped in celery-pale brocade, and a small oil portrait of a man in a turban hung upon the wall.

She watched Hayden's jaw grow slack. She felt as dazed and sluggish as he seemed to be, as if she'd suddenly fallen down a hidden slope and plunged into a dream: a fairy-tale dream, and here was the prince she'd set out to find so long ago, the prince she'd vanquished dragons for, and mortal enemies, merely conjured from thin air. She stood unmoving at the entrance to the parlor, unable to quite slide her foot over the threshold.

"Well, hell," said Rhys succinctly, smoking at her side.

He spared himself their reunion. With Zoe's first rushing step toward her fiancé, the music in Rhys had swelled, and he'd deliberately drifted away. He almost returned to the assembly hall, or even his gray familiar street, but instead he figured he'd investigate this innocuous place that housed two of his kind, plus her.

Just in case.

Most of it was properly gloomy. Curtains and shutters blocked the sun from nearly the entire upper story, and all but two of the bedchambers were stuffed with furniture draped in musty sheets. The front two chambers, the ones closest to the main stairs, were the ones in use.

One was relentlessly tidy, with clothes and personal items laid out as precisely as if a valet had stood watch with a checklist. Brushes and combs and a jar of French powder, all aligned. A jeweled snuffbox exactly three fingers in either direction from the corner of the dresser. Even the pillows on the bed were fluffed tight.

The other chamber was practically in shambles, with books and scarves and shoes littering the floor, a cloth-of-gold waistcoat tossed askew across the top of a chair. Dabs of wax from the candle on the commode spotted the surface so profusely it looked like a miniature snowdrift against the wood.

It was no great task to surmise which room belonged to whom. Hayden James was so saintly-clean Rhys wondered if the man ever even needed to bathe. Dirt probably bounced right off his gilded damned skin.

He swiped a hand at the perfectly tucked quilt upon the bed, accomplishing nothing, and drifted on.

Dressing closets off each chamber, with basins and kits for shaving placed upon stands. Square-toed shoes and stockings, and coats hung from rods. A pair of offices down the hall, apparently unused. A single water closet. Two separate sets of stairs, the one in front and the servants' skinny, crooked flight in back. He trailed along them both, from the garret to the kitchen in the basement, with chopping knives and bread drying stale upon a block, and a small pot of herbs set to grab what sun it could up high in the solitary window. A kettle of something steamy bubbled from a hook in the fireplace. It was viscous and dark; Rhys could not smell it. Not without Zee nearby.

Two rooms made up. Two *drákon* dwelling here. If there were *sanf inimicus* anywhere in this house, they were more indiscernible than he.

The voices from the front parlor drew him back upstairs, one masculine, one feminine, and he found himself following the sound of her like a compass needle returning again and again to true north.

Surely they were done kissing by now. He could easily—all too easily—envision Zoe in a fervent, lingering embrace, but stiff-as-wood James probably didn't even know how to use his tongue.

Matters were not exactly proceeding as she had envisioned.

They sat in matching flaxen-striped chairs at opposite ends of the parlor. As the room was fairly small, this was no great inconvenience, but still Zoe wished they were closer. She found herself leaning forward, perched at the edge of the stuffed horsehair seat, just trying to feel nearer to him. Just trying to feel, still, that he was real.

The dragon-boy stood with an arm resting upon the soapstone mantel behind Hayden. He kept his gaze largely pinned to the rug, only occasionally glancing up at either of them, or else pulling a finger through the knot of his bandanna. A small snapping fire burned behind his legs.

Rhys was gone. She didn't know when he'd left, only that after she'd lifted her face from Hayden's chest he was no longer anywhere in sight.

She wished the dragon-boy would leave as well. She wished Hayden would rise from his chair, and take her by the hands, and pull her back into his arms to hold her so hard it would hurt. But after only a brief, astonished embrace—sandalwood, hair powder, silk, and a faint tang of ink—he'd led her here, seated her as delicately as if she were the dream she'd imagined *he* was, careful not to jostle either of them awake.

For a long while they'd only gazed at each other. He was exactly as she remembered, exactly the same: blue eyes like woodland flowers, lips that curved upward at the corners, lending the impression that he was always about to smile. He sat with his fingers interlaced and his feet crossed at the ankles, shapely calves in plain stockings, the buckles to his garters discreetly visible, small rectangles of reflected fire.

When he finally managed to utter something beyond her name, it was to ask if she wanted tea.

Tea.

She'd declined. Her stomach was clenched so tight, she might never eat again.

"Well," he said, still staring at her. "I believe...I believe we have some *boeuf bourguignon* from the other night, if you like."

"Hayden," she said on half a laugh. "Don't you even want to know why I'm here? How I've come?"

"Yes." He blinked a few times. "I do. Of course. Very much." And there, at last—his focus returned, and he smiled at her. "Forgive me. I find myself beyond astonished. I don't know why you're here, or even how. But I'm so very—*happy* to see you."

The pain in her stomach dissolved; she smiled back at him. Then she told him.

Not everything, of course. Until they could be truly alone, she didn't want to delve into the mysteries of her Gifts, so Zoe glossed over a few of the trickier details, speaking in a matter-of-fact voice, her eyes fixed to his or else drawn to the world outside the window beside her, an uncluttered street declining into dusk, with human families taking strolls, and three boys playing leapfrog on a lawn across the way.

And since she would not speak of the Gifts, she would not speak of Rhys. He was a secret on the tip of her tongue, but somehow trying to explain him—caustic and clever, her persistent shadow guardian—to Hayden, to the strange young *drákon* with the shuttered look upon his face, was more than she wanted to attempt at the moment. It occurred to her as she spoke that she had no proof of him in any case. No proof that the presence of the missing Lord Rhys was anything beyond her lonely nights and imagination.

She'd tell Hayden later. She would.

The shadow reappeared just as she was getting to the part of the *sanf inimicus* and the dance hall. He floated straight upward through the floor, rising before her from the center of the rug with a clear smirk at her startled break in her narrative.

Hayden came to his feet in a rustle of satin; the banyan flowed about his knees. "You followed my coachman to a common dance hall? Alone? In a foreign city?"

"Prig," said Rhys conversationally, turning to face him.

"Yes." Zoe tried not to look at Rhys.

"To dance," Hayden said, shaking his head. "To hunt."

She concentrated on him more clearly, detecting the change in his voice.

"I did. To find you. Hayden, I thought—oh, I thought the very worst. I thought you were dead. That they had discovered you, and you were dead."

"And this man would somehow help you?"

"He was the last person I could locate who had contact with you."

Hayden's handsome forehead became a crinkle. "Good heavens. When I think of what might have happened to you, Zoe. If you'd been even an ounce less fortunate—"

She found her feet as well. "Nothing terrible happened."

A blatant lie, and as soon as she said it she regretted it, but it hardly mattered, because he wasn't listening anyway. He was muttering things like *such a rash risk* and *not like you at all,* and the shadow had crossed to him fully, was marking a circle around him in leisurely paces, trailing smoke in tails.

It was more than bizarre, seeing them together. Hayden, so tall and clear-cut, so very alive: broad-shouldered and warm, his wig stiffened white. The tucks and folds of his cravat glowing with the fading light in mathematical, cascading lines.

And Rhys: the same height, no wig or flour, no twilight to illume any part of him. Untamed hair. Cool and smoky dim. The horsehair chair, the embroidered cushions, the dragon-boy and the flickering glow of orange and gold from the fireplace—all still visible as he passed, only their outlines blurred by his shape.

And yet he seemed both more elegant and somehow infinitely more dangerous than anything else in the room, even as a being of mist and devoured light.

Hayden had paused to hold a hand to his head. "I suppose there's no way around it. I must send you home alone."

She tore her gaze from Rhys. "Excuse me?"

Hayden looked to the other *drákon* for support; the boy stared back at him impassively. "I'm sorry, my dear. Certainly there are— events taking place you cannot have realized, but I can't imagine you've thought this all the way through. You've become a *runner.* You're female. You're vulnerable. You've no special talents or Gifts—"

"You never told him?" Rhys arched a brow back at her.

"—only an inordinate sense of recklessness—"

"You never told him." Rhys was facing her now, grinning a pirate's grin. "Lovely sense of trust, that."

"Kindly keep quiet," said Zoe, and Hayden closed his mouth with an abrupt snap.

"I beg your pardon?"

"Darling. Did you think I came all this way for a lecture? Your letters stopped. It wasn't a far leap to assume you were in trouble. As you are *my fiancé,*" she emphasized, still purposely not looking at Rhys, "I could not think of a better person to ride to your rescue, so to speak."

Once again, his blue eyes widened. "*You* came to Paris to rescue *me?*"

"I am," said Zoe darkly, "full of surprises."

He gawked at her a moment, then, almost reluctantly, began to chuckle. It turned into a laugh: a rich, deep, mellow sound, roundly melodious and almost soothing. She remembered his laughter so well; it was one of the reasons she thought she might be able to fall in love with him.

Hayden stepped forward—right through Rhys—still chuckling, and brought both her hands to his lips.

Just behind him, Rhys had lowered his gaze to the floor; as soon as she glanced at him his eyes lifted slightly, cool green veiled with black lashes.

"I amend my statement of before," he said. "*Insufferable* prig is more like it."

She leaned forward, closing her eyes and lifting her chin. Hayden's kiss was short and hot and spiced very slightly with brandy; when they pulled apart, the timbre of his voice had warmed measurably.

"My brave girl. Why would you think I needed to be rescued?"

"Well, as I said." She gave his fingers a squeeze. "Your letters stopped."

The crinkle returned to his brow. "My letters."

"Yes! To me, to the council."

He released her hands, taking a step back. The dragon-boy behind him blew a breath from between pinched lips.

"Oh," she said. A surge of cold began a slow, slow sweep from her chest to her cheeks. She curled her fingers into her palms. "Oh, I see. Not to the council. Only to me."

"I'm sorry, beloved." He lifted his hands, repentant. "I realized in Dijon I had to mention it to them. It seemed the *sanf inimicus* had somehow discovered me, and I am the tribe's instrument, after all. I hold the council's complete trust. Their instructions came back exceedingly clear. They did not wish us to communicate. They did not wish for any stray letters to be intercepted."

She swallowed. "Not even a good-bye?"

"Not even that," he said kindly. "I apologize. I did not mean to worry you."

"Worry me," she repeated carefully, and was only barely able to check the rise in her tone. "*Worry* me." Rhys was a hovering dark shimmer at the edge of her vision; she dragged in air past the cold in her chest, spoke through stiffened lips. "But the council still received your missives?"

"It is one of their requisites."

"They never told me."

"No? I'd hoped they'd might, but—well. They have their rules, don't they?" Hayden's expression lifted into a sudden smile. He gave her a pat upon her shoulder. "Don't fret. We'll sort it all out. I'm sure when we explain to them why you left, you'll be pardoned.

No doubt they're working themselves into a frenzy trying to figure out how you managed it; we can use that as a bargaining chip for your return. I'll post a note first thing tomorrow. I'll make it very clear that in exchange for your cooperation, they must not discipline you."

The cold surrounded her entirely. It sealed her lips shut at last, preventing her from saying all the words trapped inside her, all the unwise words that pushed hard to come.

That she had risked so much. That she given up *so much,* her home and her family and her peace—the murder of that human coachman, his life fading beneath her hands—all because of them. Because of a council of ruling males, who'd cut her off from the one bright hope in her future simply because they could. On a *whim.* Because of what *might* be. And none of them had even bothered to let her know.

And him. Hayden, their willing lapdog, who only looked at her with those melting blue eyes and smiled and expected her to forgive all, his silence and his death.

No, she realized, examining that smile. She had it backward. *He* was busy forgiving *her.*

"My," murmured Rhys, sweeping closer to her side, his lips a fresh chill against her ear. "He's quite the obedient little dragon, isn't he? What an agreeable life the two of you will share."

She could not speak; the cold consumed her. She had to walk away.

He didn't follow. He wanted to; he wanted it badly enough that he drifted to the door after her to mark the colors she inflamed, the walls and furniture and ceiling brightening and fading as she passed. Only because of her did Rhys know that the curtains here were green, and the floor was beech, and the rug was Turkish red.

But her back was stiff and her knuckles were clenched; she'd flashed him a single look of black warning as she'd stalked away.

She was enraged, her fury so tangible he could practically taste it. He could scarcely blame her; James's smug pronouncements about the council, about her, were honest-to-God boorish. It was as if her fiancé had no notion at all of who she was, the fire and passion and crazed selfless valor that burned beneath her perfect union of flesh and bones.

Perhaps he shouldn't have provoked her with that final taunt about James. Perhaps Rhys would let her be. For the moment.

Besides, he wanted to hear what holy-gilded Hayden James had to say next.

Without Zee, the parlor settled into its gray dull façade. The fire, blazing so brightly only moments before, paled and shrank, pallid flames. Even the smattering of pops and crackles from the logs grew indistinct, smothered with the newly rising strains of the symphony he could not escape.

The young *drákon* named Sandu straightened. "She is very beautiful."

The boy spoke in English, a minor surprise, but Rhys kept his gaze on James, who still stared at the empty frame of the doorway where Zoe had been, not bothering to chase after her, his hands poked deep into the pockets of his robe.

"Yes," said Hayden James slowly. "She is. A veritable icon."

"An angry icon. I don't think you're going to convince her to go back to Darkfrith easily."

James smiled again, that small and handsome smile that made Rhys wish strongly to strike him across the chin.

"Perhaps not easily. But she will go."

"You should tell her," said the boy, collapsing into the chair Zee had occupied. He stretched out his legs. "She's come all this way for you. Tell her why we're here. Tell her what we've found."

Hayden's smile wiped away. "There's no need to do that."

"Why not? Don't you trust her?"

"I trust her implicitly. I trust her intentions, at least. She's head-strong, spirited. Brutally intelligent. Were she a male, runner or no, I'd have no hesitation about including her, but..."

"Were she a male, you'd be in a fix! And our world would be sadly lacking that face—and that figure."

"You are impertinent, Highness," chided James, but his tone was placid. "Zoe Lane is my wife, or soon will be, and I will not abide her in danger. Not any more than she's in already."

"She doesn't seem afraid of danger," said the boy consideringly. "She must have hazarded a great deal to find you."

"Precisely. She needn't hazard more."

Sandu gave a laugh, his head dropping back against the chair, his rough hair coming undone. "You should have seen her on the street, Hayden. You should have seen her expression as she came up to me. I thought she was going to Turn into a dragon and eat me then and there."

"She cannot Turn."

"A small miracle, I suppose. She frightened the devil out of the horse. And me," he added bluntly, raising his head to pull the tie from his hair.

James walked back to the davenport against the wall but did not sit. He touched the tips of his fingers to the sheet of paper there instead, staring down at it with his mouth pulled into a line.

Rhys drifted over, the sonata surrounding him soaring stronger and stronger, trying to lift him off his feet. Without Zoe as his anchor, this room was growing too difficult to maintain. The corners were already melting into the walls of the Soho assembly hall, high and tall, that décor of mauve and rose and cream. Crystal chandeliers burning in hot rainbows above him.

He clenched his teeth, resisting it, bending over to skim the letter upon the desk.

Sirs,

We have discovered a nest. Within it, an egg, one of our own. Two eagles alone may strike well. They are only sparrows who guard the nest.

Rhys scowled at the penned words. A code, childishly simple, but it shot a spear of unlikely frost through him nonetheless— frost, when he was already cold to the core all the time. He pressed his palm flat to the paper and saw again the effect he had upon the living world: nothing. Nothing changed. Paper, quill and ink and letters, all the same, with or without him.

The chandeliers grew more vibrant. The prisms of color, dancing right there on the back of his hand.

"Then you'll need to get her out of here before we go down there," said the boy, his voice scarcely audible now beneath the rising notes. "You won't want her in Paris when all hell breaks loose."

"No," agreed Hayden, and picked up his letter, smashing Rhys's arm into splinters of smoke; he could not re-form them. He was cracking and cracking and cracking, his entire body wisping apart. "No, you're right. I need to get her out of Paris before the operation begins."

"Good luck with her," grunted Sandu, lifting a leg to pull off his boot.

Aye, Rhys echoed silently, letting go of the parlor and the two *drákon* men, dissolving, sinking into his symphony. *Good blooming luck.*

CHAPTER FOURTEEN

She refused to cook.

Zoe stared down at the spoon she'd dipped into the stew Hayden and the dragon-boy had concocted, watching the greasy mess of it drip, one splash at a time, back into the boil of the pot. It smelled rancid; they must have had it simmering for days. There had been beef in there once. Some onions or leeks. What it had reduced to now, however, she could not say.

She dropped the spoon back to a counter. She turned around and took in once again the cellar kitchen, the dusty cupboard holding one solitary egg and a bottle of grayish oil, the half-eaten loaf of bread. What appeared to be tarragon growing sickly green upon the shelf of the window.

There was a tin of very fine Ceylon by the water basin. Boiling water was not the same as cooking, she reasoned, and the fire was already going. Tea would be bracing.

Wine would be better, but there wasn't any, not that she had found. So. Tea.

While the water heated she sat upon the bench by the servants' table. The sole illumination in the kitchen came from the fire in the hearth; it maintained a constant, meager little glow, tarnished light all along the folds of her dress. She kept her gaze willfully upon her hands, her fingers bare of rings, and tried not to notice the rising darkness of a shadow leg, trim and muscled in brown breeches, appearing very near hers.

"Pray do not speak," she said, very low.

He didn't. After a few minutes he did shift on the bench; the water on the fire was bubbling into soft little pops.

She pushed back without glancing at him. She dumped a measure of Ceylon into the ceramic teapot that had been set next to the tin, poured in the water, and capped the pot. Then she sat again, taking the bench opposite his.

"I hope you're not going to eat whatever's in that kettle," said the shadow. "It smells like glue."

Zoe lifted her eyes to his. From across the table, Rhys sent her his most bland smile.

"I'm sorr—"

"Stop talking."

"I merely wished to express my—"

"Stop. Talking."

He leaned back a little with his hands flat upon the table, looking wounded. "Zee."

She stood again and left the kitchen.

The rear stairs led to a landing just by the backroom; she found herself opening the door, stepping out into the contained dusk of the backyard garden.

Hayden and the black-haired boy remained in the house. She felt them there, still in the parlor, probably, trying to decide what to do with her.

She could leave. She could head back to Tuileries. They'd likely not track her there for days, if at all. Paris was enormous, far bigger than she'd ever even conceived. It could take them weeks to catch her scent.

Instead she plunked down upon the rear steps, common as a scullery maid, her skirts ruched between her knees, listening to the gemstones they'd buried in the dirt. Diamonds, little ones, larger ones, blue and pink and clear and yellow. They tinkled with song, lifting into light, pretty melodies now that she was so near.

The ghost of Rhys slid over one and it didn't change its tune in the slightest degree. Even diamonds were immune to him.

Only she saw him. Only she had to look upon his face and witness the emotion that burned behind his winter-pale eyes.

"Are you well pleased?" Zoe whispered. "Delighted at the turn of events?"

"Are you?" he countered, and settled upon the dying grass at her feet.

She looked away, up to the translucent purplish-blue heights of the evening sky. The stars peeking out from between the buildings marking the horizon.

"He's alive," said Rhys, indifferent. "He was happy to see you. I think you surprised him, that's all."

Her eyes had begun to tear; she would not blink against the blue.

"We should go home," the ghost said. "It's time now. He's safe. We need to head home."

For an instant she thought he was speaking of the palace. But when she looked down at him he was plucking at a blade of dried grass, his fingers pulling at it over and over, his hair falling in waves of deep brown along his face and over his shoulders.

"Darkfrith," she said.

"Yes."

She watched him trying to pinch the grass. "I can't imagine that. I can't imagine going back there."

"It's where we belong, Zee."

"Hayden is my home."

"Oh?" His tone sharpened. "Well, your home that is Hayden evidently also wishes you to return to Darkfrith. A double endorsement, rather."

The diamonds were picking up volume with the twilight; sweet, airy music that swirled about her with the sighing of the breeze.

"Is this what it will be like there?" she asked quietly. "You and I, forever and ever?"

He glanced up at her. "What d'you mean?"

She leaned forward with her hands clasped between her knees, intent. "Will you haunt me forever?"

His jaw tightened; the evening breeze took the catkins of an alder directly behind him and shivered the leaves. She could see it. Through the gloom and him. Right through him.

"Because I really don't think I deserve that," Zoe went on. "I never wished you any true ill in life. I wish you only peace in death. Why won't you leave me be?"

"I . . ." He shook his head, a blossoming of smoke. "Wait. What are you saying?"

"I can't exist with you here. Always here. I can't be expected to live my life like that. It's not right. You shouldn't be my shade, Rhys. I don't know where we go after we—I don't know what comes after our deaths. But you shouldn't be with me."

He regarded her with those chill green eyes. "Whatever happened to *I swear I'll avenge you?*"

"I can't do that from Darkfrith."

"By God, Zee," he burst out, coming to his feet. "You can't do that *anywhere*. Don't you understand? I'm not choosing to be with you. I can't help it. You're the sole light in my universe, and if I'm stuck with you, I have to guess there's a damned good reason for it. You don't know what happens after death? Well, neither do I. All I know is that when I'm with you I feel again, and I see again, and it's like there's actual blood in my veins." He slapped a hand to his chest. "In my heart. You drown the song, Zoe, you alone. If anything were to ever happen to you—"

"You might be free," she whispered.

"No." He shook his head again, smaller; his hair scarcely stirred. "No, love. I'd just be alone. Again."

"Zoe?"

She turned to find Hayden standing above her, his gaze bright as the sky, a hand spread upon the open door.

"Who are you talking to?"

"The diamonds," she answered, taking up her skirts and climbing the stairs to him. "The jasper."

"Come inside," he said, and placed that hand upon the small of her back as she passed. "Come talk to me instead."

They had found him two days beyond Dijon. He hadn't realized it was the coachman who'd betrayed him; all Hayden knew was that at some point during the night in the rustic inn they had settled upon he'd awoken to the tiny, persistent scratch of a pick working at the lock to his room. And even then he'd assumed it was just a common thief determined to ransack his luggage; France, he said, was rife with such rogues. Until he'd caught a whiff of saltpeter and nervous sweat. The oiled metal of the guns.

Hayden was full *drákon.* Although the council had instructed him not to use his Gifts unless his circumstances turned truly dire, he figured a quartet of *sanf inimicus* breaking through his door was dire enough.

"You Turned?" Zoe asked him, nursing her cup of too-strong tea. "To smoke or to dragon?"

"Oh, to smoke, of course," he said, taking a sip of his own tea. They had moved from the front parlor to the drawing room across the hall, where there were frosted-glass lamps and a settee wide enough for them both. The curtains here were heavy damask, white with saffron flowers. "A dragon would have shattered that little matchbox of an inn to slivers, even without trying."

"It was mostly spit and thatch," agreed the dragon-boy, who had shunned the pungent tea for brandy. He sat by the fire once again. The engraved glass in his hand winked in constant, cinnamon sparks.

Zoe glanced at him. "You were there?" Twice since beginning his tale, Hayden had granted the boy the honorific *His Grace,* and once, *His Highness.* Sandu was Zaharen, obviously, from that clan of Transylvanian *drákon* that so worried her own. He seemed quite young to be both a lone hunter and a prince, but there was no mistaking that air of jaded, adolescent regality about him. He even held his brandy in a studied way, the stem and cup supported between two slender pale fingers.

In any case, Hayden would not be wrong.

"I was," said Sandu. "The *sanf* were tracking your husband. I was tracking the *sanf.* Our sudden convergence was most fortuitous."

"They weren't expecting us both. We made short work of them," Hayden said mildly.

She lowered her cup. "Are they dead?"

"Really, my dear. I can't imagine you'd find any gratification in the details!" He leaned over to touch a hand to her knee and almost as quickly removed it. "Suffice it to say you need never worry about those particular humans. They shall not trouble us again."

"Yes," said Sandu, sending Zoe a short, candid look. "They're dead."

"I like this boy," commented Rhys. "I confess it. I like him more and more."

The ghost of Rhys had followed them inside. He'd taken a chair by the windows, as relaxed against the cushions as the young prince seemed to be, and up until now at least, he'd been silent.

She'd decided to ignore him. It was her only hope of slipping back into her normal life. If she refused to acknowledge him, if she refused to interact with him, perhaps he'd give up. Perhaps he'd fade away and go where he was meant to, wherever that was.

Not here. Not at her side.

When she moved her hand, the loose leaves of tea at the bottom of her cup spun in diminutive eddies. She looked from them deliberately back up at Hayden. At his profile, so golden and fine.

"Why are you both in Paris? I thought the council wanted you to reach the Zaharen in the Carpathians."

It was Sandu who finally answered; Hayden had gone stiff, avoiding her gaze.

"Because... Paris is where they are. Paris is where they've hidden their heart."

She nearly spilled her tea. "What? The *sanf*?"

"That's what we discovered that night." Hayden murmured the prince's name, but the boy only spoke over him. "Their leader is ensconced here. They're building ranks. There might be hundreds of them already in the city alone. They're preparing for something big, bigger than they've ever attempted."

"Darkfrith," Zoe guessed, then caught her breath.

"We fear it so."

Darkfrith. Cerise and the little children. Uncle Anton, gray and slow. All her kin, the village and farms and the unprotected downs . . . and that menacing phrase the cloak had captured for her back in the Palais Royal: *over two hundred sanf—*

Sandu shifted, adjusting a velvet pillow behind his back. "There's more. We discovered they're holding one of our kind. We don't know who. We don't even know why. It's not a ransom or exchange, and they're not using this *drákon* to hunt us, as they've done in the past. They're keeping him—or her—prisoner, a body bound. It could be one of your tribe or mine. You're missing your Alpha's second son and that young maiden. My own people are scattered, and we don't . . . track ourselves as you do, so it might be nearly anyone. Whoever it is, the individual seems vital to the *sanf inimicus.* Vital enough not to dispose of. Yet."

Rhys had sat up in his chair. His clenched fingers seemed to sink through the wooden arms.

"You're going after them," said Zoe, disbelieving. "Aren't you? The two of you alone, going for a rescue. Just like the heroes in a picture book."

The prince fixed her once again with that clear candid gaze.

"Of course," he said.

Hayden came to life. "And that's why you must leave. That's why I need you on the next coach to Calais. So you will be safe."

"The *two* of you," she reiterated. "Against an entire hive of Others."

He granted her a sideways look. "Do you think it an uneven match, my dear?"

"I think it's *suicide.* You've just said there might be hundreds of them here. That their *leader* is here. Don't you think they'll have prepared for our kind? Don't you think they'll be ready to defend this body, this dragon, that they want so badly?"

"They're still merely humans," said the prince with a shrug.

"Humans with weapons! Humans with a list of proper ways to recognize us! To take away our *sight*!"

"But we have the better advantage," explained the boy slowly, as if she were exceptionally dense. "We know they're here. They don't know we are. You yourself said that the one who did locate you was killed by the other man, trying to protect you. So—there you have it."

She placed her cornflower china teacup delicately upon the table before her, centering it in its saucer, and shifted to face Hayden. He looked back at her gravely, not relinquishing his own cup.

"I won't be leaving. Not without you."

"Zoe..."

"Think on it, Hayden. The *sanf* I encountered was a coachman. The man who worked for him was a coachman. I was fortunate enough to escape them both—"

Rhys cleared his throat.

"—and certainly they won't be coming after me again, but if there was one thing they both made clear to me before they killed each other, it was that the *sanf inimicus* have infiltrated the coach yards of this city, purely in search of us. They discovered me once. There is no reason to believe they will not do it again. I might get all the way to Calais before they strike. But they *will* strike, dearest. They've proven that, again and again. And when they do, I shall be all alone." She lowered her lashes, tried to look vulnerable. "Practically defenseless."

"Oh, well done," praised the shadow in an exaggerated drawl. "I knew all that sly wit and duplicity would prove handy sooner or later."

Both the prince and Hayden were glowering by the light of their smallish lamps and fire; she'd taken the wind from their sails,

174

she could see it, and could not help the slight curving of her mouth.

"I'm truly safer remaining here," she said, "with you. You must see that."

"Yes," said Hayden after a moment. "I'm afraid . . . I'm afraid I do see. You're quite right. You could not possibly leave now. Not by any standard means, and I can't escort you yet."

"Bonehead," pronounced the shadow, throwing up his hands. "For pity's sake! I should have fleeced him at cards more often. Perhaps then he might have learned to recognize a sharp."

Zoe only smiled at her fiancé, and lifted his hand to brush her lips tenderly across his knuckles.

They left her alone after that. They'd gone as a group to Tuileries and fetched her things in the deep black hub of night; she was settled in the third bedchamber of the *maison* now, the smallest of the three still adequately furnished. It had walls papered in pink and the palest yellow stripes, and brown-centered daisies painted along the trim. It was the room of a child, but she didn't mind. It lacked both a crib and even a single looking glass. The indigo cloak—all those spirits—was forced back to the windowpanes, and Zoe kept the curtains pulled tight, so that she would not have to see.

She lay in the bed and stared up at the ceiling. The prince had retired to his chamber with hardly a glance at her, but Hayden had lingered at her door, his gaze combing the girlish bedroom beyond her as if he searched for something that was not there.

"Will you kiss me?" she'd whispered, as softly as she could. She didn't see Rhys but that didn't mean he wasn't nearby.

Hayden lowered his chin and smiled at her, a soft and shy smile. Then he'd lifted his hands and cupped her face, and rested his lips against hers in what was surely the most tame, most brotherly kiss a female *drákon* had ever received from her affianced mate.

"No," she whispered. "Like this." And had wrapped her arms about his shoulders and pulled him close, pressing her mouth hard to his.

For a moment it seemed to work. For a moment his hands pushed deeper into her hair, and his chest expanded against hers, and she tasted tea this time, tea over the brandy and him.

Then he broke it off. He drew a jagged breath, lifting his head with his smile now strained, and dropped his hands to her shoulders.

Zoe reached up to grab his fingers, fierce. "Can we not pretend? Just pretend we're wed already? Do we need to wait?"

"If we do not have our honor," Hayden murmured, his eyes roaming her face, "then we have nothing."

We would have each other, she wanted to say. *We would have tonight.*

"Good night, dearest girl. You do hold my heart, you know. And it *will* be soon. As soon as we're home safe again, I promise. The very first open date in the chapel will be ours."

"Good night," she'd managed, and watched him cross the hall to his room. Shut the door.

She rolled over now in the narrow bed. She pulled the quilt up high, inhaled the scent of goose down from the pillow, and tried to fall asleep.

In the darkest corner of her very dark room, the shadow stood and watched her, unmoving. Unspeaking. Until the first blush of dawn lit the carpet of flowers at his feet.

CHAPTER FIFTEEN

O nce there was a prince. Have you heard this story before? A prince in spirit if not in title, and he was handsome and brave and bold, and more than a little charming. Like many such princes, he tumbled in and out of love with ease, and happened to leave quite a pretty trail of broken hearts scattered behind him. He was not especially kind, but he was not especially cruel, either. He had been blessed by life and forged perhaps a wee bit selfish by all that good fortune. There had never come an occasion truly to plumb his depths, and so he sparkled like a raindrop, bright and cheerful and happy to splash where he would.

Don't judge him too harshly. Born in his magical place, do you imagine you would have turned out so very different?

So this prince might well have lived the whole of his life in such a way, and then his name and story would have faded from memory; he would have been just one more dashing prince for us to amass with all the dashing others, fine-looking fellows all with the same grin.

But one day this particular prince lost his looks and his fortune with a single devious blow. He lost his light, and his hope. And he realized only then—of course!—what a waste his life had been. How foolish he was to have squandered it, when he might have been a good man all along.

He had but one chance to touch something bright again. He had but one chance to prove he was more than splash and easy charm.

This chance came to him in the shape of a female, a special female: a treasure, one might say. She possessed a heart so strong and true he could scarcely fathom the size of it.

It's a shame, isn't it, that the sole thing the prince was good at was shattering hearts?

CHAPTER SIXTEEN

She had to cook.

She'd promised Hayden and the Zaharen she'd not leave the *maison,* not until they returned from their scouting mission down to wherever it was the *sanf inimicus* were crouching. By the time she'd awoken this morning, one of them—she didn't even know which—had already gone to market, and so there was now slightly more food than that one egg and the stale bread.

But they'd been out for hours already. Hours. There was a standing clock in the main hallway by the front door, and it had long since chimed two o'clock. Three. Even the shadow of Rhys was gone; perhaps he'd taken her at her word yesterday.

More likely she'd just pushed him into a sulk.

A group of children in the yard next door were running around, squealing and laughing over the calls of their nanny. A tethered dog in the yard on the other side was keeping up a stream of steady, un-happy yips.

She was hungry. She'd already dumped their stew from the fire-place into the compost—Rhys had been correct; it reeked of glue—but she'd not found enough sand or water to scrub out the pot.

She would compose a salad; there were plenty of vegetables for that. There was little chance of spoiling a salad.

Zoe whacked the carving knife into a head of cabbage. It split in two, the pieces rolling, one of them wobbling off the chopping board; she nearly caught it with one hand, but it was fat and wet, and slipped off her fingers. A caterpillar bounced out of it onto the floor.

"Damn it."

"Gracious. Where did you learn that?"

So, at least her ghost was back. She stooped to pick up the cater-pillar, placed it in the pot of tarragon, then slapped the cabbage back upon the board. A square of sunlight slanting down from the window picked out in bleached yellow the grain of the wood, the bones and tendons of her hands.

"No doubt listening to you."

"Have you been?" he asked, walking up to her. "Listening, I mean?"

With the glow of light below him he was nearly as thick as life; she could see the slate shadow of beard in the hollows of his cheeks, the band of deeper jade around the pupils of his eyes.

"I can't really help it." She bent her head and whacked at the cabbage again. "As you seldom shut up."

"Hmmm. I hardly think I warranted that. Is your mood so sour because they've stuck you in the kitchen?"

"No one has stuck me anywhere." Another whack. "I choose to be here."

From beneath her lashes she watched as Rhys made a show of glancing around them, his hands tucked behind his back, linen ruffles to his fingers and leather boots that made no sound upon the floor. "Yes. Yes, I can see why. It's a fair paradise down here in this basement. Not dank or dismal *at all*."

She shoved the chopped cabbage into a bowl, took out the carrots she'd already washed clean, and began to slice off their tops.

"I am female." A feathery-green frond flew across the counter. "I like to cook."

"I can tell."

She put down the knife and turned to him. "You're stronger than before."

He nodded. "When I'm with you."

"You're not just a reflection now, Rhys. You have depth." She wiped her hands on her apron and, experimentally, pressed a finger to his shoulder: cold, cold resistance. Her eyes went to his; he was watching her steadily. "I can feel you."

"Yes," he said.

She took a step back. She felt better with distance between them, safer somehow. "This can't be."

"Why not?"

"You're a ghost." She tipped back her head and gave a little laugh to the timbers of the ceiling, almost despairing. "For all I know, you're an exceedingly vivid figment of my imagination."

"No. You know I'm real."

"Do I? No one else can see you or hear you, much less touch you. I look at you and I feel—"

"What, Zee?" He floated closer, his lips barely moving. "What do you feel?"

Pain, she realized. She felt pain when she saw him. Loss. She mourned the death of a man she'd not even known. He'd been beyond her, always beyond her, for both of their lives. He'd been that

181

secret enchanting memory from her girlhood and the patrician future she herself had decided to abandon. But now, with him here, with him always here, she was learning facets of Rhys Langford she'd never before guessed: that beneath his wicked humor was sensitivity. Bravery. Beyond his cocky smile was stalwart dependability. Even as a shade, even at his most galling, he'd tried to do nothing but protect her.

And she mourned him, she did. She mourned his death.

"James is a fool." His mouth thinned as he studied her, the angles of his face shining clear and dark. "He should have stayed with you last night. I would have."

She laughed again, shaking her head to disguise the moist heat in her eyes, and went back to the carrots. "Oh. Splendid. You saw that?"

He was silent. The polished blade of the knife caught the light in a brilliant, painful gleam. She had to wipe her lids with wet fingers before she could glance back at him.

She would swear there was color in his cheeks, a stain of red over the dark. He looked abashed. *Abashed,* when she had thrown her heart and her body at a man who'd rather sleep alone night after night than with her.

She stabbed the point of the knife down into the block, folding her arms across her chest. "Let me be plain. I can't go through the rest of my days like this. With you like this, always lurking."

"Zoe."

"No. It's not fair. Not to me, not to Hayden. Not even to you. I don't accept it." Rhys watched her as if she spoke some odd foreign language, a small baffled crease between his brows, as if at any moment she would begin to make sense again. "It's not fair," she reiterated, more forceful, to defeat that look.

"I believe I've heard this tune before. But guess what, Zee? Life isn't—"

"But you're not *alive*," she hissed.

"Love is stronger than death."

She opened her mouth, closed it, and tightened her lips. The aroma of chopped vegetables was suddenly astringent in her nose.

"What did you say?"

His tone was defiant, although his eyes slid from hers. "Love is stronger than death."

"This isn't *love*! You can't love me!"

"You can't make me not." He shrugged, drifting back to the hearth, and the embers of coal that shone like rubies through his legs. "Anyway, it's too late."

She gaped at him. She could not think of a single thing to say.

"You know how we are, Zee. All that dragon business about constancy and fidelity, our bonded hearts. One mate for life." He smiled gently, sadly. "For death too, I must suppose."

"No, but—"

"You're unconventional and you're loyal. You don't think or act like anyone else in the tribe, and you don't give a damn about it, either. All the other *drákon* believe there's ice in your veins but they've got it all wrong. It's fire in you, Zee. You burn so bright inside, you outshine the sun. No one else knows that but me." His smile lost its melancholy. "And you *don't* like to cook."

"You think you know me? Honestly? A few days and nights tossed together and now we're bonded?"

"Is it James?" he asked, taking a seat atop the table, kicking his feet into the air. "Because you don't love him."

If it would have made a difference to throw something at him, she would have. "Do not presume to think you understand my heart."

"Well," he said with another shrug, "you don't. If you did, you would have trusted him enough to tell him about your Gifts."

She was cold because the kitchen was cold, that was all. The sullen fire in the hearth did little to dispel the chill of September and walls of earth behind stone, and the square of sunlight bore hardly any heat.

"And don't think I didn't notice how you neglected to mention the wallet of the *sanf inimicus,* either. Were you afraid to let him know how you'd gotten blood on your hands?"

She'd presented a deliberately tame version of the night of the dance hall. She'd made it sound like the two men had destroyed each other, because, yes, it had been easier than the entire truth. And there was a part of her, an appalling, cowardly part, that worried about what Hayden would say if he knew everything she was. What he would think.

That she was mad. That she wasn't Gifted; she was cursed.

Zoe found her voice. "I'm going to tell him. And all this is simply *your* reaction to my Gifts. You never loved me before, not in all those years. Now that you know who I—what I can do, you've convinced yourself it's more than what it is. It's simple instinct."

"Perchance you're right. But the result is the same, isn't it? We were meant to be together in life. That's our law, because that is our instinct, the natural order of our kind. Strongest mates to strongest."

She took the steps necessary to stand before him. She held out a hand to him and he accepted it, lightly, his fingers cradling hers; the needles of his winter touch crept along her nerves. "This is not life, Rhys."

"No." He studied their locked hands, the pulse in her wrist, his smoky haze. "But it is still love. Just as I loved you when we were young—"

"Stop it," she whispered.

"*My* heart beats for you." He released her fingers—the pins and needles of his contact fading at once—and gave her that faint, sardonic smile. "Figuratively speaking."

"I am going to marry Hayden."

"I know. And I'm still going to love you." The smile deepened. "Sorry."

They arrived back at the house close to dusk. She'd kept her word and not ventured beyond the perimeters of the property. It was more difficult than she'd thought it would be, remaining in her place, exploring the *maison* and the back garden, thinking of all the avenues and shops and bridges of Paris she'd walked so freely only an afternoon before.

And now to be here. One house. Eight rooms. A bakery down the street offering fragrant croissants and breads and pies, all beyond reach.

Odd how she'd never felt so captive in Darkfrith. She'd never even really noticed the boundaries of the shire beyond the common sort of ways of *we don't go south of Blackburn Road; we don't go east past the River Fier.* Possibly because those rules affected everyone, young and old, male and female alike.

She'd never before come to dislike the confinement of brick and mortar so very much. And they did not return until dusk.

They were dirty, even Hayden, and brought with them the odor of muddy river. And . . . chocolate.

She met them with a lamp at the back door. Hayden touched his lips to her cheek, took the lamp from her, and handed her a paper box. Raspberries gleamed inside it, dipped into rounded jewels of thick chocolate, sprinkled with colored sugar.

He'd remembered. Her sole weakness for sweets, rich dark ca-
cao, the darker the better. And fresh raspberries at this time of year;
he must have fair combed the city for them.

Zoe lifted her eyes to his, and smiled.

Sandu had no idea what Hayden James might be waiting for. It
wasn't as if the man wasn't engaged to the most glittering female
Sandu had ever seen. And it also wasn't as if he didn't crave her: He
could see it in just the way the other *drákon*'s eyes followed her
about, how when she was near Hayden simply stopped what he
was doing to stare at her, absorbed. The fellow practically radiated
heat when she passed.

Not that Sandu blamed him. There were a good many joyful
things about Zoe Lane to stare at. He was having a deuce of a time
himself keeping his gaze from wandering to certain enticing parts
of her.

She'd been with them four days. Four days. Five nights. And
now all the rooms of the *maison* were scented of her, and all of
Sandu's clothes were scented of her, and everything she touched—
everything—smelled like wonderful female. Like honey and desire.

They'd been engaged for years, Hayden had told him. She was
still fresh as a flower for all that time—despite her own efforts
to change matters otherwise. He'd heard them that first night
in the hallway, even with his hands over his ears. Heard her
pretty whispers, her invitation . . . and Hayden had only walked
away.

It was confounding. Honestly. No doubt Hayden was tired—
he and Sandu spent each day in prolonged, serious hunt; they had
no one in the city yet to aid them—but how tired could the fellow
be? Sandu was sixteen years old; one sweet beckoning glance from
a dragon-maid as fair as Zoe would have had him tripping over his

own feet in his rush to get to her. Especially one so devoted as to chance throwing away her life for his; he knew little about the ways of the English *drákon,* but one thing he did know was that they were terrified beyond reason of leaving their sheltered shire. That they had rules against it, all manners of rules. And that breaking those rules led to punishments he would not inflict upon even the lowest of serfs in his domain.

For all their similarities to the Zaharen, the English were a different sort of breed. That much was clear.

Yet he was heartened when, in the depths of that fifth night, the smallest of sounds jolted him awake in his bed: the diminutive *snick* of a latch being released, a door softly opening—Hayden's door, directly across from his. Footsteps on the rug. And then another *snick,* another sigh of wood pressing air: Zoe Lane's door, just down the hall.

Sandu nodded to himself, glad for his friend, the sliver of jealousy that stabbed through him easily repressed. He pulled a pillow over his head and tried to think loud, loud thoughts.

Her dreams were darkly blue. She floated amid them, unable to speak, seeing the faces of all the spirits floating with her. Cerise and Thomas, both her young nieces. Hayden. Rhys. Mother and Anton and Zoe's father too—his features flatly identical to the miniature her mother used to carry on a bracelet around her wrist, white-haired, glancing eyes of whiskey gold. Everyone here in the blue was someone she knew. All from Darkfrith. All crying out to her, many weeping. Hands raised, begging for her help, to stop them from all being killed—

"No, no." Hayden's voice came clearest, his cologne choking; she could actually see it, a spangle of silver mist twirling about her, binding her like chains. "No, love. Don't cry."

She felt herself gasping for air, trying to escape the chains, trying to evade the faces, their pleas and their skeletal hands—

"Wake up," urged Hayden, so close, resonant in her ear. "Wake up, Zoe. It's only a nightmare."

She opened her eyes and he was there, flesh and heat, right above her, seated at the edge of her bed with his hands chafing her cheeks. She lifted her palms to cover his, clutching hard, still trembling, feeling the steady tension of his fingers.

"There," he whispered. In the shuttered dark his teeth gleamed with his smile. "There you are." His hands drew down her face to her neck, to the edge of her nightgown pulled in a taut line across her collarbone because she'd tossed and tossed in her sleep.

She sat up and threw her arms around him. She tucked her face into the curve of his neck and tried to breathe through her mouth, to lessen the reminder of sandalwood and chains.

"Ah, Zoe." He placed a kiss on her temple. "Beautiful girl." Another kiss, his hand sliding up to cup the back of her head; she felt his fingers tighten, urging her to lift her face. When she did, he leaned forward with new intent, his mouth brushing the corners of hers, slight, feathery touches. "You taste like rain."

She felt filled with a slow wonderment. It was like another part of the dream, so much better than the rest, but everything was still strange and disorienting, and he was kissing her more fully now, slow, teasing circles, nothing he'd ever done before.

"Hayden," she managed, breathless. "Hayden, there's something I have to tell you."

"Tell me later," he said, and pressed her back to the warmth of the bed.

He came across her at once, heavy for a moment, too heavy, as if he'd lost his balance against the spongy mattress. But then he lifted up to his elbows, and she could inhale again.

Without the wig his hair hung silky pale above her, a bare tickle against her skin. She lifted a hand, running her fingers through the blunted strands. "No, really. It should be now. Before we . . . before . . ."

His response was a lush, deep plundering of her mouth, his tongue a sudden flavor, musk and more brandy and him. Urgency.

"I'm Gifted," she blurted, as soon as his mouth lifted from hers. "All manner of Gifts. I can Turn invisible, Hayden. I can read minds."

He smiled against her cheek, his body stretched over hers. The covers were a wad of quilting between their legs.

"Amazing," he whispered, and pushed his pelvis against hers. "So amazing."

He felt heavy again, oddly ungainly. He was pulling at the ribbon drawstring of her gown.

"Did you hear me?" She caught her hand in his. "*Invisible*. Like this."

He did pause then, lifting his head to stare down at her, his head cocked. The bedchamber was gloomy but it was certainly enough for him to see her—or not, at the moment—if she could see him. His fingers appeared suspended, curled around the empty space between them.

"*That,*" he said, husky, "is quite a trick."

He released the ribbon and her hand, found her chin, nuzzled it with his mouth. Heat and sensation: another kiss across her lips.

Zoe felt a tingle of annoyance. "It's rather more than a trick." She turned her face away, visible once more. "I don't understand you. I thought you'd be—angry, or astounded, or at least want to . . . discuss the . . ."

He had stilled, that ungainly weight, that sharp sandalwood scent. He lay propped above her, saying nothing, his heart drumming directly over hers.

"No," she breathed, incredulous. She pushed at him, hard.

"No," she said again through her teeth as he rolled off her, right back to the edge of the mattress, where he sat, silent and inert, a block of wood.

"Is it you?" She scrambled free of the covers, shoved a hand against his shoulder; he accepted the force of it, didn't move otherwise. "*Is it?*"

Without warning, Hayden slumped forward, his hair dangling to his face. His torso lifted into a long, hoarse shudder; when he straightened again, he stared bemused about the chamber. He didn't even see her there, on her knees right there beside him.

"Hayden," she said, composed.

He looked back at her.

"Are you here now?" she asked.

"Zoe." He gave a little shake of his head. "Why are you in my room?"

"I'm afraid you're in mine."

He came instantly to his feet. He smoothed a hand down his chest—he wore a nightshirt, his legs bare, and she knew now there were no drawers beneath it—and backed away from her.

"Don't be alarmed." She spoke soothingly. "You were sleep-walking, I think."

"I was? I say, that's . . . I've never . . ."

She scooted to the end of the bed, making certain her shins were covered. "How do you feel? Are you well?"

"I don't remember any of it. My dear! I beg your pardon. I fear I must have been far more weary than I even realized. Was I . . . did I do anything to—er, to offend you?"

"Not in the least. I awoke when you touched my wrist. That was all."

He pressed back against the door. He regarded her without moving, a golden-haired stranger who had embraced her with such passion only minutes before. There might have been a darker shadow beside him, to the left; a trick of the night or something more devious.

The annoyance from before spiraled deeper, twisting more into anger and a curl of unexpected grief, so she added, "But you may stay if you like, Hayden."

"Dearest girl." He reached for the knob behind him, caught himself short and sketched a curt bow. "I apologize most sincerely for all this. It won't happen again."

He was a spot of brighter gloom in his voluminous shirt, there and gone with the closing of her door. Zoe fixed her gaze to where that deeper darkness had been, now vanished as Hayden was.

"No," she agreed, clenching her fists. "It surely won't."

She waited sitting up in her bed, unable to sleep now in any case, an oil lamp burning a small yellow flame upon the bureau in the corner. Outside roosters were beginning to crow; she'd opened the curtains and the shutters, and the skyline of Paris was burning pink and orange. Cathedral bells clanged and clanged, challenging the roosters.

"Rhys." She shaped his name with hardly any sound. She thought it, she felt it, and cast the cloak for him, dragging back a wake of blue nothing.

"Rhys. Come to me."

There were clouds in the heavens. They were green on top, green with fire-painted edges.

"Rhys Sean Valentin Langford."

She felt him before she saw him. Felt the air change, felt her body change, tiny hairs standing on end, an acknowledgment of his winter presence.

He was by the window. The colors of the dawn misted through him, mother-of-pearl through his outline of smoke.

"That was unkind," she said, just as quiet as before.

He looked away from her as if bored, toward the daisies on the wall. His arms were folded across his chest. Linen shirt, silver waistcoat. Those leaves of embroidered holly.

Just like Hayden's riding coat, she'd stitched that waistcoat herself. She remembered it well; his sister Lia had commissioned it one Christmas, years past, and Zoe had chosen for it the deep green thread she thought would best go with his eyes.

"Promise me you'll never attempt it again."

He shook his head.

"Promise."

"No. I won't promise." He spoke forcefully. Unlike her, he was free to be as loud as he pleased. "Why should I?"

Her temper began to unravel. "Because it's *wrong*. It's *wrong* to—to toy with me that way. To meddle with my affections. With *him,* as if he's nothing more than a puppet!"

"I'm not toying. I'm dead serious."

She paused. "Was that supposed to be humorous?"

"If you like." He sounded surly.

"Well, I *don't*." Her fingers curled against the sheets. "I don't like any of this. I've told you that you need to leave, and you respond like *this,* like it's all a game to you, like nothing in this world matters to you but what *you* want, and what *you* desire." She tossed back the covers and climbed free of the bed, her nightgown a ruffled restraint at her ankles.

He watched her come close. He watched her with eyes that now better matched the ethereal clouds. "Was it so unpleasant?" He was a lord, or had been, and he looked it still: regal and proud and handsome enough to steal the very light from the sky. "Tell me, Zee. Was it?"

She lifted her hands, frustrated. "It was a lie. So yes, it was unpleasant."

He dropped his gaze. "Not for me."

"You must never do it again, Rhys. I mean that with all my heart. Never again."

He tipped his head without raising his gaze from her feet. His lips made a mirthless smile. "We'll see."

And he disappeared before she could speak another word. The view beyond the window blazed clear again.

Against his will, by the haunting of his shadow music, he began to dream it: a life with her. Darkfrith, with her. Children, with her. By their living laws she was already his, and Rhys found it easier and easier to slip into the reverie of that notion.

Sitting with her upon the banks of the lake. Walking through the woods with her, the snow. Leaping to the stars with Zoe Langford laughing on his back.

Sleeping with her. Wrapped in long ivory hair every night, skin to skin, heat and pleasure. The taste of her lips.

Zee.

All his. At last.

CHAPTER SEVENTEEN

Breakfast was a quiet affair. By the listless light of the kitchen hearth, she'd slapped together a meal from the sole items left in the larder: poached eggs and olive oil, a crumbly white goat cheese, and sausage links fried in cast iron. Coffee and milk and the last lemony wedge of the *tarte au citron* from that bakery down the street, almost half of which she devoured herself while cooking the eggs.

So the eggs were overdone. She'd disguised it by adding more oil to them than they required, but the results were adequate.

If Hayden and the Zaharen wanted an actual chef, they should have hired one.

Both were up and dressed by the time she was finished. She was on her second cup of coffee when they joined her in the dining room. She was seated upon the bench of the bay window with a hand lifted to hold back the lace panel curtain, watching the people leave their houses, sleepy-eyed maids and wives off to buy bread. Footmen walking dogs. Shopgirls. Knife grinders hauling clunky wooden carts. Errand boys in ragged shirts and loose stockings. The sun was rising into a sharp new sky, layering shadows tinted lapis across the trees and sidewalks and everyone below.

She could not see Rhys. It was strange, though, because she could feel him. That touch of glacial cold, a subtle shiver to the air. But she did not call to him, and he never showed his face.

That was fine. Better than fine. For what she was about to do, she needed no distractions.

Hayden and Sandu fell upon the dishes she'd brought to the sideboard. The poached eggs were the last to disappear, but in the end, there wasn't even the smallest speck of cheese left.

"I'm going out today," Zoe said into their silence.

Both of them only looked at her. She was wearing her lavender gown this morning, a necklace of amethysts and sapphires that sparkled with her every breath. The matching earbobs were heavy but she wore them as well, and a bracelet of solid worked gold.

"I can't stay locked up here any longer. I'm useless and I'm bored. I want to come with you. I want to hunt. No—" She lifted a hand as Hayden opened his mouth; she could almost hear his *my dear girl* in that particularly melodious tone. "I'm going. With or without you, I'm leaving this house. And there's more. Pay close attention, both of you. There's something I must show you."

She Turned invisible. The prince started in his chair and exclaimed something in a flowing, unfamiliar language; Hayden only blinked a few times at her necklace.

She'd wanted to be clearly seen both beforehand and after. She'd wanted the jolt of resplendent jewels floating in midair, for there to be no mistaking what they were witnessing. From the expressions on their faces, her plan was successful.

Zoe willed herself visible. She looked directly at her fiancé, into his shocked gaze.

"That's how I did it. That's how I escaped Darkfrith. If we return there unwed, they'll take me from you, Hayden. They'll give me to the Alpha. To someone in his line. I don't want that. I hope that you don't, either."

"Zoe." He pushed back his chair and crossed the room to her, kneeling before her. He took her hand in both of his; the bracelet slid back upon her arm. "For the second time in too few days, you've handed me the revelation of a lifetime. You're Gifted. I had no idea. Darling." His voice sank into a hush. "I had no idea."

Rhys was there. Suddenly, a mist against the wallpaper, standing alone.

"It was a revelation to me as well," she said. "And I wanted to tell you before. Truly."

"Are there more like you?" asked the Zaharen prince eagerly. He leaned forward with his elbows on the table, his thin face alight. "More females in your tribe who can do that?"

"No," answered Hayden and Rhys together, and when she looked at him, Rhys lifted his chin and curved his shadow lips. His gaze swept her from head to toe from beneath thick lashes. "She's the only one."

It was agreed that she would go out to replenish their supplies. She'd expected that much; they would consider shopping a feminine obligation, and the prince at least appeared cheerful enough to have her take it over. But both Hayden and Sandu balked at anything more daring. They refused even to consider taking her along on their stalking of the *sanf*; they were too close; the enemy was too easily spooked; should matters begin to turn out badly, she couldn't fly, as they both could.

True, she could not fly. But if she were to decide to follow them anyway, she doubted very much either of them would notice. Definitely a human would not. But it would be ruddy cold stealing about Paris all day, through back alleys and passageways and God knew where, without a scrap of clothing to shield her.

She agreed to shop for them. She deftly did not agree to anything else but turned the conversation sideways whenever Hayden seemed about to grow adamant that she not place herself in danger: crowds, streets, the Seine, churches, docks, anything involving public gardens or theatres or musicians. That would eliminate about 98 percent of the city, she reckoned.

She was in her room, removing the jewels, when he tapped at her door.

"Come in."

Yet he hung back at the doorway, looking decidedly awkward. He wore a lawn shirt that needed bleach and a vest of dull bronze satin. She turned amid the pink-and-yellow frill of her little chamber and waited for him to speak.

"I don't know if you ever received my last missive to you. I franked it from this dot of a town near the coast. . . . It was a long while ago."

"Yes," Zoe said. "I still have it."

He flashed a quick smile. "Do you indeed? You might recall I mentioned finding something for you." The floor squeaked when he shifted his weight; he came forward only a few steps. "It's nothing much. Certainly nothing compared to what you already have, but when I saw it, I was reminded of you. I was hoping it might please you. I planned to give it to you once back in England, but I thought that now might be a better time." He delved into the slit pocket of his vest with two fingers, retrieved a ring. She caught a flicker of pure limpid blue.

"It's only a tourmaline. Not very rare, I'm afraid." He placed it in her hand, and Zoe lifted it to the window.

"It's beautiful." And it was, a gold filigree band, the square-cut stone within it purling song and light. "Why, it matches your eyes," she said, surprised.

He laughed, discomfited. "I know. How indecorous of me. It's supposed to match yours, but the shop was so small, and the fellow didn't have jet or obsidian or anything so fine a black. He had this."

She closed her fingers over the ring. "I love it."

"Do you? Really?"

"Hayden. It's quite perfect."

He let out his breath on a grin; in that instant, he looked years younger, almost boyish. "Splendid. Yes. Of course, I'll buy you something better later on. Diamonds, naturally. All the diamonds you like."

She slipped the ring on her finger, held it up between them to be admired.

"I say. It does look well on you, doesn't it?"

"Yes."

His smile faded. He stood there gazing at her, sun warming his face and eyelashes, glimmering in spears across the bronze-threaded vest.

"Zoe. I don't like this plan of you going out alone, even to such communal places. I know, I know I agreed to it, but"—he ran a finger under his cravat—"it seems absurdly risky. We know for a fact there are more *sanf inimicus* layered throughout the city. They might have sensed us already. They might know where we are."

"If that's the case," she said, "I'm hardly safer here."

"Aye. I've thought of that too." He lifted a hand, touched a lock of hair that lay across her shoulder, his gaze following the downward stroke of his fingers. "I have so many fears for you. Should anything happen to you, I don't know what I'd do."

Rhys had said nearly the same thing to her, not so very long past. The ghost of Lord Rhys, standing before her in the gloaming dusk of a backyard garden.

"Don't think such thoughts." She smiled up at him, and it was only a little forced. "Nothing is going to happen to me. I'm the most formidable creature on the Continent. You'll see."

The sidewalk of the gray street actually felt hard against his back. He found himself mildly surprised at that, that he would enjoy the sensation of pavers, a pebble digging into the tender center of his left shoulder blade. Rhys tried to recall if he'd ever noticed it before, that the street felt so genuine. That he could hear the leaves rustle on the yellow shrub and hear the wind tumble decayed filth and debris along the gutters.

He was retreating here more and more. Depressing as his little street was, he found it more palatable than the vivid colors and demolishing music of the assembly hall.

This place felt closer to life. It did have that.

He found his familiar stretch of stone and settled back. The street was bathed in daylight and the gray people passed hither and yon. Rhys took up an entire section of the sidewalk and although no one looked at him still, although not one single person glanced downward, no one stepped on him. Or through him, as the case might have been. Perhaps it was some deep-coiled human instinct, avoiding even unseen peril; none of the Others breached this space, even when they had to move around him or take a little hop over his arm or head. He lay undisturbed, staring up at the underside of the gabled hip roof overhead, and relived last night again and again in his mind's eye.

James had been such a willing vessel. Inhabiting him had been far easier, and far more pleasant, than plunging into the dying coachman or the elderly flower gent. James was healthy, for one thing. Healthy and robust, and taking control of his body had been like slipping on someone else's glove. A tight but tolerable fit. It had taken him a few minutes to get the hang of it, moving the lax arms and legs the way Rhys wished them to go. In the joy of fresh sensation—the cotton nightshirt upon his body, the blessed ordinary creaks and scents of a house bedded down for the evening—he'd nearly forgotten his true purpose.

Zoe.

Nearly, but not, needless to say, completely. And that had been the most intense joy of all.

Touching her. Tasting her. Feeling her response to him—to the Hayden/Rhys *drákon* he'd created, that sleeping body brimming to the brink with his own black passion—letting himself believe, just for those few fervent minutes, that it was only he whom she loved. That it was he she wanted to kiss. Had he been able to carry his plan to fruition, the evil symphony could have consumed him for the rest of his life—his afterlife—and it would have been worth it.

As it was, it had damn near been worth it anyway.

He could handle her anger. He could understand it, even. He'd freely admit the entire scheme had been underhanded, a despicable trick, and had he a wisp of scruples, he'd be feeling properly miserable about it all. But Rhys thought perhaps his scruples had vanished with his mortal body; he wasn't sorry in the least. He regretted nothing beyond wounding her through her discovery of him. Hayden James was a fatheaded imbecile not to have claimed her already, and Rhys regretted nothing.

Which brought him back to one of the other costs of his actions last night: He was weakened now. He had reached that state of numbed exhaustion that meant he would be prone here on this sidewalk for probably some while to come. He'd been able to slip into her world twice this morning, long enough for her chiding, and then, later, to watch her defiantly claim her powers in front of James and the other *drákon*—but that was all.

It was better to rest here a while, anyway. Let Zoe's temper smooth itself out.

She'd forgive him this, he was certain of it. She had to, he needed her to. He loved her and would not let go of her; by their nature, she was his, in spirit and disposition, and he was even willing to share her with a living dragon if that was what it took to keep her. And so she would forgive him.

Despite Hayden's admonitions, Zoe had come so very close to abandoning her word and tracking them across the city. It was a temptation that expanded inside her like a steel bubble, far stronger than she'd expected, and she'd had to sit down at a café on rue St. Denis to resist the urge to fling out the cloak and ensnare their trail of thoughts, to throw herself into the thick of their world, whether they liked it or not.

She hadn't told them about the cloak. Part of her had to admit that it was more than just that she had not found the proper time or place; she could have done it this morning, probably. She could have tried to demonstrate it by capturing the thoughts of either of them, but unless the cloak cooperated, she'd be showing off nothing. Revealing her invisibility had been a furtive sort of test; she wanted to keep her most powerful secret in reserve, hold it close to her heart just in case they tried to restrain that too.

Just in case.

The day had lost its luminous clarity already, and clouds roiled an ominous yellow-brown along the eastern edge of the sky. The wind had a bite to it, and so when she took her cup of tea and biscuits she sat inside the petite café with all the other patrons, glad for her gown and serge coat, and the gloves of kidskin on her lap. Still, she could not shake the chill that seemed determined to sneak up on her; she'd chosen a table by the grate of the fire, and only the half of her body closest to it seemed to keep any warmth.

With the chill, Hayden's ring was looser upon her finger. She fiddled with it absently with her thumb, sliding the band around and around.

The tea was tepid; most Parisians seemed to prefer coffee, and finding a decent pot of tea was difficult even amid the most fashionable of neighborhoods. She found herself gazing down at the round moon of its surface in her cup, searching for a reflection that was not there.

She remembered his kisses. Hayden's kisses. How welcome they had been at first, and then . . . how peculiar. Even as she'd embraced him, she'd felt the change in his body. At first she'd refused to acknowledge it, even to herself, because she told herself in that darkened bedroom, upon that narrow child's bed, it was what she wanted. What she'd wanted for so long: to be accepted, to be desired. And there he was, unexpectedly all that she wished. She'd known in her heart it was too good to be true.

Rhys. Wicked, wily, unconscionable Rhys, with his smoking halo and sharp green eyes, who told her openly how much he wanted her and damn the consequences. Who told her bluntly how he liked her, how their dragon nature and their animal passion bonded hearts. Who was so determined to prove their connection he'd invaded the body of a fellow clansman, and pressed his lips—Hayden's lips—to her skin, tasted her with his tongue.

Zoe brought her hands up to her cheeks. Hot color flooded them, made even the centers of her palms seem cold, but the café was nearly empty, and no one paid her any mind.

It had been so dreadful and so acutely wonderful. To be held like that, half-naked like that, stretched out upon the bed. To be stroked. To feel passion without the winter sting of his touch—

She removed her hands from her face. She brought the tea to

her lips, attempting to relish the relative coolness of the liquid: inoffensive and flavorless. Everything opposite of the confusion that boiled inside her.

She would not be so idiotic as to fall in love with a memory. That he had a sort of substance, a manner of opacity and a great deal of sweet persuasion that went with his nefarious behavior did not make him alive, or real, or worth the risk of giving him her heart.

She was *drákon,* a child of the tribe. Zoe knew her duty. She would return to Darkfrith and accept her punishment and her place in the order of things. She would not hunt the *sanf inimicus.* She would not wish for more than what she had been given. She would wed a living dragon, and live her life in her cottage by the woods, not pine for an impossible ghost, no matter how jaunty his grin.

The clouds were swelling closer. She smelled the rain in them, the thunder that ached for release. The bell over the café door gave a merry tinkle; a group of pastel-clad ladies rushed in with a bluster of wind, laughing in happy tones, exclaiming over the coming storm. Their maids waited outside, huddled in bonnets and coats.

Instinctively, more out of habit than anything else, Zoe pulled the deep blue cloak about her, then flung it out in a circle with herself in its eye.

It returned to her with Rhys caught in its folds, his light brighter and brighter, and then he was there with her. There in the chair opposite hers, just like a living man, one arm draped over the back and his booted feet crossed.

She sighed. She set down the teacup, placed a few *sous* upon the table, and rose to go.

He followed her, naturally. He kept near to her shoulder, glancing about at the brightly polished shops of imported lace and Indian silk like a tourist, then back down at her.

"Nice ring."

She gave a nod of acknowledgment, stuffing her hands into her gloves.

"From him, I must suppose."

She only sent him a look.

"What," he said, "he couldn't bother to find a black diamond?"

She paused with her back and skirts flattened to a building to allow a sedan chair past; a little brown dog staring bug-eyed out the window at her began to howl most piercingly, hushed by a woman's voice. Rhys drifted ahead, turning to walk backward when she started off again.

"Are you still angry with me?"

She rolled her eyes, kept walking. The hues of the day were browning, changing shades with the coming of the storm, and there was a mercer's in particular she wished to find before the rain began. She'd seen it once after she'd first arrived, cramped and dusty and crammed with reels and reels of intricate lace. A measure of it would do very well for her wedding gown.

To Hayden. For the wedding gown she would wear for her wedding to Hayden.

Rhys was still directly ahead of her. "Because, listen, I . . ."

She waited with her gaze on the hem of her dress, expecting any sort of new excuse or cajoling, prepared to ignore him all the way back to England if she must. But when she peeked up at him he seemed truly without words; he'd gone still, stock-still—she almost walked through him—and then moved swiftly to take her hand.

She yanked free, she couldn't help it. His slightest touch made her skin crawl with cold.

"The ring," he said. "Zee. The ring."

She pursed her lips and arched a brow, once again moving out of the way as more people brushed past, her back against the glass front of a shop.

"Did you notice James's hand?"

She shook her head, puzzled.

"The ring on his hand," the shadow persisted. "The signet."

Yes. *Yes.* Hayden was still wearing his gold tribal ring. He was! She'd seen it for days, and it'd never registered, because he'd always worn it, ever since she'd known him. Hayden had his ring. That meant—

"It was mine." Rhys combed his fingers through his hair, sending smoke up in broken puffs. "The one from the wallet. I'm sure it was. Who else's could it be?"

She shot a dubious glance at his hand, where the ghost ring still shone. He twisted it free of his finger and held it up between them, turning it back and forth in the clouding caramel light.

"But this isn't truth, is it? What you see before you is what I think I look like, what I *want* to look like. This is my favorite waistcoat, you know. These are my best boots. But I wasn't wearing them when I was killed. Taken. I recall that much. They're all still back in my quarters at Chasen, no doubt. I was, however, wearing this."

The wind gave a sudden push; the first of the rain clouds began to release, miles away. Movement flickered at the corner of her eye; a shopkeeper inside the store at her back was lighting the sconces on the wall with a taper, throwing her long, curious looks as he moved from flame to flame.

Zoe found herself walking. There was an alley coming up, an alley of muggy foul smells and cats leaping down and away from their perch upon a broken stool smashed against a wall. Rhys went first, and the cats bolted out into the street on the other side. When she stopped by the stool he lifted his hand again, focused on the ring flat on his palm; it faded to nothing. Just like a wizard's trick. Gone.

She lifted her eyes to his.

"Who knows what the truth of me is now? I had hoped—" He drew a deep breath of air and let it hiss out between his teeth. "I had hoped," he finished, curt. "All kinds of ridiculous hopes. That all this is a mistake, that I'm actually alive somewhere. Dreaming in my bed at home, and you're still back there too. That I might even be that wretched prisoner, tool of the *sanf.* But if I've been gone so long—if they destroyed my ring, kept it as a prize..."

For the first time ever, she reached for him in compassion, took his hand in hers despite the painful cold. He gave a taut smile, turned her gloved fingers over in his, and raised them to his lips. She felt his kiss, so brief and awful, even through the kid. The needles of ice gouging her bones.

"Do me a favor. Take the signet back to the shire. Give it to my brother. Let him know."

"Know what?"

"That I died well, that I didn't suffer. I don't know. Lie to him. Pin him with those tremendous dark eyes and he'll puddle like snow in July. He's only a red-blooded dragon, after all. He'll believe whatever you say."

"I will."

"Thank you." He seemed about to add something more, still holding her hand; she wanted to take it back and she didn't, but his gaze had gone fixed and distant, a flare of green against the blowing shadows.

She glanced over her shoulder and saw only the street, the shops, the rainstorm churning above rooftops.

He vanished, all of him, all at once. She was left with her arm lifted halfway to nothing, and the sensation of hoarfrost that had been creeping up to her shoulder.

The gray street had plunged to shadow just as Zoe's street had. A storm simmered here as well, but the raindrops were already falling, big fat plops of water spattering the walkways and buildings. People began to scatter, heels clicking, yanking coats over their heads, hats, newspapers, whatever they had. Rhys stood on his sidewalk and the rain fell straight through him, broke into beads through the soles of his feet. He didn't even feel it.

And yet this wasn't what had wrenched him back.

He turned a wide circle, searching. Perhaps he'd been mistaken. Perhaps he'd imagined it, that urgent *pull* that had got him here. That familiar, electric prickle along his senses that all his life had always meant only one thing. Yet nothing but the rain appeared any different: the damp buildings and the gabled roof and the shrub— hardly any leaves left—and the rat, all like before.

The rat, staring at him and then quickly to the right. The rat, running away with its tail a pink whip along the ground, into the house across the street.

Rhys looked to the right. And yes, goddamn it, there they were. James and the Zaharen boy, walking gradually toward him, cloaked, hooded, far slower and more deliberate than any of the Others dashing around them. James turned his head and murmured something; the other dragon nodded.

Rhys tried to go to them. He tried to at least get close enough to hear them speak, but he was stuck as he always was, unable to venture beyond his tiny realm. Yet it didn't matter: They were still coming to him. Right to him. James was tall and broad and the dragon-boy more slight, but there was no question that they both emanated identical crackling auras of watchful, sinuous menace.

They were hunting. Right here, on his street.

Rhys realized abruptly what it meant. He was in *Paris,* just as they were. He was in Paris, just like Zee! This was the same storm that brewed near her. The same time, the same place.

And they were hunting near *him.*

The hoods of their cloaks revealed only grim, pale jaws; their eyes were covered, their hands hidden. Raindrops shattered along their hoods and shoulders, slithered in rivulets to the sidewalk. He could practically mark their footsteps in the water, they moved so slowly.

Right as they reached him Rhys held up both hands, palms flat. They stopped. They *stopped,* just for an instant, both of them, and then as one continued through him. He broke apart, re-formed. They walked on down the sidewalk, but not before throwing quick, subtle looks at the building behind Rhys, the one with the gabled roof that he knew so well.

Rhys looked too. He saw a door, shuttered windows. He saw a pair of chimneys that let seep no smoke.

There were dots of recent solder around the lock of the door. He squinted at it through the downpour, trying to see better. Yes, the keyhole had been filled with lead. No sign or light or movement escaped the seams of the door; those were blocked too.

All ways to keep out smoke.

Great God. The *sanf inimicus* were here. He'd wager his fortune there was fresh solder sealing the windows as well. That the chimneys would be blocked.

James and the boy would have smelled the melted lead like an alarm; Rhys remembered it from life, acrid and then heady, metallic sludge with music that hardened into flat, strange notes.

He spun about in time to see them make an unhurried turn at the next corner. They were the last figures visible through the storm. After they were gone, Rhys stood alone. There weren't even any carriages going by.

And so he was the only one who heard the voices rise and cut short from the interior of the solder-sealed house. The only one who saw the door give a little shake, as if someone on the other side tested the lock.

He leaned a step toward the house. The music surrounding him reached a painful new pitch, hurting his ears, but to his very great astonishment, he managed it. Another step. Music rising. Another, like dragging his feet through quicksand. The weedy walkway to the front porch, up the steps to the bleak gray door. He stopped to rest a moment, his head spinning—was it too bloody much to ask for a little potency in death?—then pressed his palm flat to the wood. He felt the resonance of its substance, not real wood but an echo of it, almost as stiff as life.

The voices inside had lowered to hushed babbles; he could make out no words over the song in his head. He thought he heard a woman, more than one man. He thought he smelled—heavens, he smelled—drenched wood and humans and the tin from the solder, something dry and spicy like herbs. And beneath all that... the weak, dim perfume of *drákon*.

Rhys glanced around him, curled his fingers around the bronze-plated latch, and gave it a heave.

She was in the lace shop, desultorily surveying layers of fragile webbing, listening to the rain pattering the roof, sweeping strong, then faint, then strong again, soporific. A horde of people had ducked inside with the first pelting drops; the men clumped together at the windows, water from the hems of their coats dripping into puddles, staring out and speculating about the duration of the storm. The women had dispersed throughout the tall wooden racks of goods, doing precisely the same as Zoe. Fingering the delicate threads and knots of the reams, pretending they would make a purchase.

There were only a merchant and his young daughter to assist. A stout lady in a beaded aubergine hat had cornered them both, demanding to be shown a length of bobbinwork from Portofino her cousin's sister-in-law had described to her. The merchant kept lapsing into Portuguese; the woman spoke only emphatic French. He was having scarce luck convincing her she was in the wrong shop.

The daughter stood to one side with her head bowed, a silver chain around her neck the sole splendid gleam in the store.

Zoe'd not been out in rain since she'd left England. She'd not even attempted it, especially after what had happened at the coffee shop in

Palais Royal. She stood as far back from the windows—the dripping men, the front door that opened and closed each time with a spray of wet wind—as she could. Like everything else right now, the lace shop was plunged into that caramel gloom. She had no umbrella or parasol. If she was quiet and still, she could likely linger in the rear of the shop for a good while, hopefully at least until the worst of it passed.

"Zoe."

He appeared to her in the midst of a waterfall of long pale lace, a dozen dangling ribbons unspooled from a wire rod above them, draping down into his head and chest and shoulders.

She inhaled a swift breath with a hand pressed to her heart, but that was all. The shadow glanced about them quickly, then looked back to her.

"You need to return to the *maison* right now. Pack your things, and leave. I'll come to you when I can."

Her lips formed, *What?*

"Just do it. Wait—don't even go back to the house. Go to—go to a hotel. Do you have the funds for that? Someplace common. An inn. Anywhere but where James and the boy know you've been, or imagine you might go."

The door to the shop opened again; the ribbons of lace inside Rhys twirled languidly in the rush of new air.

"What's happened?" Zoe whispered. "Did they find the *sanf*? Is Hayden in danger?"

"I'll tell you later. Honest to God, Zee, you've got to do as I say."

"No, Rhys, *you've* got to tell me—"

He left. Just like before in the alley: an instant, complete vanishing. If she'd blinked, she'd have seen none of it.

Several of the patrons were glancing back at her, muttering to each other behind their hands. She realized she'd spoken her last sentence in her normal voice, straight to a line of crisp ironed ribbons, some of them still swaying an inch from her nose.

She did not wait to leave the shop. She closed her eyes and summoned the cloak with all the power her fear and anxiety lent her, and it came, indigo and deep and shimmering with the force of her will. She heard the voices from inside it. She felt the touch of countless hands, plucking, pulling, all along her body.

Find them. Hayden and Sandu.

Folds of heavy blue ballooned in waves across the shop. They devoured everything: the people and the ribbons and the woman in the hat, the rainfall and sodden scents and shying horses outside, everything physical, everything of carbon and mineral earth, smothered into silence.

From the infinity of blue before her came a pinprick of new light. It rotated in lazy, radiant spokes; it dazzled and expanded, blinding. Zoe lifted her arms to it, thinking, *hurry!* and the pinprick became a window, and the window became a door. Beyond the door was the light that was Hayden, the colors of his body flaring around him in orange and red and azure. They were the colors of his dragon self, but he and the prince were still in human form—naked, both of them naked—creeping along the hallway of an unlit corridor—two men and a woman in a mobcap with a palm over her mouth waiting around the bend in the corridor. The woman clutched a bowl of pale powdery something but the men were armed with guns. Rhys stood before the turn, frantically attempting to speak to the *drákon,* shoving uselessly at them both.

She did not bother to wonder why Hayden and the prince didn't sense the Others, or what Rhys was trying to do. She only ran from the lace shop, following the streaming arrow of the cloak, the bending, luminous colors of *drákon* that rose from a point east into the sky bright as a rainbow as the rain slapped down.

211

CHAPTER EIGHTEEN

S uppose you were made a prisoner inside your own body. A mind without the ability to control physical limbs; a heart without the ability to beat. Suppose you were bound in painful cold iron—yes, painful, even for one of us—and your sole relief was the flight of your spirit, away, away from the miserable dark grave that actually encompassed you.

Toward warmth, say. Toward other spirits like you, or the living light of the one you loved.

Suppose people who knew how to do such a thing used their Voice to command that you remain frozen in your peculiar agony. That they used the chips and glistening dust of a magical diamond to ensure that you listened, that your body remained helpless, no matter how far your spirit roamed. And the closer your spirit returned to your actual, physical self—whatever remained of it—the thinner it became; the two separated measures of you cannot fluently share the same worldly space. Our natural state of being fights to reassert itself: Either you combine again with your body to dwell in the frosty isolation of your slow death, or you abandon it once more, you soar apart. Those are your only choices.

You'd be better off keeping away, wouldn't you?

No matter how strong your Gifts, no matter how much you willed it, you would not escape the diamond dust and the iron, and the wicked, wicked song they sang. Such was the nature of the malevolence of *Draumr*.

Draumr controls us. He who controls any fragment of *Draumr* controls us, in small ways or—with enough of the pieces—large.

True, as a species we're varied in our strengths. For some *drákon* the shattered stone sings stronger and for others weaker; for many of us, even as shards, *Draumr* is unbearable to the touch. Others still may touch it without pain but fall yet under its spell.

For all our variations, it remains the one horrific, common flaw we cannot avoid.

That is...most of us. For every rule, there is an exception, you know.

That's what Lord Rhys and Zoe Lane were about to discover, along with their illustrious companions.

CHAPTER NINETEEN

He could not occupy Hayden's body this time. He tried. He could not occupy any of their bodies. They couldn't hear him, they didn't see him, and when he tried to push his way into them, it was like they were made of stone. He gained nothing. They didn't even slow. James and the boy had discovered a weakness to the house—Rhys hardly knew where, perhaps a chink in a pane of glass, a ball of tar melted loose from the roof, anything—and had Turned and rematerialized here, and they were slinking straight into a trap.

He wasn't even sure how he himself had gotten in. He'd wanted it, wanted it urgently, and here he was.

He tried speaking to them, he tried shouting. The two *drákon* only edged forward, because to them, he simply was not there.

Rhys pounded the wall in front of them. He wanted to rip out the shabby wood, he wanted to rip down the ugly house, a prop, a set that looked and felt as false as cheap stage scenery at the Haymarket. He was sick of being unseen, he was bloody sick of being a poor remnant of himself. The rage and resentment bubbled inside him like red-hot lava, and a *child* would have been of better use, an *infant* would have done a better job of warning them— there were *sanf inimicus* around the corner and a dim-blooded dragon somewhere below, and now, when he most needed words and touch he had neither, and his kinsmen were about to be slaughtered.

He felt the lava beating in his head. He felt his vision waver; he did not want this, he'd never wanted this—let Hayden James live, let him live and go back to Zoe and keep her safe—

James took another step. He was throwing a significant look to the boy—who grinned back at him with his lips peeled over his teeth—when the woman darted out, gave a single hard shake of her bowl: A cloud of rye-colored dust choked the little hall.

They could not Turn. The powder shot through Rhys, sifted like silt through the air, and for a few precious seconds neither James nor Sandu could Turn; there was no way to see clear to anything but grit.

One of the men stepped out in front of the woman, lifting his pistol. His finger squeezed the trigger. A white flash, a new instant dark.

James grunted and slammed against the wall, and the boy behind him lunged forward.

Rhys moved to catch Hayden James as he sank to the floor, but his shadow hands only slid through him.

She shed her clothing as she ran. Hat, gloves, shoes. She darted past Others hunched under awnings, past snarling wet dogs. The colors in the sky drew her on and she'd never been so fleet in her life. A pair of fiddlers on a bridge hunkered together beneath their overlapping umbrellas; they played a duet of lively, quick-pattering notes, and Zoe ripped at the bodice to her gown as she passed them, let the lavender merino go floating out behind her to land in the brown frothy rush of the Seine.

The music ceased. Both men stood up and shouted after her; she didn't slow.

The corset was easy. Chemise. The stockings—she did pause then, only long enough to yank them into tatters. If it hadn't been raining so hard she would have been truly invisible, but even she could see the water striking her legs and torso, separating around the shape of a sprinting woman.

Sidewalks and streetlamps with yellow snakes' tongues of flame. Shops and beggars and shiny painted doors. The cloak and the colors of Hayden led her into a maze of twisting back lanes; across the peaked roofs she could see the cloak now taking the tapered shape of a whirlwind, violent, swirling stars; it curved and bent like a funnel cloud fixed to the roof of one particular house.

Rhys was nowhere to be felt or seen.

She reached the front door to the dilapidated place marked by her Gift, kicked at it—once, twice, three times, until it split enough that she could tear at it with her hands. Wood splintered and metal shrieked and Zoe slapped the water off her skin and crawled inside the hole she'd made, faced the darkness of the unknown ahead.

He could not see. James and the Zaharen *drákon* were gone. Rhys was encased with utter night. He could not see, and he could not move; everything was bitter cold and ebony. One instant he'd been reaching for James, marking the blotch of blood left upon the wall behind him as James's body slid to the floor—and then the next, he was here. Stuck. Powerless.

He had a sudden sharp memory of the dead *sanf* coachman

leaning over him, the pale gray eyes, the sour smile, but when he tried to focus on it more clearly, it dissolved into dirt.

He tried to breathe, but his lungs were crushed beneath a mountain of iron and ice. He tried to fling himself to Zoe and even that didn't work. He had descended into the earth. He was in the company of worms now.

Worms, and the music. *That* never stopped.

The air inside the house blurred thick and gritty; it smelled like a bakery. Like wheat, she realized, or rye. It clogged her nose and clung to her damp skin in particles, revealed her in a thin layer of dust: her stomach. Her breasts. Her arms and thighs. Zoe rubbed at it as she moved, breathing past her teeth, managing to roll most of it from her body into little balls that littered the floor at her feet.

The scent of dragon blood pulled her ahead. Thumps and shudders, one so strong the very walls trembled. She heard no voices, no shouts. There was a battle taking place but it was silent except for the creaking of the house. The floor bouncing with an impact that sent shivers through the soles of her feet. Pottery breaking.

And then, finally, a woman's scream, high, then low, then gone.

She ran on her toes. The place was small and miserable, more narrow than even the *maison,* and reeked of fear. She passed doors open to empty rooms, no life inside, not even spiders or mice; she ran all the way to the doorway framing the kitchen—pausing only long enough to note the blotch of dragon blood she'd scented before, swiped down a wall—and there before her was more flour drifting in the air, across pots and pans and kettles and the dead man upon the floor by the entrance, and another man with a pistol aimed at the lanky young prince of the Zaharen, who moved with a twisting, deceptive grace, dodging the aim of the gun through the dust.

A woman stooped over the man on the floor. She was clutching at his shoulders, her mouth still open and her eyes streaming cloudy pale tears, when Zoe walked in.

She stepped past the human woman and over the body of the *sanf.* She walked straight toward the one with the gun, lifting a hand before her—she could see it as if it were not her own, the floured contour of Zoe's invisible hand, the floured flutter of Zoe's invisible fingers to draw the attention of the Other. Hayden's ring of blue and gold, still lustrous enough to shine.

And it worked. The man's gaze flitted to her, and in that instant the prince had him, pushed him off his feet with a hard *whap* against the stone hearth. The gun flew from his grip and hit the floor. It discharged. Zoe couldn't help it: She cringed and shielded her eyes. When she could hear again, the woman was still screaming, and the man by the hearth was covered in a great splash of blood.

"Be quiet," commanded Sandu in a velvet dark voice. "Be still." The woman cut short with a sobbing sort of hiccup, then a whimper. She collapsed over the man before her and buried her head in her arms.

"Where is Hayden?" Zoe asked above the ringing in her ears.

The prince had knelt, skimming his hands over the crimson-wet body of the *sanf inimicus* before him, and to his credit, he didn't waste time asking stupid questions about why or how Zoe could be there. He merely raised an arm and pointed toward the far corner of the kitchen, still searching the body.

Hayden leaned against the counter amid a great spill of flour and broken crockery, staring at her, coated with powder. His legs seemed to buckle, and he crumpled in a slow, queer way down to the floor, never taking his eyes from her face.

"No. Oh, no."

She was there in time to prevent his head from striking the

stone. She settled him against her lap, not even noticing the small, neat hole in his upper chest until the wet heat of his blood slipped along her folded legs. The bullet must have traveled all the way through him.

"You're alive," she said. She willed herself seen. "Hayden. You're alive."

"Hullo." His lashes drifted closed, then open again. He squinted at her, and the flour around his eyes caked into lines. "Where are your clothes?"

"He needs to Turn," said the Zaharen, who had crossed to them.

"Yes." She touched a hand to his cheek. "Turn to smoke. You'll be fine then. We can fix you back at the *maison*."

"No." He moistened his lips. "Got to . . . find the other dragon. He's here. Somewhere."

"His Grace and I will do it. You Turn."

"Not yet."

"You should listen to me now, my friend." Sandu squatted before them, regarded Hayden gravely, his face streaked with sweat and flour. "I'll find the *drákon*; I smell him too. I'll take care of the female and the men. But if you don't Turn now, you'll bleed to death, and what good will you be to any of us then?"

Hayden rolled his eyes back to Zoe's. "Turn," she urged. "Please."

He went to smoke, a sudden silky lightness. He twirled up before them both and hovered, not leaving.

He wouldn't go, she knew that. Not until she and the prince did too.

Sandu rose to tuck his hair behind one ear, regarded the woman shivering on the floor. She was dressed as a servant, in a plain tan gown and stained apron, her cap with short starched ruffles. A cook, Zoe would guess. There was something more about her,

219

though. Something odd. Perfumey, even through the choking odor of gunpowder and fear.

"She's one of mine," said the prince, matter-of-fact. His hands were at his hips; he spoke to Zoe and Hayden without looking at either. "Feel it? She's of dragon blood. Extremely thin, hardly a thimbleful. That means she's Zaharen."

Zoe stood with blood dripping down her knees as the boy went to the woman, drew her up with both hands.

The cook gasped something in a patois Zoe didn't understand. She clutched at the prince's forearms with frantic fingers and finally spewed words of pure Parisian French. "Monster. Beast. Devil!"

"Tell me where the other one is," said Sandu, Persuasion again drenching his words. "The one like us. Tell me now."

The woman pressed her lips together and shook her head, then let out a howling sob as the prince pried her hands from his arms.

"You know who I am. You must obey. Tell me now."

"I won't. I can't. They'll kill me, they'll kill my son, just like they did with that driver—"

"Wait," said Zoe, and sent out the cloak in a slow, easy puff around the panicked woman.

She saw darkness. She saw rough wooden steps steeply descending. She saw a place with limestone all around, and a wine rack. No windows. An empty bottle rolled against mortar, a glint of olive green against a stone wall. The harsh, disagreeable aroma of mushrooms and mold.

"It's a cellar," Zoe said. "She's trying to hide something in a cellar."

The cook let out a moan. Once again, Sandu didn't ask useless questions. He only did a quick survey of the kitchen, the walls, the scarlet-and-white-dotted floor. He flipped back the sole circle of rug in the center of the chamber. There was only stone beneath it.

"There's no access here to a cellar."

220

"There must be somewhere."

Hayden writhed down before them, twisted into corners, around the open doors of the larder, out again to the fireplace, the pantry. And then his voice came from inside it.

"Here," he called.

"Turn back to smoke," ordered the prince, but he was already wrenching open the pantry doors. Flour shook in a small powdery storm from his hair.

The pantry seemed to contain neither a means to a cellar nor Hayden. Zoe saw shelves of bundled herbs, rounded cheeses sealed in wax. That was all.

"Back here," Hayden said, still unseen. He sounded muffled. "There's a keyhole behind the dill. It's a false back."

She remembered the key from the wallet, the key that would open only a certain warded lock.

"Turn *back*," complained the prince. "I've got to smash it. You're in the way."

Perhaps the wood here was thinner than the front door. Sandu shattered it with one kick, and this time the cook tore at her hair beneath her cap before collapsing into sobs again.

"Who else will come here?" Sandu asked her, brushing a sliver of wood from his shoulder. "How many other *sanf inimicus* dwell in this house?"

"None. None, I swear. These two are the only—" She broke into that patois again, shaking her head, then switched back to French. "No more."

The prince sent the Zaharen woman a crystal-hard look. "You will remain here. You will not move until I give you leave."

"*Nu,*" she cried. "Noble One, *nu, nu...*"

"But you will."

Zoe Turned invisible—it seemed somewhat more modest than not, even with the flour still covering her—and followed the prince into the cave behind the pantry, stepping gingerly around the sharp particles of wood.

There was no light but what filtered from behind them. Halfway down the stairs Sandu paused, shook his head. Mumbled something in Romanian.

"What is it?" Her voice came out a whisper; she was trying not to inhale too deeply. The mold stink grew stronger and stronger.

"That buzzing. It's maddening, like bees in my head."

"What?"

But he was descending once more, quick as a cat; she followed the line of his bare back, paler than the darkness swallowing them.

Hayden was a cloud at her side, brushing cool against her shoulder.

The prince made an inarticulate sound of discovery. She hurried, missed the last step of the stairs but recovered. Hayden flowed ahead, reaching Sandu before her, becoming man by the prince and the darker thing he knelt by on the floor.

"I need a light," said Sandu, lifting his head. "Never mind. Let's just get him out of here."

The thing was long, covered with a blanket. Hayden pulled it off, and there *was* a monster beneath.

It seemed immobilized. Hands raised to its chest, fingers clawing at the air—but instead of fingers they were talons of long, twisting gold. Clothing rent, legs askew. There were manacles around the wrists, manacles that gave off an oddly pale blue shimmer, even down here. The face was frozen into rictus; a wide, blistering red scar cut along one cheek, all the way down into its neck. More gold threaded the filthy dark hair matted to the floor. The monster had clearly died in great pain; it was dreadful to look upon, anguished and petrified and very nearly unrecognizable.

"Rhys," she said, but this time her voice completely failed her. She wet her lips and tried again, an explosion of sound.

"Rhys."

And bent down to grasp those whetted claws.

Hayden swayed a little beside her; his hand gripped her shoulder. "My God, she's right. It's Rhys Langford."

"Lady Amalia's brother?" asked the Zaharen. He was holding both hands to his head.

"Yes."

"He's not dead," Zoe muttered. She had moved her palms to his chest, felt the faint electric thrill of *drákon* still pooled in him, no heartbeat. "He's not dead, yet he's not breathing. I don't understand."

Sandu had begun to stagger back. "The manacles. Don't you hear it?"

"No." She glanced up, from Sandu's face to Hayden's, and they were both looking sick. "What's wrong?"

"Break them," said the boy, right before he listed sideways. He hit the floor with that particular, youthful elasticity, in bends, only barely managing to catch himself with one arm before collapsing all the way. His voice went hoarse. "Quickly, please."

Hayden simply fell over. Just like that, fell over, a great relaxed shape flat on the floor in the dark, still bleeding, and she looked back at the pale blue-studded metal cuffs—were those diamonds? why didn't they sing?—took the nearest one in her hands and pulled it apart.

It hurt. The iron was colder than ice, far colder than anything of earth should be. It dug into the flesh of her fingers and cut and screamed as she pulled, and finally tore along its joint. She dropped it at once, then picked it up and tossed it away from all four of them. Went to the other manacle and pulled and pulled again.

When it was finished she was bleeding, tiny nicks and cuts from the raw metal, the diamond shards digging into her skin. She threw that one away as well, wrapped her hands around Rhys's wrist and rubbed hard.

"Wake up. Everyone, wake up." She took up his other cold wrist, twisting around at the same time, trying to see if Hayden moved. "*Zut alors! Merde!* Wake up!"

Rhys's arm jerked free of her grasp. She drew back, startled, but both the taloned hands had risen toward her. She felt claws whisper through her hair, the zing of gold curving around the back of her neck. He pulled her down to him, lifted his head, and mashed his lips to hers.

It was icy. Not the winter ice of his shadow touch, and nothing at all like the sweet, warm kisses she was used to from Hayden— not even passionate ones she'd gotten when Rhys had disguised himself as Hayden. This kiss was icy like the cellar, icy and prolonged and tasting of desperation. Deliverance. She needed to breathe and she could not; his tongue invaded her, his claws kept her imprisoned, and even still she could not bring herself to hurt him to break free.

It was Rhys who dropped his head back to the limestone, panting raggedly, muttering in a broken, wretched voice, "It's you, it's you, Holy Mother of God, I can't believe it's you, but it is, a miracle, it's you...."

"Zoe?"

Hayden was sitting up, staring at her. She wiped her hand across her lips, shook her head, unable to explain.

And then the human was upon them.

In the long, unpleasant days that followed, after she'd replayed the moment over and over and over in her mind, she realized that he was the man she'd seen the cook sobbing over in the kitchen— not dead, only asleep or pretending. He must have been creeping down the stairs when both Hayden and the prince had fallen unconscious. He must have discovered the iron manacle she'd thrown as Rhys began his kiss.

The Other was able to steal up upon them all, even fetid with the smells of city and blood and man, and by the time she saw him there at the foot of the stairs, it was too late.

Hayden saw the *sanf* as well. He went instantly to smoke, a rush of vapor aimed like a blade straight at the human, but the man clutched the manacle in both hands and barked in French, "Disperse! Do not re-form!"

She watched, baffled, her heart pumping, waiting for Hayden to Turn back, become dragon, leap and kill the Other—

But he didn't. He remained smoke. He reached the man and curled apart harmlessly against him, drifted up to the ceiling, and vanished.

Vanished.

She stared wildly at the *sanf*. "What did you do? What did you *do*?"

The man pointed at her. "You! Lie down! Stop breathing!"

She reached him in three steps, raised a hand.

"All of you," screeched the *sanf*, backing up rapidly, "all of you stop—"

The connection of her fist to his cheek shattered the bone; she felt it, felt the man's skull break apart, his neck snapping to the side. He tumbled to the floor and did not move.

She was there anyway, dragging him up by his lapels, shaking him so hard his head lolled against his shoulders and his wig fell off. "What did you do? *Tell me what you did!*"

A shadow came forward: Sandu, not Rhys. He took the manacle from the stair step at the dead man's feet.

"It was this," he said quietly. He held it pinched between his thumb and finger as if it burned. "Just this."

She glared at him, still clutching the *sanf.* In the cellar darkness beyond them something new stirred. It was Rhys moving along the floor, his claws making small *scritch, scritch* noises across the stone.

"It's a kind of poison," explained the boy. "Poison in the form of a fragmented diamond, embedded in this metal. Do you know the story of *Draumr,* Noble Zoe?"

"No." She released the body of the *sanf inimicus,* clutched at her stomach before bending double, then dropping to her knees. She was visible again; she was sick and empty.

"You're the only Gifted dragon I've ever heard of able to resist it."

"It's only *chips!*"

"It is the remains of the most dangerous stone in our history. I can't even imagine how they got it. I'm sorry." He bent down before her, placed the manacle carefully at her knees. "When *Draumr* calls to a *drákon,* even in this form, we comply. Hayden James won't be coming back."

CHAPTER TWENTY

Rhys was a problem. Despite the danger of discovery, they had to wait until dusk to escape from the house of the *sanf inimicus*. Fortunately, it was less than an hour's wait; the rain still fell in drumming dark sheets, and that helped as well.

The prince had dug up clothing in a bureau in one of the upstairs chambers, ordinary, innocuous clothing, and now he was a workman in wool and cleated shoes and a brown felt hat, and Zoe was dressed in the cook's spare uniform, which ended at her ankles and hung from her frame in massive folds.

There was nothing else of use in the house. No papers, no wallets upon the men. There was the cook to contain and Rhys to spirit away and—despite what the woman claimed—no means of discovering who else came here, what other faces the *sanf inimicus* might hide behind. They could not split up and they could not loiter. They had to leave.

Yet they also could not put fresh clothing upon the body of Rhys Langford. The rags he wore were pungent and held together by threads, yet his limbs were frozen—he could barely hobble—and the golden claws punctured all material. Dragon attributes, their scales and fangs and talons, were forged far stronger than even steel. By the time Sandu was able to hail a carriage for them, Zoe had given up attempting to hide anything but the claws. She wrapped him in a blanket from head to foot and sat stoically beside him in the coach, staring at the red-eyed cook across from her who was *drákon* and not, their knees bumping with every joggle, all four of them sodden. Silent. The only noises came from the joints of the carriage and the thundering storm—and the horses, which balked and neighed all the way back to the *maison.*

And the manacles, she supposed, although to her they were still quiet as a dead calm lake; even the iron had ceased to whimper. They lay wrapped in a sheet, tied in a fat bundle on the squabs beside her. Every now and then she noted Sandu's troubled gaze resting upon it from beneath the brim of his hat.

Rhys leaned heavily against her. At one sharp turn he nearly fell into her lap, wheezing as he tried to get upright again without using his hands. He struggled at first but at the next bend gave it up entirely, sagging. Zoe accepted his weight, pulled the soaked blanket tighter around him when it began to slide off. A solitary bright talon caught against her apron, tore a jagged rip through the middle before he shifted his arm.

The *maison* had not a single candle lit. They entered it without light, through the back, and the diamonds and jasper sang arias of jubilation at their presence.

Zoe lit the candles. She lit the fire in the parlor hearth. She warmed her hands before it for a long minute, feeling the steam beginning to form in the clammy mess of her petticoats and skirts, then turned around and faced the others behind her.

The cook, sans cap, rocking inelegantly in a chair with the knuckles of one hand pressed to her mouth.

The raven-haired prince standing sentinel beside her, still regal in his simple workman's garb.

And the monster, a broken shadow upon a chaise longue, his feet deformed, his legs unable to straighten. The scar drawn down his face an angry hard line. Hair hanging lank along his cheekbones, that very dark brown now oddly streaked with strands of bright silky metal. He was bony and ashen and frightening. Only his eyes remained unchanged from the ghost who'd haunted her, from the boy she'd once kissed: pale, winter green that watched her unwaveringly.

"What will you do with her?" Zoe asked in French, jerking her chin toward the cook.

"Take her home, for now," replied Prince Sandu. "Get her back home."

Zoe felt herself smile, a horrible smile, arctic and unkind. "Shall we not punish her first?"

The woman closed her eyes, kept rocking.

"Is that what you wish?" asked the prince, unmoved. "It is your right."

She kept her smile, gazing at the woman.

"Zoe," rasped the monster in his broken voice.

"Shall I?" She stretched her fingers by her sides, felt the fire behind her begin to rise and gain strength. "Shall I, female? Shall I offer you what you deserve? No doubt there's a great deal we may learn from you before . . . matters are concluded."

The cook didn't answer, her cheeks apple red, her knuckles blanched. Her rocking increased. Now that Zoe knew what she was, she could feel the woman's deep white panic, the spiral of blind, total fear that cinched her heart and clogged her mind. A true *drákon* never would have surrendered to such blank sedated fear. A true *drákon* never would have betrayed her own kind.

"But I don't know, I'm undecided," she said gently. "I do have a certain sympathy for your position. You say you have a son. It's a great pity. Yet perhaps I don't like you well enough to kill you when I'm finished with you. Perhaps I like you only enough to make you suffer."

"Zee," said the creature who had been Lord Rhys. One of the clawed hands twitched against his chest. "Stop."

"Why should I?"

The monster shook his head. "It should not be you."

The woman had bent over completely, hiding her face between the skirts at her knees. Her hair was sand-colored and wet and fraying from its braids. Zoe gazed at her, then gave a flick of her hand.

"Fine. Live." She looked back at the prince. "I'm leaving. Don't follow me."

"My lady, it's not safe—"

"Do you imagine," she said, in the same gentle tone of before, "that I care even the slightest jot about your opinion? I'm not asking permission, Highness. I'm leaving. I will return. That's all you need know. If you've left for your home by the time I get back, Godspeed." She moved to the doorway, paused with one hand upon the wooden frame. She spoke her next words to the red-and-cream runner in the hallway; she didn't face the parlor again. "Make certain you take her with you, or I won't be responsible for the consequences."

The Palais des Tuileries was also unlit. The rain remained steady, which made it simpler for her to walk there. She'd shed the cook's gown and moved unseen along the streets, but they were nearly deserted anyway, despite the fact that it was a Wednesday and the bells of the cathedral upon the Ile de la Cité were ringing over and over for the midnight Mass.

The gate into the royal gardens had a new lock upon it. Zoe cupped the weight of it in both hands, water beading and rolling along the metal. It was shiny and thick and each little piece had been fit together like a clever puzzle. The king's crest was stamped across the front. The bolt felt warm against her rain-cold fingers; she hooked her thumbs through the loop of it, gave it a swift jerk.

The lock broke into its pieces, and without nearly the fuss of the iron manacles.

Her path through the gardens felt familiar enough that she hardly paid attention to it. Her feet knew the way. She passed hedges and faceless eerie statues, fallow flower beds and the entrance to the labyrinth. Her favorite door into the palace was a hidden servant's entrance set behind an overgrown yarrow, still unlocked. She eased inside.

It was vast. So vast. How could she have forgotten it that quickly? She went from invisible to seen with scarcely a thought, no longer worrying about footprints, or sound, or human eyes peering past windowpanes. She was small as a flea in such a space.

There was no one else about. Tuileries greeted her as it always had: with marble hush and the promise of echoing solitude. Even if someone were to discover her footprints, she'd be indiscernible before they could speak a word.

Her apartment was just as before. Clearly no one had discovered it since she and the prince and—

Her apartment was the same. The bed, stripped of its covers; on the night they'd come, she'd returned each piece to its rightful owner. The broken mirror, still propped massive and hulking against its wall.

The fissure of silver that marked the divide in the glass. The stark-faced woman on one side, and the deep bottomless blue on the other.

She stood motionless a moment, taking it all in. Rainfall

peppered the lead gutters outside, cascaded down the slick walls. It penetrated the stone palace, changed the song of the foundation from sleepy to sleepier, notes that suggested undiscovered quarries far and away, mountains untouched, rivers undammed. A world flowing free.

Zoe walked across the chamber. She knelt before the mirror, her palm pressed to the cold flat glass. She felt naught but that: the cold, hard and unforgiving.

Her head bent; her forehead touched it. Nothing.

Her breath clouded it. Nothing.

Even the usual spirits were gone; nothing bright moved before her. She gazed at an endless span of dark cobalt blue, the silver fracture, unrelenting.

The air changed then; it went so thin her lungs closed. She could not breathe any longer. She could not breathe or think. He wasn't there. She thought he would be, and he wasn't. He wasn't anywhere anymore.

Something hot at last—her tears, chilled already by the time they reached her chin and dripped upon her thighs.

Zoe curled slowly down to the floor, one hand still braced against the glass, and wept into the crook of her arm, making hardly any sound at all.

The world hurt. It was a bitch of a thing, because it wasn't an ordinary sort of hurt, not the kind of pain he'd shrug off as a lad at school after a hard game of cricket, or a harder night of carousing. Rhys had had his share of bruises and bleary mornings. Once he'd even severed the primary bone of his right wing from a rushed landing in a burst of wind amid the downs, and that had been one of the most atrocious moments of his life.

This was different.

It hurt like someone had ground mounds of serrated glass into every crevice of every joint. Like he'd gone to sleep one night in his very prime, a twenty-nine-year-old *drákon,* and awoken an old, old man, so old his skin had shrunk and thinned and his body no longer obeyed him and little children would stare and point and run away if he beckoned to them. His hair was strange and his hands downright grisly, each a blasphemous mix of his human shape and dragon. His body was stooped. Clambering up the steps into the carriage he'd caught a smeared glimpse of his face in the window glass, and then he better understood Zoe's constant, horrified calm when she looked at him.

He was a corpse. All that time with her, he'd thought he'd been dead, and it must have been true. Nothing living would look as he did.

He watched her leave the *maison* and knew there was nothing he could say or do or hope to stop her. He even knew where she was going. The risks she took walking alone in this colossal city of peasants and nobles and poisonous enemies. Had he a wisp of the bravado he'd possessed months before, he would have leapt up, taken her in his arms no matter what she said. Let her shed her grief and fury upon his chest; he could accept her blows, her physical rage. That would have been all right.

It was her eyes that tore him apart. Her eyes, jet-black and beautiful and still brimming with all the tragic, shimmering sorrow he'd never before seen shining out at him. That last look she'd sent him before leaving, a mere sidelong glance from beneath brown lashes, and it had flayed him to the core.

He'd been wrong. He knew that now. She had loved Hayden James. She'd loved him, and now, because of his quest to free Rhys, a good man—a noble *drákon*—was gone forever.

And poor Zoe Lane. She'd be given to the second son of the Alpha anyway. Even like this, even mangled and destroyed as he was, as truly, *truly* fucking sorry as he was . . . when they got back to

Darkfrith, after all her dodging and hiding and intricate devious plans, she would be given to him.

The beast inside him—the dragon that yet smoldered as a cinder in his heart—was green and selfish and glad.

So he'd let her go for now. He let her slip back to her palace, to her looking glass of sallow spirits. He hoped that James was there, actually. He hoped she got to say good-bye, and that afterward James drifted away to his eternal peace.

It was the least he could hope for them.

Because one way or another, Rhys's future with Zoe was just about to begin.

He gazed down in unwilling fascination at his malformed hands, opening and closing the gold metal claws.

He was *alive.*

The prince and his small-blooded female were asleep when she returned. She'd checked on them, slipped into his room to be certain that what she sensed was truth: The boy was in the bed, still fully clothed atop the covers. The cook was wrapped in blankets upon the floor, her hands lifted to her face as if to hide her shame, even in slumber. A weak fire glowed orange from behind the grate.

Neither *drákon* woke. Zoe allowed the bedroom door to finish its well-oiled *click* behind her.

Rhys had remained in the front parlor. He might not have stirred since the last moment she'd seen him, hours past. His scent was nowhere but there. There was nothing in the air that suggested food to her, or drink, or movement. He was still angled awkwardly upon the chaise longue with his feet up; the blanket was a heap beside one slanting wooden leg, but other than that, nothing had changed. Ragged clothing. Jutting bones. Bright eyes and talons that rested across his stomach in ribbons of curling sharp gold.

The fire in here had been fed, so the light and shadows were better defined. He watched her in silence as she came to stand by the ash-colored chest placed near the parlor entrance. Finally he spoke.

"Did you find him?"

She closed her eyes and raised her face to the ceiling. "No."

"I'm sorry. I am," he added, when she opened her eyes and looked square at him. "I'd hoped . . . for your sake, Zee. I'd hoped he'd reach you."

"Well. He did not."

The monster seemed to retreat into the shadows of his longue. In this shifting dark he seemed closer to what he'd once been. But for the taloned glint of metal where his hands should be—but for the dim streaks of dragon silk in his hair—he might have been Lord Rhys again. Thinner, yes, more watchful, but still he.

"Perhaps he will later."

"Why? Do you suppose time is measured differently in death?"

He didn't rise to her baited tone. "I don't know. Perhaps."

"Perhaps." She smiled and lifted her arms to tug her sleeves straight. She'd taken the trouble in the back room to drag on the cook's gown again, and the material clung heavy and damp. "Everything perhaps," she said to the sleeves. "Perhaps he'll come to me. Perhaps he'll speak. Perhaps he'll haunt me as you once did. Would you ever even know? Perhaps, perhaps." She skimmed her nails along the surface of the chest. "Perhaps he'll even forgive me."

"Forgive you? For what?"

She let out a laugh. "I don't know. Any of it. All of it. The entire bloody fiasco."

"Zoe. None of this was your fault."

"Aren't you the gentleman still."

"No," he said. "I'm really not. And none of this falls to you."

She tipped her head to rest against the mahogany frame of the entrance. "I like you better when you don't lie."

"I'm not lying."

"Then you're in worse condition than I'd thought. Have they robbed you of your wits along with your fine looks?"

"Supposing I ever had any, then no."

Her lips began to quiver; she pressed them tight, and when they were back in her control, spoke again. "The very last thing he saw of me was our kiss. Do you realize that? The last time he looked at me, and I was kissing you."

"Ah," Rhys said quietly. "Yes. I admit those first few moments of rejoining the living are a bit fuzzy to me now, but I do recall that. I was kissing *you*, Zee. Not the other way around."

"And it's so easy to perceive the difference from a distance. In the dark."

"Of course it is. James wasn't stupid. You'd never have betrayed him, no matter whom you loved. He knew that."

Despite her best efforts, a tear leaked from the corner of her eye. She ducked her face and swiped it away.

The monster's ruined voice turned acerbic. "Does this amuse you? This self-imposed flagellation?"

"Oh, certainly."

"It does not me. Pathos does not become you."

Zoe slid a menacing step into the firelight. "Say that once more."

"Pathos. Does not. Become you."

Her words thinned to a breath. "Why you self-besotted, small-minded little boy. How dare you judge me? How dare you imply all this—all my feelings—his *death*—is an act?"

There it was—that smile, that damnable arrogant smile, and it sharpened his face just as it always had. It made her fingers itch to slap him.

"Yes," he whispered. "I'm to blame. Come over here, Zoe. Come over here and show me what you'd like to do to me."

She trembled at the edge of her intentions. She stood there and trembled, her hands balled into fists. He only smiled at her.

She took a step back into the safety of the night. She loosened her hands, expanded her lungs, and slipped into the striped chair closest to her. The one she'd sat in before, only days past, when she'd been reciting to Hayden the story of how she'd tossed her life upside down and come to France.

"Listen," she said, crossing her ankles. "Do you hear it?"

The monster tensed. "What?"

"The music, of course." She fished into the pocket of the apron, withdrew the bundle she'd taken from Sandu's room.

He'd stuffed it beneath his pillow. It might have made a difference had he not slept so deeply; it might not have. Either way, she was getting what she wanted. Removing the manacles from him had been as easy as slipping her hand beneath his cheek. He'd sighed and lifted an arm to his head but by then she was finished. Prince Sandu had returned to his dreams before she'd even tiptoed back to his door.

Foolish child. Had the cook the slightest degree more valor, she might have stolen the manacles instead.

But they were still tied snug in their sheet, firmly in her possession. She worked at the knot, let the corners fall across her lap in great folds of wrinkled cotton.

"Here they are. The secret to your internment." She lifted her eyes. "Tell me. What do they sing for you now?"

Rhys gazed back at her, unblinking. "Opera. German. Dreadfully overwrought."

"How nice."

"Clearly you haven't been to many operas."

She regarded the torn iron cuffs in her hands. "No, you're right. Like most of our kind, I've lived my life according to rules imposed by others. Rules to keep me where I am, rules I must abide without question. Opera never figured very prominently in any of it."

He never moved; the parlor seemed clinched in an absolute stillness. Even the fire dimmed. "I can take you there, Zee. London. Edinburgh. Even Vienna. Opera and theatre, street festivals, games, whatever you like. I can show you all you've missed."

"Hmmm. I suppose you could. Or...I could simply ignore all those rules and take myself."

She lifted up both manacles. The rolling sparkle of blue diamonds seemed blinding against the rest of the tame darkened room.

"Listen," she said again.

The monster made a slight, serious curve of his lips. His eyes locked to hers. "I swear I am."

She opened her mouth and spoke the words she'd practiced all the long walk back through the rain. "You will never again fall prey to this spell. Should *Draumr* sing to you, any fraction of it sing to you, should anyone who holds it charge you, you will ignore it all. Never, never again will you hear its song or give yourself to its commands. From this moment on, I will it. Let it be."

For a good while, nothing else happened. The ravaged, glinting creature upon the chaise longue still only stared at her.

"Did you think I meant to do you harm?" Zoe asked, lifting her chin.

"Not for an instant."

She stood, crossed to him, and dropped both manacles into his lap. "In that case, you're more naive than I ever imagined. Congratulations. You're free."

No, beloved, Rhys thought, watching her walk away. *Not nearly.*

CHAPTER TWENTY-ONE

"It's no longer secure here. I think you must both come with me."

The dragon-boy clasped his hands to his elbows and leaned across the table with an ease Rhys envied: such a simple move, the fingers compressed, the stretched spine and the working jaw. He'd wager the boy never considered for an instant how he did it, what muscles needed to labor instead of atrophy. He studied the taut, unblemished face of the prince and remembered how it had felt to rub his own fingers over his chin. To feel unscarred flesh. To touch without severing anything within reach.

That was before the cellar, of course. B.C., he'd decided to call it, in another one of those spurts of inappropriate black humor.

B.C. Before he'd spent months lying motionless against ice-cold stone, every fiber of his body tensed, withering into slow starvation.

Before he'd been struck down and scarred and stuck in this weird, in-between state of dragon and man.

Before. Everything was beautiful, everything was better before.

Except for one. One thing had improved: He wasn't going to spend the rest of his life alone. He was going to spend it with a creature whose grace and bravery surely canceled out all his own fresh new flaws.

Whether she liked it or not.

Morning sunlight warmed the narrow dining room of the *maison*. It lit through the lace curtains in fanciful pieces, fell along the table to highlight the white ceramic serving dish of buttered eggs and burnt toast they all shared. The manacles were here as well, one resting on the chair between Rhys's legs, the other in the coat pocket of the prince. It seemed an equitable compromise, at least in the eyes of Prince Sandu—who'd been right displeased to discover them both missing this morning.

Zoe had only ignored him, dismissing his complaints with an impressively Gallic shrug. Neither she nor Rhys mentioned her spell of the night before. He didn't know the reasons for her silence but he knew his own. By not sharing what she had done, it became a precious secret that bound them. A gift from her to him—the first she'd ever handed him—and Rhys was going to treasure it.

And it seemed to have worked. He no longer heard the symphony. Even when his skin brushed the iron, the sharp little stones, he heard nothing. He'd never, ever been so pitifully grateful in his life to have silence ringing in his ears.

Zee had made the breakfast. None of them trusted the Zaharen woman to concoct their meal, and blackened toast was a small price to pay, he reckoned, for safety. Rhys had devised an awkward yet effective manner of getting the food from his plate to his mouth: After several messy tries, he'd eschewed the fork and knife for the end of one bladed talon. Since then, he'd cut himself only twice. Handling his cup of coffee, however, was more hazardous. He'd had very little coffee.

But the eggs and toast were like manna. He savored every bite.

His future bride and the cook ate in silence, seated across from each other at the table. Neither made eye contact with the other.

"The lease here is done in a few days anyway," continued Prince Sandu. "With the *sanf* all about, we never wanted to lurk in one place very long. You will be welcomed in my castle. And there we may together invent a new scheme against our enemies." His crystal eyes lit upon Rhys. "You're the brother of Lady Amalia, who was our guest so many years past. She was the daughter of the Alpha of your tribe. As his son, do you have the authority to speak for him?"

"Yes," Rhys said.

"No," said Zoe. She placed her fork beside her plate. "I mean, no, Highness, I won't be traveling with you."

The boy flicked his hair back from his cheek with a pale finger. "Are you certain? It's far by human means, of course, but if we fly, we'll be there in days. It's a strong sanctuary. A fine place to regroup."

Zoe addressed Rhys. "Can you Turn?"

"I don't know." He stirred a swirl into the leftover butter on his plate. "I have not tried."

He was afraid to. Stupid, cowardly, mortifying. He was afraid. He didn't know how he would be able to bear losing one more slice of himself.

The iron cuff against his leg still felt cold through his borrowed breeches. Rhys wore the clothing of Hayden James now, only slightly ripped; the dragon prince was too slight, but James had been about the right size. If Zoe had noticed or minded the garments, or his hands' effect upon them, she'd had no comment about that either.

"Even if he managed smoke," she was saying now to the prince,

241

"his dragon will be as wounded as he is. I doubt you'd fit that female and me both safely on your back, Highness. Much less a third person."

"Then, very well, we may hire a carriage."

"No," she said again. "Thank you. I'm staying here."

The prince leaned back in his chair—ah yes, so easy, another mechanical contraction of muscles, no spasming, no pain—and then lifted his voice to the cook, saying something to her in his native tongue.

"Da," she whispered, her eyes glued to her plate.

Sandu lifted his coffee to his lips, blew at the steam, and spoke in English. "I told her to forget what I'm about to say." He took a taste, set down the cup with his lips puckered; it was bitter black, and there was no cream or sugar or even honey left in the house. "Here is the problem: I cannot control the female forever. My Gift is good, but perhaps not as strong as some. I spoke with her last night, enough to realize she was taken from my hills just for her blood—and that due to a traveling father, she speaks a rudimentary French. She swears only three men ever came to the house—one was killed days earlier; I assume your fellow from the dance hall—but she cooked for many. I need to get her out of Paris, back to my castle. She's a weakness for us. No doubt she has information that she isn't even aware she possesses. Any small memory may help. In time, I can access it, or someone in my clan can."

"So your strategy is to leave Darkfrith to their mercies?" Zoe asked. The sun beamed behind her, spreading fire through her unbound hair, scintillating gold over silver. She had that same slight, chilly smile as last night, lovely and fearsome together.

"No, my lady. The *sanf* are shrewd enough to remain fragmented as a group. Hayden and I learned that much from the first ones we encountered. There is a leader, he is here in this city. There is a plan. Yet no one man—or woman—seems to have been given enough information to stitch all the fragments together. I will not abandon your family, Zoe. I pledge it now. But my initial hunt was meant to last only a week. I'm the Alpha of the Zaharen. I must go home to them. I must rally them. And I must get this female away from Paris." He reached for his coffee, reconsidered, and returned his hand to his lap. "And you two should come with me."

Zoe's eyes went to Rhys. "You may. If you wish."

Rhys managed, with great effort, not to grimace as he shifted in his chair. "Surely. And what do you imagine *you'll* be doing whilst I'm relaxing in this fairy-tale castle?"

"I will be here," she answered calmly. "I will be killing *sanf.*"

"My, that's absolutely splendid." He dug his fingers into the table to sit as high up as he could; the wood ripped like paper beneath his claws. "Do you even remember that night at the dance hall? Do you remember at all what happened? The two men? The knife?"

"I remember everything," she said, impassive.

"Really? Because I could have bloody sworn you just said you'd be tripping about, killing the *sanf inimicus,* when I couldn't even get you to bloody smother a dying man who was doing his damnedest to kill you first! But *now* you're ready? *Now* you're lethal, willing to murder in cold blood?"

"Yes. Now."

He nearly smacked his palm to his forehead but caught himself in time. "Zoe! This isn't what he would want!"

She shoved back from the table so quickly her chair tipped over. "Don't tell me what he'd want."

"Why not? I can't speak his name? I can't imagine myself in his position? I love you! And God help him, if Hayden ever loved you, he wouldn't want you in danger like this!"

She stared at him with her cheeks gone bloodless and her eyes so black he thought he'd see eternity in them. She looked like she wanted to spit in his face. Then, without another word, she turned around and left.

Rhys unstuck his hands from the table. The gouged wood shone in long, pale scars against the otherwise warm cherry stain.

"You'll agree I managed that nicely." His claws clicked against his plate. "It bodes well for our wedded bliss, don't you think?"

Sandu was staring at him with his brows drawn into a frown. "You were at the dance hall with the *sanf*?"

Rhys sighed, wishing for more coffee. He stabbed a piece of toast instead, lifted it to the light. "It's a long story."

"I believe I have time." The prince glanced back at the cook, who watched them both now with wide brown eyes. "Oh. Yes." He switched to French. "You're to forget all that, as well."

He found her in the back garden. She felt him approaching from the hallway, felt his living warmth, the odd, unexpected whisper of gold that wafted about him now. More significantly, she heard his sliding, mismatched pace upon the floor. He could not walk well. It must hurt, putting weight upon his feet.

Yet he came to her. She was seated on the steps again because there was nowhere else dry to sit. The garden had been devoted either to grass or gangly tall herbs; it had no benches or chairs or even flat stones. So she sat upon the steps.

The rain had swept to the south around dawn. Droplets dewed everything before her, grass and twigs and leaves, darkened the trunks of the trees. If she angled her head a certain way, the sun lit the beads of water into thousands of round perfect jewels.

At least the fence around the yard was high. No one would easily see them, not unless they crept up to press an eye against the slats.

"Please do not say you've come to apologize." She'd wrapped

her arms around her knees, interwoven her fingers hard to keep herself fixed.

"I haven't. My parents told me never to lie."

She narrowed her eyes at the colors of the alder, tan and red and brown. "Laudable."

"And fruitless. Lying can be marvelously useful, especially if you're good at it, as I know you've already discovered."

"You're not going to change my mind."

"Am I not?" He sank down two steps above, slowly, in jerks. "As you wish. Listen well to the opinion of an educated lady. That's what my mother used to say."

"Did she."

"Yes. She liked you, you know."

She turned her face, gazed deliberately at the mangled mess of his right foot on the stair above her. "Now you're lying."

"No. Honestly. Even when we were young, she thought you had ... a certain zest of spirit. It was Father whom you scared. Mother was all out for you."

Zoe dropped her forehead into the cup of her palm. "My sister was in love with you."

"Was she?" He sounded much brighter. "Excellent. Er, I mean ... how nice."

"You are as insubstantial as the specter I thought you were, Lord Rhys. You feel nothing with your heart. You test nothing with your depths. You say you love me, but I think it must be merely the reflection of my face. My Gifts. I don't know how I can be expected to live the rest of my life bound to someone who doesn't even know my favorite color. The name of my childhood pet. The ages of my nieces."

"It was that rooster, wasn't it?" he said, after a moment. "I recollect that. You called him a pet. Nasty thing. Kept attacking me, even if I was just strolling in the remote vicinity of your cottage. I vow it hid in trees just to ambush me. I never harmed a feather on his malicious little body, but by God, he hated me."

"Yes." She rocked a little, started to laugh, but it choked in her throat. "All right. You win. We're meant to live happily ever after."

He eased down another step. "Is your favorite color blue?"

"No. Definitely not."

"Ah—wait. I do know. You don't have a single favorite color."

She felt something inside her fall into silence. Waiting and still and arrested.

"It's three colors," Rhys said. "Gold, silver, and pink."

Zoe lifted her head, scooted around in place to stare at him. "You found my diary."

He lifted his terrible hands. "No, love. But I've seen you, the other side of you. Your dragon self. Those were your colors."

"What are you talking about?"

"From before, when I was a ghost, and you were my light. I saw you once as a dragon in the palace. You were asleep." He looked down, curled his fingers closer to his palms. "Gold and pink and silver. We'd look very well together, I think. As dragons. In that ghost world."

The children next door had been set free into their yard. The dog on the other side was gone, but high-pitched laughter and shouts began to punctuate the clear morning air.

"I do not know the ages of your nieces," the monster confessed in a low voice. "I don't even know their names. I left the minute details of our tribe to my father and my brother. It seemed to matter more to them. I was a flippant fellow, Zee. You know that. I was more concerned with the cut of my coat than the ways of the shire. Mostly."

She surprised herself with his defense. "I don't think that's true."

"No? You're too kind. But it is true that I went adrift for some while. I let the shallows move me, when I should have not."

A little girl next door let out a furious screech, then a babble of words. Another girl shrieked back at her.

"We're all meant to learn our lessons," Zoe said at last, under the screaming. "If you drifted, at least now you have the chance to head home."

"Yes." Metal ribbons at the corner of her eye; the soft, slight pressure of his hand upon her shoulder. "I'd like that. I'd like to go home." His talons skimmed her dress. "Will you come with me, my heart, my compass and anchor, Zoe Langford?"

She did not answer. In time, as the sun climbed and climbed, as the shadows shortened and the children tired and returned back inside their home, he rose. And then he left.

The prince departed that evening. He truly meant to fly, something that would have been unthinkable back in England, but he would carry a satchel and the female Zaharen, and claimed they'd reach the borders of his realm within days.

The backyard was too narrow for a grown dragon to take flight, and the front was far too open and visible to all the other homes. So the four of them climbed up into the garret—even Rhys, though he arrived minutes after the rest of them—and waited for the last of the twilight to thicken into true night.

No one spoke. Enough had been said already; she'd refused over and over to leave Paris, and the prince had finally given up asking. Rhys had made it clear he wasn't leaving if she wasn't. And that was that.

The cook maintained that petrified stillness she had perfected whenever Zoe was near, the prince's hand on her arm. Rhys lounged against a box shoved against the canted attic wall. The slant of the ceiling nearly matched the curve of his back.

Zoe amused herself briefly imagining the councilmen's faces should they hear of this: an unshielded dragon atop an unshielded roof, soaring off across an open city sky.

"I think now," said Sandu, breaking their silence. They'd opened the skylight to monitor the heavens; he was barely visible, a face and vanished hair, a sheet wrapped around his shoulders for propriety. He wore, of course, no clothing beneath it.

They climbed out to the roof, first the prince, then the cook, then Zoe and Rhys. The great blue bowl of heaven was cloudless. Stars fought the yellowed haze of the streetlamps below them in fierce prickled dots.

The prince made his way to the most level section of the roof. He glanced around him, took in the hills and mighty spires and steeples of the horizon that was Paris unfolded.

"Come to me whenever you wish," he said to Zoe and Rhys. "If you need me, come to *Zaharen Yce.*"

"Yes," said Rhys. "Thank you."

The boy inclined his head. He lifted a hand to the cook, said something in Romanian, and released the sheet.

Before it even finished rumpling to his feet, he Turned to dragon. In the space of a heartbeat his human shape was gone, smoky twists that expanded, re-formed into a being of silent, glistering magnificence.

He was ebony with bands of sapphire and deep purple shaded along his sides, silver-dipped talons and wingtips. Zoe's people were more colorful, living rainbows in the sky, but the prince of the Zaharen had a sober, serpentine beauty she'd seldom seen.

The dragon turned his great head and gazed at the cook. They could not speak in this shape; they had no vocal cords to command. But the woman moved forward without hesitation, picking her way across the shingles, carrying the satchel. She climbed onto his back as if she'd done it a hundred times before, settled the bag against her stomach, and dug her fingers into his mane.

"Farewell," murmured Rhys, and the prince nodded in return, tensed his powerful haunches, and leapt from the roof.

A sharp wooden clatter from below: shingles tumbling free, striking the cobblestones.

Neither Zoe nor Rhys looked down. They watched Sandu instead, his beating wings, his sharp ascent, the skirts of the cook flapping hard around him like laundry stolen by the wind. They watched until he was nothing more than a speck against the indigo heavens, a black star in the east that gradually shrank to nothing.

By mutual, unspoken agreement, Rhys slept in the prince's old room. If it could be called sleeping, which he didn't think it could, as it really didn't involve anything like rest, or dreams, or blissful relaxation. It was far more a matter of him attempting to get flat upon the surface of the bed, small fluffy feathers kicked up every time he moved, tickling his nose and sticking to his lips, because no matter how he tried, he could not stop his talons from piercing the mattress.

He had pulled a quilt across his chest. He felt too cold and then too hot, too restless, but knew better than to attempt to rise and pace or read or brood alone in the dark. It had been far too much work just to get here, right here, in the center of the bed.

So he remained as he was. He kept his claws embedded in the ticking because it was easier than not, and he was tired of accidentally cutting his skin.

Zoe was in her room. He felt her. He couldn't tell if she slept either, but at least she was in the *maison* tonight. He'd half feared she'd want to start her hunt at once, that she'd wait for nothing, especially not him.

But after the prince had left, they'd shared a small meal and each retired, no more than five words spoken between them.

He was relieved. If she'd wanted to leave tonight, he would have had to find a way to stop her or else stay by her side. And he honestly didn't think he was capable of either at the moment.

The prince's room contained a looking glass. Nothing so

ominous as the one back in Zoe's palace, just a small square mirror mounted in pewter, set at an angle upon the chest of drawers. He glimpsed no other faces in it but his own. His own was surely alarming enough.

He hadn't realized it was there at first. He'd walked by it, caught the motion of his reflection from the corner of his eye, and instinctively turned.

He didn't know the creature there staring back at him. It looked like him, but some exaggerated, gruesome version of himself. He'd brought his hands to his face, touched his palms lightly to his cheeks. Stubble—that was familiar. And the shape of his jaw, that too. Same eyebrows as always, black and straight. Same nose and eyes. A series of shallow nicks across his lips from before he'd mastered breakfast.

His hair, that dark vanity of his youth, now a mix of limp human strands and gold metal dragon.

His earlobe was torn. He'd worn an earring before, an emerald on a hoop; he supposed the *sanf* had stolen that as well. And he was emaciated. Their kind was lean in general but if he brought the lamp in his hand close enough, he could see the outline of his skull. He must have been without food or drink for months, without breath, all that while.

Worst of all was the scar that began above his hairline and ripped all the way down the right side of his face, halfway down his neck. He was lucky not to have lost an eye—or his head.

The fight in the woods. The sanf *coming after him with swords and knives and bullets, and a hood. The spell of the diamond sinking over him even as he fought them, telling him not to Turn—but he was— look at his hands, he was—and someone clouted him in the face with a sword—*

He'd backed away from the mirror. He had not looked into it again.

Rhys centered himself better in the bed, closed his eyes. He thought of Darkfrith. Of the woods and the lake, and the falcons and gannets that would sometimes venture to hunt fish in the River Fier. Crickets, serenading him from the bracken. Waterfalls. Swimming, weightless. Diving like smoke through the cool waters...

His eyes opened. His body clenched, and more feathers puffed free.

After his discovery of the mirror, alone in this room, he'd tried to Turn to smoke. He'd tried three times before it worked, and even then, he'd only been able to hold it a few minutes.

Smoke should be so easy. Smoke was the most elemental of Gifts, and it should have been easy. It had not hurt, per se—not like his human body did. But he hadn't been able to hold it. Against his will, he'd felt himself gathering weight again, felt his limbs solidify, felt the floor beneath his feet.

Three more times, he'd done it. Each time he'd been able to remain vapor a little longer than the last. But when he'd tried that extra fifth Turn, nothing had happened. His Gifts were numbed.

He closed his eyes again, tried to relax the knotted muscles of his back. At least he was clean again: with his Turns, all the dirt and grime of his imprisonment, the dried sooty sludge from the rain, had been left behind.

His hair, he thought with a trace of self-mocking humor, must look much better. He supposed that was something.

Paris was an unquiet beast. He heard no crickets here, no soothing splash of waterfalls. He heard humans. Many, many, humans. He heard dogs and cattle and chickens, and somewhere far overhead, a flock of geese honking lovelorn to the moon. He was certain he wasn't going to be able to sleep, not even in the midst of this soft bed, and so when he awoke at some undefined time later, he thought he must have simply been lost in thought for too long.

But it was darker, and it was more quiet. Not so many sounds of people. Not even animals. Just breathing. His own, a deep, slow, rasp that scraped from the bottom of his lungs. And Zoe's, lighter, more even, no rasp at all.

She sat beside him on the bed, unspeaking. He felt the curls of her hair brushing his arm.

"Zee," he whispered. He didn't have to whisper, it wasn't as if anyone else was going to hear them, but she was here, and she seemed naked, and his first raging instinct was quick hard lust— followed instantly by guilt. "What's wrong?"

"Nothing." She whispered as well. She leaned closer, touched her fingertips to the quilt; he felt that, all the way through the cotton. How her fingers bunched the material and dragged it slowly down his chest.

Perhaps he was asleep after all. Perhaps he was dreaming. Only an idiot would think to lift his hand and wrap his claws—gently, very gently—around her wrist to stay her. But he did it anyway.

"What are you doing?"

"I can't imagine you're that obtuse." He thought he saw her smile, a little smile, hardly there. She did not release the quilt. She pulled it farther down, all the way past his stomach. And his hand did nothing to stop her. His hand only moved with her, not resisting, no longer a part of his best-of-intentions resolve.

"I really don't think this is what we—should be doing right now," he tried. He swallowed, fighting the incredible sensation of her fingers rubbing a circle against his skin through the cloth. "You're tired. You're grieving."

"This is what you wanted." She turned her wrist until his fingers opened; she used both arms to inch closer to him, leaned her face down to his. "All those nights you watched me. All those times you stared at me, tried to touch me. All those pretty words about love. You said you wouldn't lie."

"You weren't listening. I said I was proficient at lying, actually. So listen now. This isn't what I want."

She came so close her lips met his: sweet, so sweet and warm; short, teasing contact that rippled pleasure all the way down his body. He felt himself arch with the power of it, rising to her.

"I don't think you're proficient at all. You're doing a terrible job of it."

"The circumstances," he gasped, trying not to move or inhale, "are somewhat intimidating."

"Are they? Good." She kissed him again, full and hard on the mouth, with her hair fragrant on his face and her soft tongue tasting his and Rhys lost himself. He pulled both hands free of the mattress, and goose down floated about them like snowfall.

Easy as silk, she slipped above him, rubbed her bare skin to his. He felt her breasts crushed to his chest, her nipples peaked. As carefully as he could he raised both arms to embrace her, to urge her closer still.

It was the best, best—God, the most amazing dream ever. All his pain forgotten, drowned in her touch, in her heat, in the heavy curtain of silver that hung between them. He wanted to run his fingers through the strands and it killed him that he could not. He wanted to stroke her as she was stroking him, her hands hot and urgent all up and down his body—and he couldn't, he wouldn't.

Because he might hurt her.

Because he might bring her hurt.

"Zoe. Zee. Stop."

She cupped his face and held him for her kiss, and despite himself Rhys felt his neck strain as he reached up to kiss her in return. When he couldn't breathe any longer, when he thought he'd black out with the hunger for her, she turned her face and pressed her lips to his cheek. To the scar.

"I'm not going to do this with you now," he said, as quickly as he could; he wanted the words out while he could still speak them. He squeezed his eyes closed so he wouldn't see her face. "I love you, and you're not ready, and I'm not going to do this."

"This is just another way to love."

"No." He turned his head away from her. "This is one of the most sacred ways. It's meant—between us, between mates, it's meant to be sacred."

He felt her chest rising and falling against his. "More pretty words. Where were your principles the other night, when you were in another man's body while with me?"

"It's different now."

She stilled.

"I love you," he whispered again.

She rolled away and off the bed, gone in a tempest of stale-smelling feathers. He still couldn't bring himself to look, so he only listened as she walked, very swiftly, out of his room.

When he finally woke up the next afternoon—he thought it must be afternoon, judging by the shadows—the *maison* was empty. Zoe's belongings were missing. James's belongings were missing.

Even the diamonds from the garden were missing.

He couldn't believe it. He did not want to believe it. She'd actually abandoned him.

Rhys stalked a final circle around her room: the neatly made bed, the washbasin and chamber pot empty, the drawers of the bureau and the door to the closet politely closed, everything left tidy as by a houseguest departing who did not mean to return.

"Right," he muttered. "We'll just see about that."

CHAPTER TWENTY-TWO

She gave the diamonds away, one by one. She ventured down the back lanes of St. Antoine, boulevards that grew smaller and more crooked with every step, buildings pushed and crammed together so tightly that the only way to tell one from another was by the changing colors of paint. Wan-faced Others stared at her from stoops, out from windows. When she wandered too near a cluster of grubby children gathered around a spinning top, they surged toward her, hands reaching.

Zoe gave them each a gemstone.

A man with a red beard who was missing an arm and smelled of beer.

A girl with a baby on her hip and a toddler behind her crying soul-sobbing tears.

An elderly woman.

A toothless young man.

The last diamond, heavy and round and colored canary yellow, went to a gray-haired fellow surrounded with cats—he'd been feeding them before she walked up, feeding them painstakingly the crumbs of something from a greasy sheet of waxed paper. All the cats scattered, and the old man looked after them without trying to call them back, his hands trembling.

She took up his nearest one, pressed the diamond into his palm, and then added a *louis* for good measure.

It took some time after that to trace her way back to a street respectable enough to house a grocer's market. A few of the very first children she'd encountered recognized her as she walked the other way down their lane, cried aloud and stampeded across the cobbles to her, and persisted in begging even after she told them she had nothing more to give.

"Madame! Madame!" followed her for blocks, and those children picked up more as they went, starveling boys and girls trailing along behind her like she played a magical pipe to lure them.

She had dressed too well for this faubourg. It was difficult to judge sometimes; everyone in Darkfrith was the same, barring the marquess and his kin, all the villagers were the same. The same fine houses, the same clean streets, the same fresh foods and imported wines in every home, even the farms and shepherd's huts.

Paris was not like that. Perhaps there was no other place on earth like that.

She was wearing her last French gown, salmon-pink satin with yards of deep orchid lace, and even with her shawl of plain wool she would have done better with the cook's second frock, but when she'd arisen this morning she hadn't known what she was about to do. She hadn't thought through anything beyond leaving the *maison*, removing herself and her belongings and everything that had belonged to Hayden. Even the diamonds he'd buried. Even the jasper, which she'd already thrown into the river as far as she could.

Zoe waited until she and her entourage of urchins reached an especially narrow passage, one with tilted buildings looming so far over the street the upper floors had been propped in place on stilts and all trace of the sun was blocked. As soon as she stepped fully into the shadows she whirled, raising her arms and Turning invisible, rushing abruptly toward them with the most unearthly howl she could manage.

Every single child stopped, stared, and screamed, fleeing in all directions. She was alone within seconds.

Not quite alone.

"They'll have nightmares for years," predicted the being who had been smoke just an instant before. She became seen, turned about, and found him leaning naked against a peeling house that cast some of the deepest shadows. "I'm fairly certain there's a reason the council frowns on that sort of behavior."

"They may add it to my list of transgressions." She looked him up and down. "What about Turning in public? I'm fairly certain *that's* forbidden too."

"Rebels, the both of us," he said with a shrug. "But at least I'm dragon enough to face my consequences."

A woman bent out from the open window above them, peering around to discover the source of the commotion below. Zoe ignored her.

"You're saying I can't face consequences?"

He slanted forward a bit, raised his hand and waved up at the woman, who stared at him with her mouth agape before hastily withdrawing inside. "I'm not the one who ran away."

"No. *You* have permission to leave Darkfrith, remember? Glorious son of the Alpha, et cetera, et cetera."

"I'm not talking about Darkfrith." He scowled at her. "I'm talking about now."

"Now? Right now I'm about to go procure us some foodstuff. In case you failed to notice, we suffer a rather severe lack of domestics to serve us. I haven't run away."

Another woman appeared in the Dutch half doorway across the street. She glared at them, shouted a name back over her shoulder.

"Your things were gone," Rhys said, straightening. He limped a step toward her, his hair falling longer than she last remembered, a look on his face that pierced her like a rapier. "Everything. All of it. After last night, after what happened—I thought you'd left."

"So you chased me all the way here? I don't know if I should be more insulted or impressed."

"Be impressed," he said, after a moment. "Your scent is exceptionally subtle. A snowflake in a blizzard. I'll have to douse you in rosewater every morning just to find you for luncheon back at Chasen."

A man pushed the woman in the doorway aside; he had the aspect of a butcher, a close-shaved head and burly arms, a shirt streaked in red rust. Zoe tucked down her chin and began to walk. Rhys stepped back into the shadows and went to smoke, a hovering wisp above her.

"I wouldn't desert you," she murmured. "Kindly don't make the same mistake again."

He lowered, became a brief, twining mist about her face and shoulders, almost stroking, before rising above her again.

As apologies went, it was nearly sufficient.

That night, she took him back to Tuileries. It was where she had already reestablished her former suite, resheeted the bed, redraped the mirror. Better to leave the *maison* before it was to be turned over to its landlord, who had no idea who they were, anyway. She could not envision maintaining the illusion of beclawed Lord Rhys as an ordinary man in a Parisian hotel or country inn. They needed privacy. The *sanf inimicus* would be well aware of them now, so they needed a place no *sanf inimicus* would think to look.

And there was a deeper truth she would not say aloud. She needed to escape the last hints of Hayden: her memories of him in each chamber of the *maison,* sandalwood yet lingering. It had been difficult enough to enter his room: the comb and brush and aquamarine-rimmed snuffbox. He knew how she disliked his habit; he'd made certain never to indulge in front of her. She'd been unable to bring herself to touch the pillows on his bed, where a single golden hair still shone. She'd shoved all his possessions into his portmanteau and stored it far back in the closet of the palace apartment. She would return everything to his parents. She would keep only his ring.

Since she'd been here last, a pair of swans had taken up residence in one of the garden ponds. Zoe was sorry to see them go, silent and massive, taking flight across the liquid silver surface like water-dragons, long necks stretched and wings of thick perfect feathers.

She and Rhys watched them together, outlined in moonlight. The back of his hand touched hers; he kept it there, unmoving until she nodded toward the palace and drew him onward.

He was displeased about the solitary bed, she could see that. But she wasn't going to sleep on the floor and told him that if he wanted to, he could, and he was a fool to even consider it.

"Your virtue is safe from me," she said, dry. "I shan't trouble you again."

"*Mine* is safe," he muttered, still glowering at the bed. "Most reassuring."

She walked to the closet to find her nightgown. "Sleep where you wish. You might sample a hundred different rooms here before anyone discovered you. But this bed is comfortable."

"Is it feather?" he asked, lifting his voice a little, but she didn't trouble to answer. She knew he could smell the down as well as she, and better feathers than straw.

When she emerged again, he was exactly where she'd left him, only now he was glowering at her.

"Can't you see? I can't sleep beside you."

"Stars above! I told you I'd leave you alone."

He hunched his shoulders and angled his body away from hers, his gaze fixed churlish to the crimson walls. "It's not that." One fisted hand slowly raised into the lamplight; gold glimmer and blades. "It's this. I don't want to hurt you. If I'm asleep, I won't know what I'm doing."

"You won't hurt me."

His eyes cut to hers. "Your faith is gratifying, if extremely misplaced. I'm not a light sleeper. You did see the mattress back at the *maison,* did you not?"

"I did. And I also see this." She walked forward across the chilled floor, the folds of her gown flowing and rippling behind her. She lifted his hand daintily, mindful of his talons, and held it up between them. "They're shorter now. Did you notice? Your hair is longer and more brown, your claws are shorter. Even your eyes seem a deeper green. And that's in just a few days. Soon you'll be much better, I think."

He stared down at his hands, marveling. "You're right. They are shorter."

"Just sleep on your side," she said, and crossed to the lamp upon the floor, blew out the flame.

Darkness. The same shrouded gloom she'd grown used to since she'd left her English home, far more comfortable and known than the little girl's room at the *maison.* The smells of the palace, the antique curtains and bed, the tapestry above her like a pale patterned magical carpet, sending her off into dreams.

She fell asleep before Rhys made up his mind, but awoke in the night to feel the heat of his body against hers: chaste, his back pressed to hers, the soles of their feet barely touching, a single sheet covering them both. It nudged her out of that deadened, exhausted place where she'd been hiding: Never before had she lain in a bed with a man, any man. It felt foreign and wrong, and at the same time ordinary and exactly right. She had the drowsy notion she'd awoken to him like this, the two of them like this, so many times before she'd lost count, and yet it must have only been because he'd been her shadow, her familiar. The spirit that had watched over her and discovered her dragon reflection without her even knowing.

And now he was no shadow.

He wore no nightshirt to bed, only breeches. He wore no cologne, and so his scent was purely his. Zoe curled her fingers into her pillow and inhaled it: Rhys. Summer woods and smoke. Nature and grass and outdoors. Enticement.

He spoke into the darkness, his voice so muted she barely heard it.

"I don't want to hurt you."

She twisted around, allowed her hand to briefly brush his waist. "Then do not."

She waited. She did not move again.

He rolled over. He lifted his arm and placed it across her, just beneath where the gown pulled taut against her breasts. She felt his breath upon her cheek, only slightly uneven, and then the pressure of his lips: a kiss that was also chaste and yet not, because it wasn't on her mouth, but his arm lifted and pushed at her a little, and his body curved toward her a little, and his feet retangled with hers.

All she had to do was turn her head. Not even very far, just a fraction. She kept her eyes open and gazed at the canopy of the bed, the tapestry of purple roses and vines, and as he bent closer she allowed at last that small motion of her head, tipping toward him, and he leaned up and found her lips with his.

It was a gentle thing, so light and skimming, and yet it warmed her in a way that all the gold she'd ever worn never did. He savored her, faint, delicious kisses at the corners of her lips, her chin and nose and eyes, his cheek scraping hers, because he was still unshaven.

He began to lean more heavily against her. He drew one arm up by her head to support himself and allowed the other to slide along hers, his hand flexed, the warm skin of his biceps and forearm tracing the shape of hers through her sleeve. His leg lifted, angled across her stomach, gliding slowly up and down as he kissed her, and the hem of her gown rumpled upward until her bare knees and shins touched his.

She felt the whisper of his hair along her neck, that faint tickle of metallic silk. She reached up and wove her fingers through it, enjoying its heat and satiny weight as he closed his eyes and rubbed his cheek back to hers. He learned her without using his hands, exploring the delicate hollows and curves of her face with lips and eyelashes, his scent intoxicating. She was melting from it, melting from the inside out.

And he was changing too. She stroked her hands down his back to the sudden rougher edge of his breeches, traced the circumference of his waist from back to front. Wool and linen. Hard buttons. His hips finding a rhythm against hers, the leg curled over her scissoring tighter, aligning his body over hers, one knee between her own.

She'd seen him before without clothing, more than once, and if he could summon even a sliver of their time together in the house of the *sanf*, he'd seen her nude too. There were still mysteries between them, the interlocking of their bodies, her gown and his breeches; the gown at least had a simple solution. A few slithering moves and she had it over her head, wadded into a new pillow against the gilded headboard.

He had arched over her as she'd moved, allowing her the space to disrobe, but that was all. Now he lowered himself again, and she felt the fresh heat of his chest to hers, his mouth moving from her temple to her ear to her neck, to the winged curve of her collarbone. Lower, to the underside of her breast, his tongue drawing circles against her, smaller and smaller luxurious circles. Her pulse matched his circles, thumping and thumping in hard, anxious beats, and when he closed his lips on her nipple at last her heart skipped and the flutter of breath trapped in her throat became a moan.

He suckled her, a hard pull and a brightness that shot all the way through her like a comet. The gold of his claws scraped the gold of the bed, and the music of their clashing rose in her head; Rhys at her breast and the metal songs in her ears; she could not seem to drag in enough air. Her hands were working at his buttons, her leg lifted to bring him closer, and he broke off with a gasping that matched her own.

"No, no. Let me."

His hand moved between them; the bone buttons popped free, one hitting the sheets and the rest bouncing to the floor. He rubbed his face between her breasts and his palm up and down her arm.

"Sweet Zee," he said breathless, smiling. "Lovely girl. I think I might need some help for this next part, actually."

She put her hands upon his shoulders, pushed until he sat up. Zoe rose to her knees, kept her eyes on his—a faint gleam of color, framed with lashes darker than the night—and drew her palms down his chest, let her fingers catch against the loosened waistline. She tugged the breeches down to his hips, down to his thighs, pressed him back against the mattress lightly with one hand and finished the job, tugging the tan wool all the way down his legs.

When it was done she had a moment of dreamlike uncertainty: There he lay, beautiful still in his animal way, with his hair a dark-and-bright flag against the bedding, and his arms spread wide and his legs crooked around her hips. Rhys Langford. And he was looking back at her with that smile that was both knowing and aroused, as aroused as his body; Zoe lifted her hand and covered her eyes with her fingers.

She felt his legs encircle her waist, muscled warmth, strength that pulled her back down to him. His arms came up too, wrapped around her and held her pinned to the length of him. When he arched his hips into hers she opened her mouth to the hard curve of his shoulder; he tasted of salt. He made a low hum in his chest and used his wrist to guide her lips higher, to the bottom of his jaw, whiskers and the scar, all the while grinding against her. All the melting inside her seemed suddenly concentrated in her loins. Where she felt that male part of him, satiny and hard and demanding.

But she didn't know what to do next. Silly, spinster virgin—untouched for all her years, untouched despite all her best efforts—and she didn't know what to do.

Rhys did. Of course he did; there was nothing virginal about him, she'd known that forever. He wasn't smiling up at her any longer. He was watching her through those lowered lashes, breathing as if he'd just run a sprint. She moistened her lips and looked back at him, and he blinked once, a slow and lazy blink.

"Am I awake?" he asked.

"I hope so." She sounded breathless herself, the shyness stealing her words. "Or this is a very frustrating dream."

"You are the most wondrous, miraculous—you know that; I know you do—but Zee, if this is a dream—"

She lost her nerve, hid her face against his shoulder.

"This is how I wanted it," he murmured, holding her. "When I was dead. This was all I wanted. You, with me. To touch you again. To do this..."

He tensed, gathered her closer, and rolled them together, so now he was on top and she had the rumpled bedding beneath, and the mattress must have ripped anyway, because there were tiny feathers dusting them both, caught in the mess of their tangled hair.

"To do this," he whispered, and cradled her head in his hands as he pushed into her, into the center of her heat, his eyes closed.

She stilled, feeling him, the strange and brilliant sensation of him filling her, stretching her to hurt: She couldn't move, she was afraid to move. He was inside her, and she'd never, ever thought it would feel like—

"This," he breathed, moving in and out in slow, languorous thrusts, turning the hurt into the worst pleasure imaginable, an aching, throbbing pain that spread white fire through the core of her, that had her opening her legs wider and digging her fingers into his back.

"I love you." She barely understood him; he'd buried his face into her hair. "I love you. I love you."

It was a chant, a song, rawly beautiful in his broken voice, a rhythm that matched his body's, and he moved more quickly now, plunging deeper, pulling that white fire within her into a taut coil. She was drawn thin with it, she was desperate for something she could not name. She turned her head from his, searching, held in place by her hair where he pinned it with his arms.

"Love," he ground out between his teeth, and pressed at once so hard and so deep within her that her entire being lit and burned and she cried out in surprise, a soft startled sound that curled across the floor and walls to die in echo, just as she did.

Rhys collapsed against her. His skin was slick, his heart racing. She felt that, the pounding in his blood, just as she felt his legs against hers and his face and his talons that curved up and around her head like a spiked metal sunburst.

He did not lift himself from her; he felt heavy but not crushing, supple and warm and welcome. She was floating, astonishingly re-laxed, gliding into smooth liquid dreams before he moved, and even then it was only his lips, a bare kiss at the top of her ear, and words she could make out only because she was asleep now, she was finally dreaming. . . .

"Someday you'll love me too."

He'd hurt her. He knew that; in the morning he found the blood that marked him, and her, the small dark smears on the sheets and between her thighs.

Zee was a virgin. Naturally, she was. Ice and proper prim on the outside, she'd rebuffed more men of the tribe with just a single, level look than he'd been able to count. Yet her eyes kept betraying her. Poor Zoe; she'd probably never even realized it. No matter how cool her words or demeanor, those exotic black eyes always prom-ised pure, wanton sensuality.

And last night that promise had transformed into truth.

He hadn't only hurt her. Rhys had given her pleasure as well. Even like this, even as a miserable scrap of who he'd once been, he'd found the way of her, things he'd known for years because of all those daydreams: how to kiss her. How to stroke her white skin. How to move inside her so that her lips parted and her head arched back and her throat worked, all because of what he was doing to her. All the things he could do to her.

How to feel that rising release that wanted to shatter her, and him. To coax them both into that place.

Rhys felt as if his heart was a dry well that had been unexpect-edly reflooded with life. He overflowed. He lay next to her and nuzzled his face into silver-glossy hair, and let the waters pour through him.

Let them spill over.

CHAPTER TWENTY-THREE

The hive of the *sanf inimicus* reeled only very briefly from the discovery of their losses: the house they'd secured breached; the Romanian half-blood they'd persuaded into servitude stolen; the Frenchmen they'd recruited so carefully murdered.

The body of the beast in the cellar missing. The precious shards of diamonds that guarded him taken too.

It took them almost no time at all to abandon the house. They'd scrubbed out the blood from the floorboards, wiped down the walls until there was no trace of flour or dust. They'd removed all the boards and shelving of the false pantry to restore, more or less, the original entrance to the cellar. They'd rehung the door.

They would leave no element of themselves behind. Their enemy was cunning, and they would not be caught so short again.

The woman named Réz shuffled slowly through each chamber, her nose lifted to the air, her withered fingers tracing nooks and crannies, the hard corners of the wainscoting. When it was done, she pulled the hood of her cloak low about her face and stepped outside.

Her carriage awaited at the curb. She trundled closer, sighed at reaching the bottom of the lowered steps—and the horses in their restraints rolled eyes white with fear.

When I asked her later what she'd felt as she'd entered the ruined house, tasted the leftover emanations of the *drákon* who had ransacked it, the shock of grief that lingered like a preternatural slap over the one who had perished there, her answer was: naught. She'd felt naught.

Our Gifts are tremendous burdens. You will discover that among us, for all our grandeur, there are those who cannot survive beneath their weight.

CHAPTER TWENTY-FOUR

Sunlight flared red behind her lids. Zoe turned over, reached for a pillow to pull across her eyes, and gradually, in that sliding strange world between deep sleep and full awake, realized why there should be no sun on her face.

Because she wasn't home. She wasn't somewhere safe. She was in Tuileries, and she had ensured that the drapery was very firmly closed the night before.

She opened her eyes. A shadow man stood against the window, contoured in light, spreading the tall heavy curtains with both arms.

He turned in place and looked back at her. Yellow sun proved what wasn't shadow: the curvature of a cheekbone; the hard, smooth arc of a shoulder. The muscles of his stomach, rippled and flat. He wore the breeches again, had tied the corners into a knot to keep them fixed without buttons.

Before she could tell him to do so, Rhys let the curtains fall closed in a pall of spinning dust.

"Awake yet? Come with me. I have a surprise."

He did not give her time to figure her regrets about last night, or wish for a moment alone, or even to do more than toss on her nightgown—which she did, swiftly, using the cool crumpled linen to momentarily hide the heat rising in her face. He kissed her as she'd emerged from the neck hole, kissed her hard and then soft, his lips like velvet, the cuts that were healing still tasting a little of blood. Then he wrapped a hand lightly about her wrist and led her out of the apartment.

Down the silent, grave hallways of the palace, the bare green tiles. He didn't head toward the servants' stairs, the way she always went, but instead to the main grand staircase, with its black iron design of fleur-de-lis topped with a sickle-curved rail of gold-plated brass, the royal coat of arms set within the iron every six treads.

They went down together, one step at a time.

There were windows meant to illume the space, grand, imposing windows, but they had been sheeted, and so they descended three full levels by uncanny, impure light, her gown billowing with a draft of unseen air, Rhys's hair a mussed drape down his shoulders.

Past galleries of slender pillars and wide arches, ormolu garlands draped along the walls. Faces carved into the decorative friezes gazing back at them with blank stone eyes.

She'd been here before, but only in the dark. By day it seemed more haunted; through the cool solemnity of the open atrium she could easily imagine the long-dead Others who'd lived here, who'd touched the banister as she did, who admired the ocher-banded colonnades and intricate shining details of the garlands.

Zoe could not prevent her periodic, nervous glances toward the gloomier corners. She was ready to Turn if she had to, she could shed the nightgown quickly. They were so very open to discovery. Yet Rhys limped his way down the inlaid marble steps with an élan that was almost cheerful. She wouldn't be surprised if he started to whistle.

A thin, scorched aroma teased her nose, stronger, then weaker, wafting once very close before disappearing altogether. Smoke—not dragon smoke, but ordinary smoke from ordinary wood. The occupied chambers of the palace were still quite distant. Perhaps one of the groundskeepers had lit a torch outside.

Rhys had moved ahead. Like her, he kept a hand upon the banister, but gripped it harder. His limp was growing more pronounced.

At the bottom of the staircase he angled to a sealed doorway to the right, double doors, and she knew what was behind them as well; she'd visited every room on this level at least once, and this, she recalled, had been a parlor.

It *was* a parlor, but surely one for a queen, for the floors were a mosaic of sky blue and pink marble, and the arabesque flourishes covering the walls had been done in pure silver, still singing bright to her ears but long since tarnished to black.

There was a picnic laid out upon the floor. A blanket with china dishes—fruit and bread and sliced roast. An Oriental teapot that smelled of warm chocolate, and two thick plain ceramic mugs.

"I know how you feel about cooking," Rhys said.

"How did you—" She only just stopped herself from glancing down at his hands. "Where did you get all this?"

"Here and there." He smiled at her—oh yes, that special smile; her heart gave a little squeeze—and backed into the chamber. "Have you been to the kitchens in this place? One might house the entire English militia in a single corner. Even with only the few, poor hardscrabble souls living here, there were plenty of delicacies to choose from."

"You stole it?"

His lashes lowered; his smile grew more wry. "Let's say *pilfered.*

It sounds more debonair, don't you think?" He lifted his hands and flexed his fingers, and his claws blurred in a cascade of wicked symmetry. "Call me cynical, but I doubt they would have volunteered it, beloved, no matter how sweetly I asked."

"But how did you manage to . . ." She remembered the odor of woodsmoke. "You set a fire."

"Just a small one."

"Rhys!" She caught herself, lowered her voice. "You set a *fire* to draw them away?"

"You're welcome. See all the trouble I go to for you?" He came forward at her look, held her gaze in a straight green reply, then leaned in to buss her cheek. Soft, soft, like bluebell petals, a bare tempting brush of sensation.

"A *fire*," she murmured, shaking her head. "What a madman."

"Excruciatingly small. Hardly any grass burned, I promise."

She surveyed the meats and fruits and the peony-painted pot and thought of how much work it must have been for him to get it all here. How he must have made three trips at least in his mangled human form, and the kitchens were nowhere near the queen's elaborate pink-and-blue world.

The bread was so fresh it sent out waves of yeasty perfume. Her stomach gave a loud rumble.

"Lovely timing," her shadow said, and lowered himself to the blanket. She stood there watching him, watching how his face went blank and his muscles clenched, his arms and back and calves, how his claws dug ten pointed holes into the immaculate marble floor. When it was done he released a breath and looked up at her. His scar seemed reddened but that was all. She saw not a trace of the pain that must have racked him left on his features.

"My lady. Won't you dine with me?"

She gathered up her nightgown and sat beside him with her legs tucked under, close enough to feel the heat of his gold, because like everything in Tuileries, the parlor was cavernous, and her body was chilled.

She was glad to have the cook's uniform after all. Its tan-and-brown stripes would make her blend better with the teeming crowds of peasants, and it was going to be easier to hide amid them than in the extravagant pockets of nobles who picked their way about the city like jeweled birds hopping through rubble. She could stoop her shoulders and stuff her hair beneath a cap, and if she kept her face lowered, she would gather hardly any attention. Especially with a measure of dirt rubbed upon her cheeks and neck.

It was brilliant. No matter what Rhys said.

"It won't work," he insisted stubbornly. "You're still too pretty. You can smear yourself with all the mud from here to the Seine, and I still won't believe for a moment you belong in that woefully hideous frock."

"I'll keep my face down."

"And I'll see the nape of your neck. And your hands. And your chin. And your lips. It's no use, Zee. Everything about you screams of aristocracy."

"That's ridiculous. I'm the daughter of a seamstress."

"You are Lady Rhys Langford," he said, coming up to her. "And it shows."

It was the first time he'd used the title the tribe would give her—that all of English society would give her. It pricked at her conscience and made her take a sliding step back from him, averting her gaze.

She was going to hunt. Nothing he said or did could change her mind about that. She'd accepted his body last night, his caresses, but that was all. It granted him no dominion over her, despite what he believed.

And still . . . the beauty of last night, the joy of discovering true physical acceptance, had been a rare revelation. Their merging. That devastating conclusion. Whenever she found herself slipping back into daydreams about it all, her blush rose again, and she'd swear—she'd *swear*—he felt the change in her, pinned her in a cool green gaze and sidled close. Close enough that, if she wished, she could lift a hand to trace the curves of his lips. Enact a slender motion of her arm to have it brush his. His essence of outdoors, that warm summer scent, wrapped around her in constant invitation and desire.

And she did desire, she did. As sure as if he'd lifted a veil from her eyes, Zoe saw herself more clearly now than ever before. He'd been right, all those days ago: She burned inside, more vivid than the sun. A hard, steady burn that kindled only for him. She wanted his touch. She wanted it in the most intimate places on her body, and she wanted his tongue in her mouth, and she wanted him inside her again. If she let her imagination fly too far, her blood peaked and her nipples hardened and even the pain between her legs seemed insignificant.

She'd never felt this way for Hayden. It was a niggle of discomfort crawling through her, a small ugly truth: never this way for Hayden, nor any of her other suitors over the years. None of them had had eyes of winter and jade, or a smile so staggeringly sweet it eclipsed scruff and grief and scars. Only Rhys.

But last night had lifted into morning, into right now. She was bathed in daylight, hard autumn daylight, and last night was done.

Zoe was going to hunt. She was going back to the Palais Royal and use the cloak and finish what she'd begun in the house of the *sanf.*

Rhys, of course, was determined to go with her. She'd already presented her arguments about why he should not:

He was weakened.

He countered that by Turning back and forth from man to smoke, ten rapid times in succession.

He was noticeable.

Not with the proper garments, he replied.

His body, she said.

He bent and touched his toes, ten times again, and she'd had to bite the inside of her cheek against the agony he concealed with that proud, blank mask.

His *claws,* she said.

Easily hidden beneath a blanket. Elderly gents were often wheeled about by their nurses in chairs.

His hair, she pointed out. His brown-and-*metal* hair.

"A wig," he'd answered. "A nice, dodgy, old-fashioned sort of wig, I think, with horsehair and lots of stiff curls. I'd wager there's a good one somewhere in this monster abode. And a rolling chair," he'd added, before she could open her mouth again. "You can wheel me about. Pretend you're going to pop me over the riverbank into the rapids." His tone softened. "Honestly, Zee. You can't possibly believe I'd let you go alone. Not when you have me. But I'm an old goat, you see. I don't need a cook. I need a nurse."

So they removed the apron from the dress. They had no scissors, and of course, did not need them. Rhys used the smallest finger of his left hand to sever the threads.

By the time they'd worked out the details, it was past teatime. They were seated upon the bed, both of them, and Zoe was so absorbed in using her fingernails to tweeze free the last, frayed threads left from the apron from the bodice that at first she didn't notice his silence.

She looked up when she rolled the crick from her neck, and only then realized he'd been staring at her for minutes with his hands cupped atop his knees, his expression pensive. That lock of chestnut down his forehead, still rakish and charming, a clash to the more sinister reality of his scar.

"This isn't how I thought it'd be," he said in an undertone.

She let her hands fall to her lap.

"I wanted a different life for us," he said. "I wanted peace for us. A home together. Babies. Laughter."

"There has been an *us* for approximately twelve hours," she said. "A bit too soon to become maudlin, don't you think?"

"There has been an *us* since the day I first beheld you. Yes, I realize you don't believe me. All those girls, all those years, and I didn't even know myself how much of myself I'd lost to you. Given, rather. I don't need you to believe me. But it's true."

"I don't wish to discuss this now."

"When?" he asked calmly. "After tonight, when we may both meet our fates? We're not playing skittles and tops here, Zee. You desire to challenge our most earnest enemy. You're determined to strike a blow, no matter the cost."

She compressed her lips and pinched at the last white threads.

"I want you to know that I support you," he said. "In this, in all your heart's dreams. I know you loved him, and a part of you needs this. I'll do what I can for you. But God's truth, if it comes down to a choice of hurting the *sanf* or saving you from yourself, I'm going to choose you. It's domineering and unfair and reeks of our tribal ways. But I want you to live, no matter what. I would do . . . *anything* to ensure that you live."

"Why don't you just knock me over the head right now?" she asked without looking up. "Save yourself some trouble. Hood me and bind me and trundle me back to England. It's been done before."

"Not by me," he said.

She pushed the cook's gown from her lap. She uncrossed her legs and slid off the bed, walking toward the door, veering to the mirror, touching a hand to the sheet that still covered it.

She would have sworn she could hear the chorus of voices swell from behind it. Could see the darkness shifting, small lights drawn into coronas around the tips of her fingers.

Rhys had managed to come up behind her without noise. He touched his hands to her waist, lightly, diffidently. She felt his head bend to hers, his exhalation at her temple.

He did not speak. He moved his lips to her hair. She turned in the circle of his arms and met his gaze.

He was wild and not, a green reflection of the woods, of home, and not. Because he was here too, he was a shadow creature tortured into the light, and he gazed at her with such a sober wild clarity it sent quivers of awareness crawling all along her skin.

"You should stay here," she managed, her voice a thread as small as those from the apron.

"No."

Her fingers had found his own waist; she had changed into the salmon-pink satin but he still wore no shirt, only those breeches, torn and knotted, because she hadn't had the courage to go into Hayden's portmanteau and get him anything else.

His skin burned her. He was hot, very hot, still too slim. He felt as if he were a man cut from paper, so brittle and impermanent as if he might flame to ash at any moment. Wintry cold or sizzling heat, there was never anything temperate about Rhys Langford. His passions ruled him. He'd decided that this was love, and Zoe knew he'd never change his mind. She would be the one for him for the rest of their lives . . . however long that might be.

"Please," she said. "Please stay."

"I can't. I'm tied to you. Don't ask again."

He kissed her, and this time there was nothing soft about it. It pushed her back against the mirror, a small bump of the frame against the wall. He shoved his body against hers and spread his legs, trapping her, talons jabbed into the garish red silk.

Her body arched in instant response. All the memories from last night, all the burning white heat that turned her face to his, that had her tongue meeting his. She tasted him and reveled in it: He was not paper, nothing insubstantial despite the bones of his ribs and the twisting claws. He was still *drákon,* his mouth open over hers, the breeches shifting down his hips as he pushed against her again and again.

She craved him. She wanted to taste him, to feel him. She wanted his scent on her and hers on him; there was an animal inside her after all, and the animal wanted to bend down and submit to whatever he desired. However he desired.

His mouth devoured hers; they were breathing each other, clinging to each other. When he drew a hand down between them she felt only a tug and a catch, heard the popping of stitches.

The bodice of the *robe à l'anglais* split in two. She wore no corset beneath it—she'd lost her final corset to the rainstorm—but only a chemise, thin and also a little ripped, cool air like a shock after the touch of his skin.

He yanked the bodice from her. The sleeves were tight and they caught on her arms, but he pulled them down and down until her arms were free again, and she wore only her torn shift and the skirts. He shoved them both to the left, away from the mirror, and when she tried to step away he pushed her back against the wall, gold barbs stabbed through petticoats and pink satin, hauling them up to her thighs.

She raised a leg to his hip, her stockinged thigh to his hip. She found the knot in his breeches and yanked at it, cinching it tighter, so she pulled and pulled until the fabric split down the seam on the other side, and she could grasp his shaft.

He made a strangled sound in his throat. He held motionless, trembling, as she wrapped her fingers around him and began to stroke, using first her fist, then her fingers, and finally her nails—deliciously, delicately, scraping his skin, then soothing it, tracing the crown of his head and the tender underneath as if she'd always known how to do it. Always known his body and his wants, and how to make him thrust into her hand with his eyes closed and his mouth drawn tight. His claws scoring furrows into the wall, ravaging her skirts.

She guided him between her legs. She urged him there, remembering the way of it, her hands around the hard muscles of his but-

tocks, and he slid back and forth in her slickness, that small strangled sound turning into a rasp with every breath.

He bent his knees, brought his palms to her shoulders and
thrust up deep into her, lifting her to her toes. The hurt came
again, quick and hot and wet...and then easing into something
better, a dark licking flame eager for more of him.

He put his forehead to hers. They moved in silence, neither
speaking, only the smack of their skin filling the air, perspiration
beading down his face, onto hers. Strands of dark and gold hair
clinging to her neck. Moisture between her breasts. One twisted
clawed hand shifted from the wall to scoop behind her waist; he
bent her there, bowed her toward him, and she nearly lost her balance until he grunted and shoved even deeper inside, lifting his face
to the ceiling with his eyes now closed, something that looked like
anguish hardening his features.

She stood on the balls of her feet. She kept her fingers clenched
into his shoulders. She could not move otherwise without tilting
them both off-balance, and Rhys knew it. He had mastery of the
moment and used it, pumping in and out of her, using his body to
rub against hers, the crisp curls of his groin, the center of her
caught in some terrible tight torment that wasn't letting go—

She tried to turn her face away but he wouldn't let her, bending
close to suck at her lips, her breasts bouncing, then crushed against
him. She couldn't move, she couldn't fight him. He had control of
every aspect of her body, shifting from hard and fast to slow and
deep, deeper, and without warning she felt that rising within her
once again, spiraling white flame.

Zoe tore her mouth from his; she could not breathe, and she
needed to breathe because she was about to incinerate; she was the
one made of paper—

Rhys paused, only long enough to hear her low, desperate

moan, then pushed so far into her the wall surely buckled, and she no longer touched the floor at all, and someone's voice had risen to a gasping, wordless plea.

"Yes," he growled. "Yes, yes, Zee."

She climaxed, her body clenching around his, shuddering, and he pumped and pumped and came inside her with a sudden stiff push, flooding her without sound, only his breath harsh and frantic in her ear.

Her toes gradually sank back to the floor. He waited until he could speak again, until they could both speak, and then ran his tongue up the line of her neck.

She shivered. His teeth closed over her earlobe.

"You *will* love me," he whispered.

"Unlikely." She closed her eyes, opened them, and struggled to find her sense in the sex-scented gloom of the crimson chamber. "*That* was my last decent gown."

He convinced her to delay their leaving. He convinced her with words and his hands, and finally with the remnants of the food he'd stolen for her, slivers of roast beef and apples that he fed to her in bed. He knew if he delayed her long enough, she'd give it up for the night. Her plan required daylight and respectable people surrounding her in the fashionable quarter of the Palais Royal.

Let it grow dark. Let the sun set. Let him have one more day with her in the flesh, one more night, before their lives were tossed back to the fates.

Rhys lay with his head pillowed upon her stomach, enjoying the unhurried rise and fall that shifted his view: the bed and window, the ceiling and window. Bed and window. Ceiling and window.

The apartment had grown dim. It had been some while since either of them had spoken, and he wondered if she'd fallen asleep.

"I should go," she said just then, as if she'd read his mind and was determined to dash all his hopes. He realized, oddly, that perhaps she had.

"Not yet."

"There's no reason not to."

"There are a thousand reasons."

"Name one."

"Me. I don't want to go tonight."

The rhythm of her breathing never changed. "We could do this every night, I suppose," she murmured. "Laze here. Eat and sleep like a pair of satisfied house cats."

"Make love," he said, hopeful.

"Cats," she said again, determined. "And naught would change. Our world would slip by us. Our people would fight without us."

He said nothing.

"But they would not win. They need us. We hold a key now. We know the *sanf inimicus* now, their weapons against us, a portion of their plans. We may be the ones who turn the tide. But to do that, we must leave this place."

Rhys allowed his lashes to drift closed, his fingers exploring a rent in the sheets he'd made before, gradually widening the tear.

"You know I'm right," Zoe said.

"Aye. But not tonight."

She sucked in an impatient breath and his head rose sharply with it. He rolled over, snagged the sheets again, plucked free his claws, and rested on his elbow as he gazed down at her.

In her bare shift she was girlish and lovely, her skin fresh as cream, her lips dark rose. All that glinting silvery hair, surrounding her like winter wind spun to silk.

"Why do we even need to leave this room?" he asked.

"I told you—"

"No. You read minds, Zoe. You gather thoughts. You told me

that. I've watched you growing these last days. I've watched your Gifts expand. Why do we need to go anywhere but here? Can't you find them from right here?"

She gazed at him, arrested. Opened her mouth, closed it. "I don't know," she said at last. "It's only worked in close proximity before."

"I wasn't close," he pointed out. "And you found me."

He saw her comprehend it, saw it and felt it too, a sudden profound chill to the air, the unexpected awakening of her potential. She lay there as fetching as any maiden, and above and all around her he felt the soundless, bottomless depths of her power gather, invisible wings that brushed the air and stirred the molecules.

Her eyes went black. All black, pure liquid, just like that time at the dance hall. It was scary as hell and even more beautiful; he could not look away from her.

She didn't seem to notice. Those shining jet eyes seemed focused on a point beyond his comprehension. She was seeing things he could not, he realized. She was *knowing* things he did not know.

The velvet curtains rustled. The sheet across the broken mirror rippled and shimmied, trying to pull free. He felt the brush of those wings glance his face—

—*malevolent dark, stinking water and dripping tunnels and*—

Zoe blinked; her eyes went back to normal. She turned to him in the bed where he lay frozen, trying not to smell the decayed scent of earth and rot that had rushed over him with the touch of her Gift, no, not ever again . . .

"I know where they are now," she said, her voice hushed and low and still luscious with power. "You were right. It was easy. I know where to find the heart of the *sanf*."

CHAPTER TWENTY-FIVE

Kimber,

I'm alive. Hayden James was killed by the Others. All three emissaries are dead. Zoe Lane Langford is with me. I'll explain all when I get back. I hope.

—R.S.V.L.

Paris was one ravenous city built upon the back of another. Above the earth it bedazzled: marble façades, slate roofs, breathtaking palaces and cathedrals and ancient walled cemeteries brimming with statues and bodies. Hospitals and monasteries, faubourgs that housed the deprived and the prosperous and everyone in between. People flocked to its opulence, lamented the state of its water and its roads, were overwhelmed by the abundance of theatre and science and public restaurants. There seemed little to rival it in all the civilized world. And tourist or native-born, most people who traveled its streets gave no thought to that other place. That world that still existed, crouched and hunched, beneath them.

The other city had no official name. It was a running sore below the paving stones and filthy wide river, miles and miles of underground tunnels and rooms carved first by Roman hands, then Frankish, Carolingian, French: the bedrock chipped and sliced and hauled away to the surface to supply all those generations of buildings and bridges.

Les carrières. The quarries.

They had been abandoned for centuries. Water pooled in milky puddles, made lakes and grottoes of entire portions of the hidden city. Where it didn't pool it merely leaked, or dribbled, seeping and plopping from above to below. Always seeking below.

Some of the tunnels had collapsed beneath the weight of the behemoth above them; great sections of Paris were progressively sinking, and all the timber joists to be found would not prevent it.

Most of the entrances to the quarries had been forgotten over time. There existed still a few more obvious apertures, usually by way of Gothic crypts, especially in Montparnasse, but by and large the populace of the upper city had overlooked its origins, and the warren of tunnels lay dead and dark.

But for those that formed the easternmost edge.

The passageways there spoked from a hub in eerie resemblance to the pattern of the streets above. The hub itself had once been a massive field of tightly grained limestone, but that was before Charlemagne. Its excavation had left a chamber the size of a granary and roughly the shape of a rectangle, with side tunnels leading away, both up and down, all across the city, toward walls of yet-untouched stone.

It was cold in the tunnels, but on this particular night it was colder above the ground. Fat gray clouds had enclosed the city, and the first snow of the season had started to fall.

The flakes drifted nearly directly through the twist of smoke that slithered above the sidewalks of la Vallée. They continued their path downward to catch along the shoulders and hair of the woman who walked just below the smoke. A servant out very late, or a tavern girl, with a woolen coat but no hat or muff, no hint of cosmetics or jewelry, not even a simple ribbon about her neck. She was scurrying along the lanes with her chin tucked to her chest, clearly in a hurry.

It was nearing midnight. The stalls of the poultry market she passed were empty. Feathers of all sizes and colors littered the ground, cupped the snow to create walkways of bumpy white. The flakes helped mute the stench as well; they muffled all the worst aspects of the city, hid the piles of garbage and stained roofs, dropped in quiet, drifting beauty along the wealthy and the poor in equal measure.

The woman slowed, then stopped. She hesitated, looking around her, then retraced her steps back to the poultry stalls, began to forge a new path through the virgin white.

The odd twist of smoke followed her, a smudge of gray above her head.

Zoe moved guardedly through the wooden stalls of the market, switching her gaze from the indigo cloak that writhed in its funnel ahead to the sticky mess at her feet, damp feathers clinging in lumps to her shoes and hem. She shook her skirts every few feet, glanced back behind her, and was pleased to see the snow falling quickly enough to muddle her tracks.

The cloak beckoned her forward. It had chosen a point upon

the ground, the tapered end of it skipping and hopping, whipping back and forth in a random small circle without disturbing a single chicken feather.

She walked up to it, crouched, and touched a hand to the earth. The smoke that had been a twist rushed down beside her and took a new shape: a man, a dragon-man, with a curved back and bent legs, and talons that scratched the dirt.

"Here?" he asked, frowning at the scratches.

Zoe nodded. She knew they both heard it, the subdued song of limestone made hollow by the open space behind it, about as big as a trapdoor. Everything else around was solid stone beneath packed mud.

She stood, kicked her heel against the earth. The song wavered, then resumed.

"Allow me," said Rhys.

She stepped back, and he curled his hands into fists and pounded them both against the ground.

The song broke. Rhys hit the earth again, and again, and when the stones crumbled apart they both heard that as well, and then they saw it: a hole opening up, snowflakes and feathers tumbling down into the sudden darkness, disappearing.

"You know what I miss?" sighed Rhys, peering down into the opening.

"What?"

"The smell of peaches. Ripe peaches. There's nothing that evokes warm days and starry nights, leisure and happy times more than the aroma of freshly picked summer peaches. And plums. Plums are good too."

She glanced up at him.

"This"—he aimed a talon at the gaping hole—"is about as far from that smell as I can imagine."

"Agreed," she said. She stood to dust the snow off her lap. "Shall we go?"

"In a moment. One last thing." He faced her, flakes gathering on his bare skin, speckling his hair, white fluff across his eyelashes. It was coming down harder now, much harder, and she had to blink a few times to clear her own vision. "I know I've told you how much I don't want you to do this."

"Rhys—"

"And I know you're dead set on it anyway," he continued, speaking over her. "It's one of the things I love about you, Zee. Normally. That you think for yourself. That you don't adhere to any sort of conventional behavior for a female, even a female dragon. So now I'm going to tell you for what may be the last time the one thing I hope you'll remember of me: I would give up all the summers of eternity for you. I love you. Forever and my summer days, I'll love you."

She cupped her cold fingers to his cheek. "This won't be the last time."

"Well." His lashes lowered and his mouth curved; he turned his face to kiss her fingertips. "Just the same."

Her hand dropped. "I didn't love him."

His eyes flashed back to hers, and she swallowed.

"You said that I did. But I...I want you to know that's not true. I wanted to love him. I tried and tried. He was a good man. He was kind."

"Yes," Rhys said, and nothing more.

"But no matter how hard I tried, it just...didn't happen. Maybe, had we been given more time..." She wiped the snow from her eyes. "So no, I didn't love him. But he was still mine. That's why I'm here. That's what this"—she pointed at the hole—"means to me. He was good, and valiant, and he was mine."

Snow fell in dots between them, a curtain of endless dots.

"Then that makes him mine as well," said Lord Rhys, and shook the flakes from his hair. "Let's go."

Had any of the *sanf inimicus* inhabiting the quarry tunnels come upon them, no doubt they would have been startled to see a single candle in a lantern bobbing along by itself in the air, an excess of smoke drifting behind it to crease along the bumps and knots of the ceiling.

But they encountered no one. Not the first mile. Nor the next.

She followed the cloak, swishing and flicking ahead of her, a living thing now, deep blue and yellow stars, voices murmuring in chorus, whispering to her, *hurry; no, don't; yes, hurry, it's time.*

The limestone had been chiseled in great sheets from its base, but the floors of the tunnels were littered with splinters and flakes, and she was afraid she was beginning to leave a trail of blood behind her, for all her invisibility. She looked back and saw nothing but water puddles and sharp changing shadows. If she rinsed her feet, she'd leave prints for certain. So she tried to step lightly and went on.

Her strategy had evolved from simple vengeance into more complicated duplicity. She had instructed the cloak to take her to the leader of the *sanf inimicus.* Zoe would identify him, wait for him to be alone—and he would be alone at some small moment, she was certain of it—and then she and Rhys would abduct him. Smuggle him out together, out of the quarries, out of Paris, all the way back to Darkfrith.

Let the council have him. Let the Alpha work his tender mercies upon the human who had caused them all so much grief. She wouldn't shed a tear.

And if perchance the man proved to be...disagreeable, or impossible to transport, Zoe would kill him. She would picture in her mind the face of the dragon who had pledged twice to wed her. She would remember Cerise, and the shire, and she would snap his neck.

That seemed an excellent plan too.

Up ahead, the cloak loosened its arrow shape, widened and thinned until it blocked the entire passage as a diaphanous veil. Through the spirits she caught a glimpse of a different sort of light, less mobile. It was a rushlight, fixed to the wall.

She paused and glanced at the smoke beside her. Rhys Turned to man, winked at her, and went back to smoke.

She blew out the flame of her lantern and set it against a wall. She crept onward, up to the veil, straight through it, and for the slightest second—as the world plunged deep blue and she tripped forward into infinity—she heard the voices again, clearer than ever before: *yes! go!* Then she was through it, back upon solid stone. She stopped to lift her hands to the rushlight to get warm, then wrung them down her hair to ensure no stray droplets of water would betray her.

A line of torches ahead, each one a bright cherry of light, until the tunnel ended, and she walked into a vast cavern of stone, minute, refractive glimmers from veins of quartz sparkling through the shadows. The ceiling was domed and uneven, and reached so high along the far side she could not see the top.

It was a living chamber. It had been furnished with fixtures and rugs, an agate-topped card table with matching chairs, a teak dining table with carved phoenixes winging up along the legs. Three satin settees. A painted golden screen in the Chinese style, brushwork depicting birds upon branches, a river rushing below them. A gilded candelabra burning with a dozen white candles. There was even a harpsichord, amber-colored wood and ivory keys, flowers painted in a pretty plait upon the sides.

A bed loomed by the Chinese screen, a big one, with four

mahogany posts and ocean-blue covers, furs strewn haphazardly along its base.

But for a single, elderly woman seated upon a bench at the foot of that bed—and all the gossamer songs of the quartz bespangling the limestone—the cavern appeared to be deserted. There was no scent of Others anywhere nearby.

Zoe was invisible. Rhys was close to it, hugging the area around the final torch. Yet the woman turned her face toward them anyway, a sheen of gray-white hair bound into a coronet, shoulders straight, her hands frail and elegant. She lifted a small golden watch fixed to a chain about her neck, checked the time, and let it drop. In her other hand was a teacup; she raised that and drank from it, and Zoe realized right then, from all the way across the cavern, that this woman was a dragon.

Not faint-blooded. A full *drákon.*

"Will you take tea?" she called, her voice wavering across the silence.

Zoe froze.

"Yes, I can feel you," the woman said, nodding. "Don't make me get up. These old bones, you know."

Before Zoe could move again, before she could think, a spiral of smoke bloomed around her, brief warning, then shot past, transformed into naked Rhys before the elderly female. He walked casually to the bed, picked up one of the furs, and wrapped it around his waist.

"Tea would be delightful," she heard him say. "How kind."

The woman made a motion toward the stand by the bed, where a service was arranged. Rhys took a cup, poured from the pot, glanced around him as if to discover a place to sit, then remained standing. He lifted the tea to his nose, appeared to inhale.

"It's not poisoned," said the woman, sounding amused. "If I'd sought to poison you, Lord Rhys, I would have done it long before now."

"You're English," he said.

"I am."

Zoe began to steal forward into the cave. Rhys was sipping at his tea, pattering on in his damaged, cordial voice.

"But I don't know you. I know everyone from the shire, but not you."

"Are you certain about that?" She smiled up at him, and her eyes crinkled. They were blue, Zoe saw. Not the faded, chalky blue one might expect of a human her age—*but she's not human,* whispered her mind, *she's not human, is she?*—but an intensely rich blue, like the heart of a midnoon sky.

Zoe weaved around the candelabra, stepping quietly upon the rug beneath it. She cast the cloak at the woman and had it bounce back to her at once, untouched.

Astonished, she tried again. And again, it rebounded, as if it'd struck a rubber wall.

"Mmm, no," Rhys was saying, a brow lifted, shaking his head. He rested his weight upon one leg and held the teacup with his fingers splayed, a gentleman at his leisure with talons poking in every direction. "Don't recall you. Sorry."

The woman rocked back upon her bench, still smiling. Her gown was blue as well, an old-fashioned powder blue, with a stomacher and embroidery. "Now, that *is* a disappointment. A girl never forgets her first kiss, but I suppose you males are more fickle than that. And you were always such a flirt."

Zoe went motionless once again. Rhys slowly lowered his cup.

"I beg your pardon?"

"I'd fallen. I'd scraped my chin. It hurt like the devil, and then you were there. Right there on the street in front of the silversmith's, the dark and dangerous second son of the Alpha. Oh, how my heart skipped! Even then you were quite the handsome rogue. You smiled at me and told me not to cry. But it hurt, you see. So you bent down, and you kissed it better. You wiped my tears away with your thumb. That's all." She tasted her tea. "That's why I kept you in the basement. That's why I haven't killed you, the way I'm going to kill the rest."

For a moment, he only stared at her. "What are you talking about?"

"Oh." The woman gave a cackle. "I forgot to mention that I was only eight years old at the time. Old enough to know better than to cry, actually, but you were so tender. It was the first time you'd ever truly looked at me. *Seen* me. Such eyes, and that smile! I was swept away. I'll tell you this, I adored you for years after."

Rhys limped back to the stand by the bed, replaced his cup amid the little pots of sugar and cream. The woman watched his every move.

"My name was Honor then," she said evenly. "Honor Carlisle. And that was my first kiss, trifle though it was."

He had turned to see her. He was scowling down at her, his black brows drawn into a slash, his jaw grim. Candlelight flickered over him, highlighted muscle and sinew and the gloss of his hair.

"I'm Réz now," said the woman. "I have reached ninety-one years of age, and my name is Réz."

"I beg your pardon," said Rhys again, still polite. "One does hate to contradict a lady." He gave a short bow without taking his gaze from hers. "But I don't think that's possible."

"What, to be this aged and still this fine-looking?" She laughed at her own wit, and it was a surprisingly youthful sound. "Dear me! And I thought you were the brother with the sense of humor. I'm a time weaver, Lord Rhys. I discovered that right before my fifteenth birthday. Right after I was stolen from the tribe."

292

"A time..."

"Weaver. Yes. Well, that's what I call it. As far as I know, I'm the only *drákon* with such a Gift, so that means I get to invent the name. Time weaver. Sounds impressive, doesn't it?"

"Extremely. You know, I believe I do recall the incident before the silversmith's. You were pushed, weren't you? Another girl pushed you."

The woman's smile faded. Her gaze was vivid blue.

"And your hair was...not blond. Not red. In between, sort of coppery. The color of..."

"Sunset," whispered Réz. "My mother said it was *sunset*."

"Little Honor Carlisle. I say, how you've changed. Why don't you dispel the last of my doubts right now? Go ahead...weave me some time. Prove to me what you're saying, because frankly—and I'm sorry to be rude—frankly your story reeks like a load of ripe horseshit."

Zoe had been circling about the cavern, making her way closer and closer to the woman. Her scent might indeed be subtle, but the animal in Réz was going to sense her sooner or later, and realize that there was not one *drákon* before her but two. Zoe needed to be close enough to strike when that moment came.

Réz seemed unoffended by Rhys's bluntness. "I'd really rather not," she murmured, sipping more tea. "It happens that there are some unpleasant consequences when I do it. Little bits and pieces of me gone missing. I try to save the weaves until I absolutely need them."

"Now isn't one of those times?" he asked, again with that lifted brow.

"Not yet." She set the tea upon the bench beside her, put her hand into the pocket of her gown. Rhys Turned at once to smoke, and the woman glanced up at him, took her hand from her pocket with her fingers curled around something dark and glittery.

"Did you think I was going to shoot you?" she asked mildly. "Please. Turn back to your human shape, my lord."

That was when Zoe realized that Réz held one of the manacles. The manacles embedded with *Draumr.*

It was impossible. They'd separated them, given one to the prince and kept the other, and theirs was still back in the palace, Zoe was sure of it. She'd made sure, right before they'd left. And Sandu had to be halfway home by now—unless the cook had turned on him—had managed to hurt him, force him back to the city—

"Return here, Lord Rhys," commanded the old woman, and after a barely discernible hesitation, he clouded back to the ground, resumed the shape of a man.

No. No! He was supposed to be immune. Was it a trick? Was he only pretending? He was gazing at Réz and she was gazing at him; he didn't glance in Zoe's direction at all.

"Thank you. Now I'd like to address your consort. The female. Come forward, my dear. I need to see you as well."

Zoe looked wildly about the chamber—the distance yawned before her and she was still too far—if she ran at her, if she ran quickly—

"Right now," barked Réz in a sharp new voice, "or else I make your lover suffer. I'm most creative. You really don't want to test me."

Zoe willed herself visible. She was by the harpsichord, one hand pressed to the wood.

"Ah." Réz raised her white brows. "There you are. I've heard about you. Read about you, rather. Zoe Lane. Invisibility. That's a useful Gift too, I must suppose. Except for right now, of course."

"Why are you doing this?" Zoe asked. "We're your kin. Whoever you are, we're your family."

Réz came to her feet, clutching the manacle with both hands. Two spots of color burned high in her wasted cheeks. "Family. Is that what you think? I had a family, Mistress Lane. I had a husband, and a child. And now they're dead—they will be dead, they will be born and they will be dead—" She cut herself off with a snap of her teeth. "You are not my family."

"Did you kill the prince?" she asked quietly, and took a step closer. Rhys was still unmoving, watching the woman without blinking. "Is that how you got the manacle back?"

"Kill him?" The color began to fade from her face. "How little you know, girl. Kill him, indeed—when all this has been for him. Ever him. No, Prince Alexandru of the Zaharen is quite well at the moment. I'm going to take this fascinating bit of iron from him three days from now in the luxury of his castle. He won't even know it's gone for a week. *Time* weaver," she spat. "I *told* you." She cocked her head toward Rhys. "Lord Rhys. I regret to inform you your presence is no longer required. I want you—"

"No," said Zoe, with another step.

"—to Turn to smoke. Do not Turn back."

"No," screamed Zoe as Rhys went to vapor, a cloud of gray lifting and thinning against the stratums of radiant stone above.

There were men in all the tunnels. He supposed he'd not heard them before, not smelled them, because of all the stone surrounding them. He'd never been so deep within the earth, never been so encased in steady music besides that of *Draumr.* But the songs of the limestone and the quartz combined created a weirdly deadened effect, and Rhys only realized that he and Zoe were surrounded by men after he became smoke, and the music lessened.

Holy God. The head of the *sanf inimicus* stood below him, and her minions were everywhere. She'd known they were coming. Somehow, she'd known. And Zoe was alone down there amid them all.

She had gone to her knees, staring up at the last spot she'd seen him, veins of quartz glinting and glinting against the dull dark.

She'd folded her hands over her stomach and stared, just like in the cellar. Just like with Hayden.

Réz clucked her tongue. "Yes. Love is terribly painful, is it not?"

She could not speak. She could not move.

"I want you to know," the woman said, "how very tempting it is to let you live and be my messenger. That was my original notion for you. I thought I'd feel a touch of affinity for another female of the shire burdened with a singular Gift. I was going to tell you to tell the English *drákon* that I'm coming for them. I *will* come for them. I did not create the *sanf inimicus,* you see, but I certainly did revive them. Yet it occurs to me now, Zoe Lane, that I may send my message just as effectively by letter. The post these days is fairly reliable. Perhaps I'll include a lock of your hair."

Zoe gasped a breath; it choked in her throat. "Are you mad?"

"Yes," answered Réz serenely. "I think I must be." She smiled. "I told you there were consequences to my Gift. For every glory, a price. Isn't that what the council used to teach us? Stand up, my dear. Do stand up. You don't want to die on your knees."

Zoe climbed to her feet. She faced the old woman. Rhys did not reappear.

"I'm not so ill informed as to think this will work on you," Réz said, lifting the manacle. "I did a little research after you thieved back my creature in the basement. That's yet another fine Gift of yours, young Zoe, immunity to *Draumr.* So I'm going to have to destroy you the human way. With a bullet. Or an arrow. Whichever gets you first." She tipped her head to the black rounded entrance nearby; the twists of her coronet shifted between gold and gray by the candlelight. "Do you know why I chose this place for my home? Because of the music. You think it's soft at first, but it's deceptive, and distracting. It's nearly solid, you see. Nothing beyond it reaches you easily, not scent or sound. Go ahead and Turn invisible, if you wish. My men will hit you anyway."

CHAPTER TWENTY-SIX

Zoe vanished. She went unseen, sprinting at the same time, bending and turning and racing toward the pale blue figure that was her
enemy, who had murdered Zoe's two *drákon* and her heart. She felt
her lips curl back in a silent snarl, heard the sudden commotion of
feet scraping stone, hammers cocking and the creak of strings from
bows, but before she could even finish her dash to the bed a deep
gray column of smoke fountained from the ceiling to the floor, became a man standing behind the old woman with one arm around
her chest and razor-sharp talons jabbed up high against her throat.

"*Hold,*" he bellowed in French, a single word that crashed
through the cavern, gained pitch and echo, and deafened. He stood
tall and straight, and his eyes glowed poisonous bright green; a
thread of scarlet snaked fast down Réz's neck. "Hold or I kill her
now!"

Like a marionette on strings, Zoe did as all the others: She stopped in place, staring at the wrinkled woman and the taloned man, the light gliding over them, shifting and changing.

"Zoe," said the dragon-eyed man, and she finished the distance between them at a jog, still invisible, touched her hand to his arm.

Réz's gaze shifted. She seemed to see Zoe standing before them; she smiled once again, beatific.

"*Adieu.*"

She blurred. There was no better word for it; she was solid one second and a blur the next, and the next second after that, Rhys's claws closed upon empty air.

Réz was gone. Not invisible, not smoke. Just gone.

"Well," said Rhys, stepping back. "That didn't go right."

Someone shot at them. Zoe ducked and Rhys Turned back to smoke, and the bullet whizzed by and pinged against the stone wall. As if that single retort had tightened all the other fingers, pistols fired from all corners; gunpowder sparked; arrows whistled past, up and down, puncturing the bed, the golden screen, the harpsichord. Zoe's thigh.

She cried out and collapsed to the carpet, rolling, clutching the shaft of wood. It was perceptible even if she was not, three rows of bright yellow feathers, and nearly at once a hail of new fire came toward her.

She rolled. She screamed and broke the feathered part of it from her leg, tossed it away—but a bullet found her hand, and another ricocheted off the floor, spraying chips along her body.

Without noise, without wavering, a shadow formed above her. It was huge; it blocked out all the light and the arrows, it crouched over her and fashioned sounds not from its own throat, but from the thrash of its tail belting the Others, from its claws—metallic claws, razored claws—scraping sparks along the limestone, digging trenches, swiping at men. Shrieks and blood, more gunfire, bullets that bounced off him and struck stone. She lay on her back and stared up at his belly, the scales that glistened there, thick and glassy and emerald, shielding them both from the worst of the assault.

The dragon reared, still thrashing, and began to move, taking out everything in his path. She heard wood splintering, harpsichord strings twanging in a jarring medley. Zoe maneuvered to her hands and knees and crawled with him, she didn't know where, but it was clear they couldn't go much farther like this. He was too large to fit into any of the tunnels.

She scrambled out from beneath him. He'd drawn them both near one of the black open entrances, and she scratched at the floor with her fingers, dragging herself upright. She hopped on one leg and kept her shot hand close to her chest, pressed against his neck so he'd know she was there—hot, his scales burning hot, and humans yelling behind him—slipped around the pair of men frantically reloading their guns and hurried down the passage.

She felt him Turn to smoke behind her, but he didn't follow. Zoe stopped, grimacing, reeling against a wall, and from inside the cavern came fresh shouts and then a rumbling. Stones falling. Heavy stones, their impact shaking the earth. A rush of limestone dust devoured the two men with guns, began to boil toward her.

She lurched away again. When she glanced back she saw at last a trail of blood behind her in the final, clouding light; as it left her body it became visible, slick and dark against the paler stone.

She clutched her good hand to her thigh and forced herself to move faster. The dust became plumes overtaking her, choking, and then one of them Turned into Rhys. He scooped her up into his arms and ran.

It was ungainly and very swift. Zoe dropped her head to his chest and closed her eyes and let the deadened stone air wash all along her, wash all along until she hooked her arms around it and drifted away.

He took her back to the palace. It was the only place in the city he knew besides the cellar and the *maison*. He got her in by the last squeak of dawn, laid her down upon her bed, and was glad she'd passed out, because getting the barb of the arrow out of her leg was a vicious enough affair, especially for a creature with claws. Only one of them should be weeping over it, and he reckoned since she never woke, it might as well be him.

But he was glad she didn't see.

Her blood swamped his senses. She was whiter than the linens, whiter than lilies or the snow he'd trampled through. He'd purloined a bottle of cognac from one of the apartments belowstairs, saturated her wounds with the alcohol, ripped up the sheet she'd used to hide her mirror of souls, and bound her leg and her hand. At least the bullet—he assumed it was a bullet—had gone straight through the flesh of her palm.

He'd stuffed pillows beneath her leg, laid her hand upon her chest, then taken a moment to bend over to catch his breath, breathing in the scent of very fine liqueur and blood and her, his forehead pressed into the bed by her ear.

He thought woozily that he might never touch cognac again.

She was alive. She was breathing, she had a pulse. She was alive.

One of the arrows had nicked him beneath a scale on his shoulder; compared to everything else he'd been through, it was no worse than getting pinked in a duel. But he cleaned that too, to be safe, and all the little scrapes and cuts along her feet and the left side of her body.

Rhys spent the remainder of the dawn and all the next day sitting upright beside her, the near-empty bottle cradled between his thighs, fighting sleep. When he wasn't looking at her he was looking at the mirror. The crack slanting through it. It seemed normal to him again, just two pieces of broken glass over a mercury backing, foxing along one side. No sign of the beings he knew dwelled inside.

"Where were you bastards," he muttered, as the afternoon light began to push against the velvet drapery. "Where were you last ruddy night, eh?"

No one answered. Zee was asleep; the mirror was empty. He was talking to himself.

The day passed. By twilight he knew she was in trouble, because the lily-white cast of her skin had deepened into ruby at her cheeks and forehead and chest, and her breathing was labored.

He could go hunt a physician. He could go out into the streets and find one, lure him back here, bribe him into silence. . . .

There was not enough money for silence at the sight of Rhys. He understood that. He thought perhaps his claws were even shorter still than yesterday, but there was no mistaking them for anything else. They were still claws.

He'd have to find a doctor, bring him here, have the man treat her, then kill him. It would be the only way.

Even then, there was no guarantee that human medicine would work for her. Their *drákon* bodies were just enough different to make matters unpredictable. Darkfrith itself had no surgeons or physicians. They were strong as a species, resilient. When bones broke, mothers and fathers set them. When fevers struck, blindfolds were used to prevent the ill from Turning unawares. Sometimes the clan used tribal stones with healing songs. That was about it. Live or die; it would happen quickly either way.

A poultice meant to drain the heat from a human fever might be the very thing that pushed Zoe over the edge of her resistance, and Rhys had no stones to heal her.

His mind circled the question wearily, the same problem and solution, over and over. Find a physician. Bring him here. Get the medicine. Kill him.

Rhys lay beside her on the bed, atop the covers. He turned his hand over and drew his knuckles down her soft burning skin from her chest to her stomach, back up to rest over her heart.

"Would you forgive me that?" he whispered. "Would you forgive me?"

Talking to himself again. He already knew the answer.

The bronze-plated portions of the roof of the Palais de Tuileries had long ago corroded into green. She'd noticed it the way she'd noticed all the details of her sanctuary, the rows and rows of windows, the giant squared dome dividing its middle, the stately columns wrapped around its façade, chimneys wider than houses sprouting up from its ends.

But it wasn't any of those things Zoe first saw when she opened her eyes. She saw the green roof, wide and pretty against a bright blue sky, a rim of snow sugaring its raised edges. Sky blue, sea-green, white. The bronze didn't sing but it hummed, a calm and soothing drone that wrapped her in warmth.

She *was* warm, she realized. She felt air cool on her skin, and warmth where she was held. A voice was speaking in her ear.

A broken voice, a ruined voice, going from husky to nearly normal, cracking in places, just as an adolescent boy's might do.

"... in my tea, just to annoy me. And that's when I first realized I loved you."

"I didn't." Zoe sighed and cleared her throat as the arms holding her abruptly tightened. "I did not put mud in your tea. . . ."

"You did." Rhys was clutching her so hard it began to hurt; he was seated, and she was cradled on his lap, and he was resting his cheek upon her head. She felt a deep, faint tremor in his bones, quaking through them both. "Liar. We were twelve, and you did."

"...didn't put it in your tea just to annoy you," she finished. Her mouth was so dry; it sucked her words into a whisper. "I put it there to teach you a lesson. You wouldn't stop teasing me. I had to knock you down a peg."

He rubbed his face into her hair. "Poor Zee. There's never a chance of that. Ask any of the elders. I'm deuced hard to train."

"Like a colicky mule."

"Exactly." He took a breath as if to say something more, but only released it hard. The trembling grew stronger, then, slowly, began to fade.

She blinked again at the roof, her mind still processing what it meant. They were outside. On the roof of Tuileries. With all of Paris spread before them, the great crowded city dappled white beneath the arching sky.

She stirred against his grip. His arms loosened slightly, enough for her to sit up—and instantly regret it. Pain shot up her hip, spread like fire ants through her right hand.

"What are we doing here?"

"I wanted—I just wanted you to be outside, in the sun. Away from all that gloom and dust. We're beings of the firmament. I thought it might help."

"Help?"

He kissed her temple. The scrape of his chin was actually painful. "You've been out for a while, love. Two days."

"What? Are you serious?"

"Never more."

She leaned back in his arms. He was whiskered and red-eyed, his brown hair blown into knots with the wind, rolling into tangles over his shoulders; the golden dragon silk wouldn't tangle, and still rippled free. "You look like hell."

"Now, see, were I less of a gentleman, I might point out that you've looked better yourself. Lucky for you I'm so well-bred. I'll say merely that you're quite fetching in that old sheet. And the lack of blood to your face lends you a fashionable air of malaise." He tried to smile but it was like a clay mask cracking apart, brittle and bleak. He gave it up, shook his head. "God, Zee. You scared the life out of me. Don't do it again, I beg you. If there's any mercy at all in your heart, you'll never scare me like that again."

It came back to her then, all of it. The quarries and the arrows and the dancing shadows. The madwoman who claimed to be one of them.

"We lost, didn't we?" she asked quietly.

"Lost? I'd say not. We're still here, aren't we?"

"Rhys."

"Zoe." He gazed back at her, grave. "We're still alive. A great many of them are not."

"How can you be certain?"

"Unless humans have developed the ability to allow solid stone to pass through them unimpeded..."

"Oh."

"They're dead," he said. His hand curved around her cheek, urging her to rest back against his chest, claws poking through her hair. She allowed it, enjoying the fresh warmth of him, the comfort of his touch, even with the talons. "I did my best to ensure it."

"But she escaped. That woman."

He said nothing. He rocked them both back and forth a little, balanced upon the pitched humming roof. A lock of her hair flipped up over his arms, glinting against his skin.

"We've got to warn the tribe." Zoe closed the fingers of her bandaged hand, testing the ache. "They don't know about her. We've got to warn them. And Sandu—him as well."

"Yes."

"We could post letters," she said, tipping her chin to see his. "Today. Tell them everything."

"Yes," he said again.

She understood what he was not saying: that a letter would be slow. That far swifter than the post, than carriages or boats, was a dragon in flight. Even if it traveled only at night. Even with a wounded woman on its back.

It would mean her return home. No excuses, no recourse. She'd face censure from the council, Cerise's tears. Marriage and a title and stares, probably stares and sly whispers for the rest of her life. Once they knew all her tricks she'd not elude them again. She'd be watched. She'd be locked to the shire forever.

With him.

Far in the distance a flock of birds rose in a dark fluttery cloud, veered a circle and flew off toward the sun.

"Will you hate it?" he asked softly. "Will you come to hate me?"

"No. I could never... *Hate* is such a dreadful word."

"What about love, then? Do you think you might ever love me?"

Horses and coaches and donkeys below, the low of cattle being driven down the Quai, the calls of the street vendors. Notes from a solo being stroked from a violin reaching them in fits and starts along the wind. The gardens of Tuileries, empty and frozen with silence.

"Yes," Zoe said.

"When?" He'd stopped rocking.

"Just now." She paused. "Perhaps before."

She heard his exhale, felt it, the tremble in his arms returning.

"Days ago," she said, "or perhaps before even that. When you told me I didn't like to cook."

"You don't!"

"I know that, Lord Rhys of Chasen Manor, of Darkfrith. I was just surprised that you knew it too."

"Oh." The trembling turned into laughter. She slipped carefully from his arms, found her place upon the warmed metal roof between his legs, and gazed up at him, her hands upon his thighs.

He wiped at his eyes with the heels of his palms. A sudden gust sent tendrils of chestnut and gold flaring about him. Like a halo, like the smoke that used to define him. Aye, her own Lord Rhys, with lips still so sensual, and eyes that shone like summer leaves under ice, clear and bright.

"I know so many things about you." For an instant his voice returned to normal, pure and deep and smooth. "Zee Langford. I know all about you."

"I believe you," she said simply. "You've been spying on me for a while." And then she smiled at his look.

He lifted his face to the sun, his lips smiling too: a better smile than before, no mask now, no hidden anguish. Moisture wet his lashes, spiked them into stars. She traced a finger down his scar and felt his hushed attention, how his head turned ever so slightly into her touch.

"Have you ever made love on a rooftop?" she asked.

His smile puckered a little, as if holding back another laugh.

"No, don't answer that. Have you ever made love upon *this* rooftop?"

"I have not," he said, sounding very solemn despite the pucker.

Zoe ran her good hand down the sheet, soft cotton rumpled against her palm. She decided that her leg hardly hurt at the moment. "Well."

He looked at her askance. "It's very steep here."

"Yes, but we could . . . You're right. It's very steep. And there are no doors to this section. Not even a window." The wind picked up again; she held back her hair, squinting around them. "How did we get here?"

His eyes dropped. "I carried you." He lifted a hand between

them and spread his talons, and the silver snapping strands mingled with his gold. "In my mouth."

She felt her eyebrows climbing.

Rhys said, "You're light. I managed not to bite you at all."

"Oh, of course."

"It's true."

"In full daylight. A *dragon* crawling up the side of the Palais des Tuileries with a maiden clutched in his fangs." She aimed her squint at him, waiting for the jest. "I believe I've read this somewhere before."

"Don't be absurd, it wasn't daylight. It was right before dawn. That's the best time not to be seen, you know."

She only stared at him.

"Wife," he said, sober, lifting his eyes, "if it meant waking you again, having you with me again, I would have flown all about the city with you in my teeth. I would have landed at Versailles and danced a jig for the king and queen themselves if it meant you'd be well."

"Really?" She pushed more hair from her lashes. "Danced a jig?"

"A *bourrée* at the least. Listen, beloved. I know I'm not him." He shook his head when she opened her mouth, went on more quickly. "Wait. I know I'll never be him. And I know that a part of you will always mourn that. But I swear to you...I swear I'll do my best by you. I swear I..."

He seemed to run out of words. She watched him struggle in silence, a shadow-darkened man with enamel blue all around him, endless but for the birds that flew, and the clouds that swept in pale crystalline tiers, blown about the horizon.

"I love you," she said for them both. "At your best and your worst, I love you. Paris or Darkfrith. Here, there, and everywhere, I love you."

She leaned up on her knees and touched her lips to his, her un-damaged hand upon his shoulder, his arms coming around her waist. The roof beneath them hummed and hummed.

She kissed him. She closed her eyes against the sun and sky and put her heart into it, and he made a hum that harmonized with the sheets of bronze, that resonated back into Zoe and spread through her veins in something very close to complete happiness.

He drew a breath against her lips. He laughed and suddenly spread his arms wide, his face tilted back to the sun: unruly hair and a vicious red scar, his twisted feet pushed hard against the roof, his hands shining and gleaming with their blades of whetted gold.

"Then I'm the luckiest dragon on earth," Rhys said, and opened his eyes to look at her. He offered her that slow and dazzling sweet smile. "My miracle Zee. You make me the luckiest one."

It happened that the roof was not so very pitched after all. And that twilight was just as good as dawn for stealing back down the side of a palace. And that the heavy antique bed that waited inside fit two *drákon*—two human-shaped *drákon*—very well.

If the spirits in the broken mirror tried to watch her still, Zoe didn't notice. She and the husband of her heart had shifted it about so that the glass faced the wall, and the falling night embraced them without interruption, and the flakes of gold from the gilt along the bed broke free with their joy, a small shower of muted color that sang and sang as it floated down to the floor.

EPILOGUE

So now you begin to comprehend the dark wonders of the magic and earth that compose you. You flex your claws into the rich soil of our land and smell its loam. You taste raindrops on your tongue, all the dissolved minerals that become a part of you when swallowed, that expand through you and harden your scales and lend vibrant color to your body.

Beautiful child. Blessed by nature, you soar and coil and hunt the moon. You wink at the stars and they wink back at you. You dream of clouds and castles, of the diamonds that are your birthright. You Turn to smoke and let currents of air move you, as lissome as the dolphins that slice into the soundless core of the sea.

You cherish our home. Like the rest of us, you are its guardian and its savior. Darkfrith cannot exist without you.

Understand, then, the nature of the creature who seeks to hurt us. Understand her ruthlessness, her powers. She won't stop until she tears out your heart, and mine.

She has time on her side, and she will not stop.

Dear Prince Sandu of the Zaharen,

No doubt this letter will come as something of a surprise to you. We have not yet formally met, although I've seen you a few times before.

I will not trouble you long. I wanted only to say I look forward, very much, to seeing you again soon.

Yours humbly,
Mlle. Honor Carlisle
(of the English *drákon*)

ABOUT THE AUTHOR

Shana Abé is the award-winning author of eleven novels, including the bestselling *Drákon* series. She lives in Colorado with six rescued house rabbits and one big, happy dog. Please support your local animal shelter and spay or neuter your pets. Visit her Web site at: www.shanaabe.com.